WELCOMING MAD ERA

BOOK 1 OF THE REVOLT OCCULT SERIES

AM BORNFREE

CONTENTS

Vengeance is not the point; change is. But the trouble is that in most people's minds the thought of victory and the thought of punishing the enemy coincide.

- Barbara Deming

CHICAGO, IL—2015

WALKING DOWN THE STREET, SNUGGED IN HER MAROON LEATHER jacket, Madera halted. A chill brushed her ear as did the unexpected shouts from her aunt: "Mad! Mad!"

Madera peered over her shoulder.

Sure enough, her *Tia* Amaryllis stood hollering at her from the front porch of their greystone three-flat. As usual, Amaryllis' dramatism was ravenous. Burdened by cigarettes, her tone was hoarse, "Mad! Come here!"

Amaryllis was dressed in her sleeveless button-up pajamas, the dingy white ones dotted with smiley faces like teachers' stickers for good papers. Her dark hair held high in a sloppy bun above her tired face. Even from afar, Madera noted her dry skin; the texture and hue of classic sandpaper. No surprise, her aunt was dehydrated.

"I'm trying to get to class to review for my psych test, *Tia.* It's the first one of the year! Like you say, we want to be good people," Madera said, rolling her eyes.

She was already aggravated at Chicago's morning dew for frizzing up her flat-ironed hair. *Remember weather has the upper hand, and if your hairstyle fears the weather, you'll have yourself a bad hair day.* Madera recalled her mother's words. She wished she'd given herself two long French braids last night instead of heat damage. She tucked her hair behind her ears.

"That's why people study at night," Amaryllis hollered.

Little did Amaryllis know, Madera spent last night marinating in the memories of her mother. Yesterday was her mother Constance's birthday. Constance would have turned forty-two years old. She died a decade ago when Madera was only ten.

"Looks like you should've been studying last night and not doing your hair," Amaryllis said.

A part of Madera wanted to be forward with her *Tia*, but she didn't care to ride the rollercoaster of her mouth. Last night, Madera was busy listening to her mother's hum. Over the years, Madera trained her mind to encapsulate the texture of her mother's voice. Constance's tone was ample with floral accents, and Madera always loved her mother's hum.

Stopping at the greystone's gate, Madera gazed at her *Tia* and grumbled, "You sound like a mad woman shouting at me."

Madera noticed that her *Tia* wasn't hungover—she was still drunk from partying last night with her coworkers. Alcohol had a way of hanging onto Amaryllis well into the mornings. A foggy film covered her eyes.

"Oh, please. You're the one named Mad...Era," Amaryllis snickered at her own joke. "Now, come," she cajoled. "Water the plants! Get in the habit, please!"

"Really?" said Madera as she trooped up the steps to their third-floor flat. She'd dash back down the stairs if there wasn't any threat of Amaryllis pulling another embarrassing act.

The familiar blend of sandalwood incense and cooked chorizo enraptured Madera's nose as she entered the flat. She often wondered if this combination was her "home smell." Well, she was sure she'd have to add her aunt's cigarettes and coffee for the full effect. Madera peeked into the living room, anticipating an array of angry potted plants to glare at her from the short bookcase. The wild range of plant life sat with thick wafts of incense curling around them. They looked sad, especially the snake plant.

"*Pobrecitos*! You see my poor thirsty babies!"

Amaryllis adored her plants. She said enough times that she would probably die as a plant lady. The cat lady stereotype was too played out. All the plants had names too difficult for Madera to keep up with: Red Patty, the pinkish flapjack plant; Under the Sea, the string of dolphins; Mouse, the Swiss cheese vine; and Severus, the snake plant. These were names Madera remembered off the top of her head. But other names puzzled her, like, Alchemy, the spider plant, or the peacock plant named Pudding—or was it Paddle? The plants' names, and needs, could be overwhelming just like her *Tia* Amaryllis was.

Habitually, Madera forgot her watering chores, but Amaryllis kept assigning them.

"Can't I just make the coffee in the morning?" Madera headed for the kitchen.

"No. I like my coffee perfect! And that you can't do."

"But you trust me with your plants?"

Madera retrieved the water pitcher from under the sink as Amaryllis topped off her skeleton skull coffee mug.

"The point is, you said you were going to water them two days ago and you forgot. Then you said you'd do it yesterday and that didn't happen. Been trying to tell you this for twenty years. Twenty years old and I still have to remind you?"

"You haven't been telling me for twenty years. I'm twenty years old *now*," Madera said. "You've only known me for ten."

Filling the clunky plastic pitcher from the slow faucet was the worst.

"Oh, shut up, Mad! We said we'd hold each other accountable for these kinds of things. We want to be good people. So, if I have to yell your name down the street, *Lo haré*! I'll do it!" Rolling her eyes after a sip of coffee, Amaryllis leaned against the countertop. She cracked her neck side to side and wiggled her raised nose. "Why do you look all somber and shit? I heard your music playing when I got home last night. You okay?"

"Yesterday was my mother's birthday."

Amaryllis' slate gray eyes widened, "Oh, shit, you're right. Damn— I forgot! How'd I forget that?"

"You came in at one in the morning, *Tia*. It wasn't her birthday anymore. Did they roll out new wines at your job? Is that what it was?" Madera said, turning both taps on for extra strength.

"Oh, please, none of that matters!"

Honestly, Madera wasn't too upset that her aunt forgot. She didn't want all that alcohol toxicity around her mother's memory anyway. In one way or another, a drunk *Tia* Amaryllis would've turned the celebration into some theatrical event at two in the morning.

We want to be good people, Madera reminded herself. Wouldn't do any good to dive into a mental rant about Amaryllis. After all, Amaryllis was the one who suddenly changed her entire life at the age of twenty-six to raise a niece she hardly knew. Familial roommates, that's what they were. But Madera didn't have a job, and her piggy bank could carry an echo. She cleared her throat, accepting her aunt may have a reason to holler her name down the street as if she were a child, right?

"When do you wanna go to the gravesite? Sunday?" Amaryllis fumbled through the words. She scratched her head, her messy bun shaking side to side.

Madera lifted the pitcher out of the sink and said, "I went already. Yesterday morning."

True, she aimed to miss the verbal rollercoaster with her aunt, but the ride was unavoidable at this point.

"Wait, what? Without me?" Amaryllis' voice dropped.

"Yes."

Catching the time getting later on the microwave display, Madera spun around wielding the water pitcher. Amaryllis followed in a daze.

"*Ay Dios Mio!* That really pisses me off. I haven't been on top of my calendar," she griped.

Amaryllis cherished celebrating each birthday and death anniversary with candles, cake, and music. She kept a calendar on the side of the refrigerator marked with significant dates of loved ones. However, the calendar was left hanging on July and it was now two days away from October. Yet, Amaryllis made sure no one forgot May 28th, the birthday of Hilda, her late mother and Madera's paternal grandmother. Hilda died of breast cancer before Madera was born. Her annual birthday parties were the best. The living room would be cluttered with paper streamers, balloons, and the crumbs of a tres leches cake. Hilda's favorite movies would run on the TV, and the dramatic songs of Vincente Fernández transported Madera to a mythical Mexican past. Those celebratory memories felt like they were cased in Spanish Colonial picture frames.

With hurried hands, Madera poured water in each of the terracotta pots, careful not to overflow. In deep thirst, the surrounding soil slurped down the water as if a clog was loosened. Severus looked troubled with slow growth. Madera slid an index finger along a couple of its erect leaves. She thought of joy, just the simple sound of the word itself. Maybe, she hoped, Severus would receive this word and stretch its limbs out.

"Why did you go to the gravesite without me?"

Madera sighed. "*Tia* . . . look, you never even knew my mama."

"That's fucking rude!" Amaryllis took a swig of her coffee as if it were booze.

"It's not a lie."

True, Amaryllis knew Madera's mother, Constance, secondhand, from stories in the neighborhood.

"What did they say to you, *Tia*, about my mother? People that didn't know her, huh? Oh yeah, I remember. 'Constance, *la mujer* with the smart mouth and wide hips that talked shit. Right? Constance, *la morena* that your brother impregnated. Constance, *la negra* who was killed by a police officer for being out of line. Constance, the woman who left her daughter an orphan at the tender age of ten.' That's what you heard. That's all you knew of my mother."

Up until five years after her murder, Constance's name had lingered in the chatter on Chicago's West Side. Now, a decade after her death, the names of new men, women, and children taken by the steel claws of police had replaced hers.

"Listen, I get it. Okay!" Amaryllis snapped back.

Madera was still waiting for her *Tia* to admit she'd only heard side-eyed comments dipped in anti-Blackness about her mother.

"I think it's supposed to rain this weekend. Maybe sometime early next week I'll stop by to visit her grave. You know how I am. I care about those things." Amaryllis retrieved a long Marlboro Light from the pocket of her pajama coat.

"You care about what things? Visiting my mom? You never even ask me about her."

"Oh, that's not true!"

Madera remembered when Amaryllis first became her guardian. She gently probed about her mother then. At that time, in the thick of trying to navigate life as a young orphan, Madera didn't want to discuss her mother's murder. She succumbed to numbness as the trauma sat fermenting in the pit of her stomach. Every so often, triggered by a taste, a color, or a smell, Madera would share a memory of her mother. She believed Amaryllis was trying to respect her as an introvert and had let her be. Nowadays, Madera carried the need to deal with these intense feelings surrounding her mother. There wasn't any point to bring it up to her *Tia*, especially with all her drinking.

Smoothing down her hair, Madera peered at her aunt from the corner of her eye.

"I like your hair better when it's natural, right? It's better like that," Amaryllis said, lighting her cigarette. Her gray eyes, reflecting the lighter's flame, looked silver as she pulled in a deep tobacco drag.

"Yes, I think so too. But sometimes a change is needed," Madera said.

Amaryllis' eyes flinched, as if she saw something unsettling on Madera's face.

"*Ay!* Your eyes just changed colors! Wait, why are you looking at me like that?" Amaryllis inhaled her cigarette.

"Change colors! Like what?"

Madera sat the pitcher on the floor. She glimpsed at herself in the small oval mirror that hung above the living room's altar. Her eyes looked the same to her.

"I'm probably seeing things. They looked red. But now they're back looking so unbothered but bothered at the same time! It drives me crazy," Amaryllis exhaled. "I can never really guess what you're thinking."

Red? Maybe Tia's doing more than just drinking, Madera thought.

"I can't control my eyes, *Tia!* And I doubt they are red."

"Yes, I know. They're just like your papa's! He could see a child tumbling out of a moving car or a woman without a mouth and barely blink. Mysterious but . . . um, vacant. I miss my big brother. So young."

Madera did inherit those inscrutable deep brown eyes from her late father, Adan, who died in her infancy. Someone said her eyes were shields to keep others from getting too close. That description felt the most accurate to Madera. Just peculiar genetics that made perfect sense; a pair of numb eyes for someone with a life worth numbing. And with those eyes, Madera rolled them at her aunt, clung onto her backpack, and hurried out the door.

2

"RED EYES! SHE'S THE MAD ONE," MADERA MUTTERED TO HERSELF AS she stepped back outside.

Madera lived with her *Tia* on a little block sandwiched between Madison and Warren in East Garfield Park. The block was a mix of two- and three-flats, a six unit apartment building, and classic early twentieth century Chicago greystones. It was a relatively quiet block as gentrification was rapidly spreading their way from the southeast.

The predominantly African American area was becoming more diverse these days with the arrival of Latinx and White homeowners who had dropped in from suburban Schaumburg. Madera believed they moved there to be near the United Center, home of the Chicago Bulls and Blackhawks. Plus, the area had a decent view of the skyline.

Amaryllis moved from Pilsen to East Garfield Park when she adopted Madera. She scored a deal with the landlord who was an old manager of hers at a restaurant. *Tia* had more faith in the neighborhood since it was "up and coming." The area was once home to a prominent Chicago Public Housing Authority, The Henry Hornets. Any residue of those projects made Amaryllis spew out reasons to move, but she never did.

Madera picked up her pace east toward the elevated L green line train. Fortunately, it looked like she'd catch a train in decent time to get to class.

She passed the youths huddled outside the corner store as they talked about the random White woman in vibrant yoga pants who struggled to tame her crew of rottweiler pups. The pups yelped across the street, fascinated by the vintage bathtub that was transformed into a gorgeous mosaic home for fairies. One of the owners, Mrs. Sanchez, made the fairy paradise to beautify the block. Most people would say folks got along fine, except for occasional trouble—East Garfield Park was still the West Side of Chicago.

Crossing the street, Madera found it hard to not think about her mom. It was as if her mother was sending signals to her from heaven, or maybe she was right on the sidewalk beside her. Wherever Constance was, she was restless.

"Are you having a hard time getting back to heaven, Mama? I know you came to visit me last night. I heard your humming. Are you annoyed about my hair?" Madera mumbled into her gray scarf.

Climbing the metal steps to catch the L, Madera heard the rumbling train approaching. She felt a pull in her chest, as if she were being dragged by an invisible harness. Madera heard her mother's cry as she reached the platform. The cry was piercing, as if it surged from Constance's guts, or was it the squeal of the train wheels slowing down? A whirling image of police lights flashed in Madera's mind, so deep was the need to conjure up the name and face of the cop who caused her mother's demise. Madera swallowed, trying to flush away this roaring desire. It was saturating her mind as of late.

Stepping into the train, eastbound toward Chicago's downtown Loop, Madera looked for a seat in the last railcar. Suburbanites found their breaths on the first couple of cars. Being closer to the motor operator, Madera believed, gave them ease. Sometimes they'd bury their faces in phones and newspapers. Other times, they would cast skeptical looks. Most of them were afraid of riding through the West Side, especially when the train stopped at Pulaski, a street of notorious drug turf. Madera felt less judged on the last railcar, she preferred to sit there.

She sat down next to a gentleman in his mid-fifties. It was the only empty seat in the railcar. As she adjusted her backpack to sit comfortably on her lap, the man ventured a polite but firm, "Good Morning." Fellow CTA riders didn't often speak on the morning commute, but something was warm about this man. His voice was hearty like a stew.

"Morning," Madera replied.

He was a dark-skinned Black man, cheeks thick with stubble that mirrored cracked black pepper. A pair of bushy eyebrows hung above his brown eyes and a too-small Chicago White Sox baseball cap perched on his head. He held a white, wide-rimmed ceramic mug of hot coffee. Madera marveled that the coffee did not jump over its edge and burn him—or her. It vibrated with the rattling of the train, not a splash leaped out. The coffee was well trained. Its wooden brownness, a mixture of cinnamon, not cream, and a little bit of sugar, struck her as a startling match to the tone of her own skin. Madera smiled in high respect to this magician who could train his coffee. The man hadn't budged since he spoke. His gaze was focused out the window.

Where there's good energy, there's wisdom, Madera remembered her mother saying. Madera felt good energy from the man.

"Your coffee is well behaved," she said to him.

The gentleman leaned his head toward Madera and said, "That's the only way it should be."

Letting out a curious little laugh, Madera loosened her gray scarf, which now felt smothering against her neck. Maybe she pulled out her autumn scarves too soon, but this week she felt done with summer and ready for fall.

"There's a trick, you know!" The Coffee Magician gave a knowing smile. "If you want your coffee to be still without a lid, there's a trick."

Madera watched his coffee, looking for the lesson to be revealed. But as the gentleman lifted his mug to his lips, Madera sensed a dooming presence against her right shoulder, like a cryptic shadow. Shifting her head to face the aisle, Madera found a vested police officer looming beside her. His groin pressed against her shoulder. Neat and straight in his blue uniform, belt loaded with gadgets and gun, the cop emitted a scent of vinegar which overpowered the warm coffee. He was built like the Brawny paper towel man, just shorter, with a startling pair of rigid green eyes.

The policeman glowered at the man with the mug. "White Sox, stand on up!" he said.

"Officer? What . . . what's the problem, sir?" The man looked up.

"Stand up!"

A droplet or two of the cop's saliva spewed out, landing on Madera's black backpack. Shaken by the officer's bitter tone, Madera felt her head throb. Disgusted, she wiped her backpack along the seat in front of her.

"For what, sir?" The man asked.

The cop locked eyes with Madera and shouted, "Get up so this man can pass!"

"Why?" Madera asked boldly.

"Why? You do know who you're talking to! Little *girl*, get out of your seat!"

A stronger, more unpleasant vinegar stench sailed down on the cop's wet breath. Madera's nostrils flared. Did this cop really address her as a 'little girl'?

The man with the mug rose from his window seat to obey the cop's order, leaving Madera no choice but to do the same. As the train slowly screeched to a stop, she stepped aside for the Coffee Magician to pass.

All heads in the railcar turned toward them, waiting for the drama to unfold. Some commuters scratched their heads. Others sipped from their lidded coffee cups. A few zoomed their cell phones' cameras on them. It felt surreal like a high drama TV show, but then Madera thought of her mother. The scene was all too real.

Snatching the mug, the cop spilled coffee on the Magician's brown slacks. The Coffee Magician's eyes widened as the hot liquid soaked through to his flesh, but he made no sound.

With a thundering heart, blood pumped around Madera's head and rumbled into her gut. A dizziness fell over her, like a fragile veil, as if the spilt coffee cast a spell. She wanted to do something to help the man, like striking out against the cop. But how and with what?

The cop tossed the ceramic mug on the floor, baptizing nearby passengers as the cup bounced and rolled along the floor, somehow unscathed.

"You ain't gotta do all that now!" a random passenger yelled out.

"How he gonna knock his coffee on the ground? You gonna clean that up, Officer? Huh, you gonna clean that up for the conductor?" someone else cried out behind Madera's shoulder.

Reciting the Miranda Rights, the cop handcuffed the Coffee Magician. Reduced to a docile, obedient body, the man cocked his head to one side as the officer tugged him from the railcar door.

The Magician turned to look back at Madera. *Was that a wink?* Madera wondered as he cut his eyes toward the cop. "Just wait a little longer and your time will come," the Magician sang softly.

An odd thought stuck in Madera's mind: save the white coffee mug. Something about it was special. She picked it up. The mug was still warm and shockingly, not chipped. She held it against her chest as if an infant.

Like everyone in the last railcar, Madera watched through the window as the Coffee Magician's undersized White Sox's cap, the tip of his nose, and his round mouth moved down the platform. He tromped, captive, down the stairs, attached to the officer who stank of vinegar.

3

The putrid stink of vinegar lingered in Madera's nostrils until she arrived at the community college. *Fucking green-eyed cop.*

In class, Madera sat down at a long table, placing the white coffee mug in front of her as if it cradled a beverage. She lost all aspirations to dive into the study notes the instructor left scribbled on the dry erase board. Taking a second glance, all those scribbled notes looked like one sentence written over and over to Madera, *Justice for Constance Maria Miller. Justice for Constance Maria Miller.*

Questions took root in Madera's head: *What foul words did mama hear from the cop who left her to die in the street? Like the Coffee Magician, did she seem to have no choice when the cop approached her?*

Blurry figures shuffled past Madera as students gradually filled the long tables. Ten chairs each, all facing forward like soldiers, primed for a psychology test.

A pale, clammy hand darted past Madera's unfocused eyes, yanking the white mug off the table. She flinched, looked up, and then slumped back in her chair. It was just Dewy, her only friend at the moment. They met last year in an art fundamentals class. They kept catching each other's eyes every time their art instructor tried to crack a joke. It was as if they were the only students stunned by the old man fumbling over back-to-back inappropriate one-liners followed with wheezing laughter.

"Yo! Need a refill?" Dewy teased, the mug dangling from his hand.

Madera focused on Dewy's fingernails, which couldn't be mistaken for anyone else's: cracked at the center tips, nail beds freckled with greenish-brown marijuana debris as proof of his smoking habit. Madera bought him a weed grinder for his 21st birthday. She hoped it kept his fingernails from being so nasty. That didn't work all the time.

"You almost scared the shit outta me." Madera rolled her eyes.

Dewy smiled, revealing his straight, bright, white teeth. His sandy brown hair fell heavy down his neck. He looked a bit orange whenever he wore his pumpkin-colored hoodie, which he did today. Shutting one hazel eye tight, Dewy examined the mug like a detective with the other and said, "What's this all about?"

"My morning commute," Madera whispered.

Placing his backpack on the table, Dewy sat beside her. Out of habit, one which fed both intrigue and comfort, he rested his right leg against hers. Madera sought the fluttery sensation she often received from these touches, but today she didn't feel a thing.

Dewy sat the mug in front of her and pulled out his sketchbook. He had a keen eye for geometric patterns. His talent was so immense that it naturally encouraged Madera to dive deeper into her own art. As of late, Dewy was considering leaving school to be a tattoo artist.

Staring back at the mug, Madera's body temperature crept up.

Unusual, she thought, unraveling the stifling scarf from her neck, bunching it up into a sloppy heap on the table, and setting her chin on it like a pillow. If the mug had eyes, she would've been staring into them.

"What happened?" Dewy asked.

The instructor hadn't arrived, so Madera told Dewy about the train the way she often used him as a spoken-word diary. As she talked, the heat in her body spread. By the end of it, she was sure she'd been nuked for thirty seconds in a microwave. She had no clue why she was so hot. Touching her forehead, her flesh was murky like a bayou. It was as if she had a fever, yet she didn't feel sick.

"Wait? Why did you call him a Coffee Magician?"

Madera sensed a tinge of jealousy in Dewy's question.

"I told you, he kept his coffee tamed!" Madera's giggles rang out.

A classmate overheard Madera's laughter and responded with a chuckle. Madera was never really fond of her own laugh, wet and runny, like a sweet child gargling mouthwash. Many times, Madera was told her laugh was cute. She didn't like that description. She preferred what her mother said, *Your laugh is just contagious, baby.*

Madera lifted her head. A droplet of sweat fell on her scarf. She never sweated like this. She wiped her forehead with her thumb. "Are you hot or am I just the one on fire?" she asked Dewy.

"I'm not hot," Dewy said.

He swayed his leg from hers and then back, seeking the bodily sensation they teased each other with. It was a quiet, physical flirt, not quite enough to question. Madera knew he desired something more than friendship.

During one of their after-school sketch and smoke sessions, not too far from the Garfield Conservatory, Dewy confessed his lust for his friend. Equipped with their sketch pads and packed bowls, Dewy had finished doodling a bouquet of feathers and cattails on the inside of Madera's elbow. The pressure of his writing hand left an electrifying clamminess on her flesh. He admitted that on tough mornings, when the sun couldn't even wake him, the thought of Madera would get him to open his eyes, but only after stroking himself. Wedged between embarrassment and flattery, Madera laughed. She found Dewy's fondness for her charming. However, it was his grave concern for her feelings that she adored most.

"What happened at the gravesite yesterday, sweaty forehead?" Dewy teased, switching subjects. "Did you leave a note for Diane?"

"I did! I took a train *and* a bus," Madera proudly stated.

"Dope! Now Diane knows you're alive," Dewy said.

Diane was one of Constance's best friends. She was several years older than Constance and was like an aunt to Madera. Madera remembered Diane's big feet, her loud boisterous voice, and those tight hugs that rocked her back and forth. At Constance's funeral,

Madera learned that Diane buried her entire soul into researching her mother's murder. Once the case was colder than Chicago's January, Diane struggled to contact ten-year-old Madera. The state had already handed Madera over to Amaryllis then. Diane began leaving laminated letters underneath a tear-shaped rock near Constance's headstone. She left one every season. Some letters spun funny memories about Constance, some were filled with rants about the state of the police, some were poems by Nikki Giovanni. Once in a while, Diane would leave postcards of vacation spots she had traveled to. Diane would conclude every letter with, "I will always be here for you, regardless of the need."

Amaryllis was leery of this connection. She said she didn't want Madera to live in the past. Amaryllis even got a new phone number after the funeral. Madera had other theories. Madera kept Diane's letters stashed in an old Adidas shoebox under her bed. She never wrote Diane back, until yesterday.

"I got there and left before she came. You know, she always visits my mom's grave before me," said Madera.

"What did your letter say?"

"To tell me about what happened the night my mama died. I want to know as much as she knows. I need to know who killed her. It's been on my mind like crazy, Dewy. Every single cop I see or hear . . . or smell awakens my inner beast. It feels like the entire police force is my enemy."

Dewy's face tightened. "I guess it's good to fill in the holes. It all sounds so heavy though. But maybe it's good for healing?"

Like Madera, Dewy was raised by his aunt, and, like her, he had a problem talking about his mother. All Madera really knew about Dewy's mother was that she was from Colombia. Somehow these commonalities were refreshing to Madera.

Abruptly, Dewy grimaced. He inched his head back and blinked a few times. His eyebrows furrowed as he leaned in. "What the fuck?"

Madera touched her face and turned side to side as if a bee was trying to sting her.

"What?" she asked.

"Mad? Your eyes were just red," Dewy said in a hush.

The door of the classroom slammed shut. A flock of students' heads lifted followed by someone's grunt and another's sigh.

"Sorry I'm late! Good Morning! Hope everyone read chapter four. And if you did, I'm certain you revisited it again because it's one of the most challenging reads you'll have in this class. I'm sure you've looked over the notes I left on the board, right?" The instructor zoomed his eyes directly at Madera.

Did the instructor see it too? No, he couldn't have. Madera watched him survey other faces as if to decipher who was ready for the test or not.

Red eyes? Red eyes like Tia saw?

Madera knew she wouldn't make it through class. That hot feeling began spreading over her entire body. And then, straight out of her womanhood, a stream of warm, potent wetness crept out. It coated the insides of her thighs as if she were nervously dipping into a hot tub.

The instructor turned to wipe the dry erase board clean.

Sliding back in her chair, Madera glanced down quickly. She slightly lifted her thigh from the chair and spotted blood on her jeans. But her period ended two weeks ago, and she was never irregular. Why was there *blood*?

"You okay?" Dewy asked, studying Madera's face.

"I . . . I have to go. I'm hot and . . . I don't know what's going on," Madera stuttered.

Madera snatched her scarf off the table and stretched it out, beyond grateful that she was still thinking logically. With gentle haste, she lifted her bottom off the chair and wrapped her scarf around her hips. She knotted it snug like a rock climber.

"Excuse me," she said to no one in particular.

Madera realized Dewy caught sight of the blood on her jeans.

"Take care of yourself," he said.

Madera gripped the mug like a child's hand and slithered out of the classroom.

Bolting into the bathroom with its old round sinks and cracked tile floor, blood hugged her vagina and thighs as they started to itch. Pushing open a stall, Madera loosened the gray knotty scarf from her hips with swiftness. Alarmed, she didn't encounter a single drop of bloody evidence. She widened her eyes as if that would be the secret to seeing the blood. She pulled down her pants and underwear. Nothing. No blood. She wiped her front and her backside, not even a tinge of pink appeared. The blood not only stopped—it disappeared. What kind of illusion was this? Madera knew there had been blood there. Dewy had even seen it. *Right?*

For the first time, Madera didn't have a care in the world to hover over the toilet seat; she planted her butt right on the cold porcelain pot and sobbed. Her eyes released a downpour of tears. Unlike the blood, the cooling tears returned her body temperature to normal. With a soggy, tearful face, Madera couldn't imagine taking a test, certainly not after a case of mysterious, vanishing blood. This was like some kind of psychological experience found in the dark pages of her text book. What if her instructor's stare created this? Maybe she was experiencing chapter four right now. He had shamed her for not studying— and cast some spell on her? Of course, not.

Sighing, Madera wished this problem was as trivial as a bad hair day. A lukewarm shower was calling her name—she couldn't fathom the steam of a hot shower. And it was most definitely time to scrub this scalp. The emotional thunderstorm from the L train stifled her soul, and now, her body was freaking out. Again, Madera found hope in knowing her mind was intact. *Right?* That's all she needed to get back home.

4

Clutching the white mug in her hands, Madera stood in front of her altar that evening. In the east corner of her bedroom sat an old TV tray wrapped with a delicate gold sarong that used to be her mother's. Three long ivory candlesticks in silver thrift store holders stood tall on the altar. The middle candle represented herself: her hopes and dreams, past, and present. The left candle was for her mother. The right was for her father.

A frameless photo of Adan rested against his candle. The picture captured his entire body—lean with broad shoulders, perched on a stool in a garage, he sat tall with an apple in his mouth. He stared at the camera, face firm, with those penetrating, numb eyes. The photo was taken when Adan was twenty.

Since the age of fifteen, Adan had been a mechanic. He was twenty-four when his "heart exploded" at the garage. It took the ambulance over thirty minutes to reach him. Rumor was that Adan's friend Efrain, who didn't speak English, had a difficult time communicating with the 911 dispatcher. That may have had something to do with it, but Amaryllis was quite frank with Madera about her dad: *There were drugs. A lot of hiding and* pura mentiras. *Nothing but lies about what really happened. I knew he overdosed.*

Madera was just three months old when her young father passed away. She only knew of Adan from her mother's eye rolls, shrugs, and sarcasm: *A complex man. Intense. The man I met was different from the man that died so young.*

Madera first placed her father's photograph on her altar as a way of respecting her aunt. She hadn't one first-hand memory of him, but she left room in her nightly ritual to honor him and see him beyond his addictions. She hoped to channel the best of him, whatever that was. "Love you, papa," she whispered.

In front of the left candle sat a photo of her mother in a chunky bright red frame. The picture was taken about a year before she was gunned down. In the picture, Constance was laughing, her eyes gazing off-camera at someone. Shown from the waist up, she sat on a wooden dining room chair against a backdrop of brown wall paneling. Her sparkling eyes were large, and her charismatic smile was full of joy. Madera wondered what joke gave her mother such a smile— probably something Diane said. Constance's blouse was a swirl of cream and orange, and it always led Madera to crave a Creamsicle. Constance's velvety, sepia skin shimmered. Her hair was slicked back in a high bun set off by simple, little pearl earrings.

As always, Madera saved her last moments at her altar for her mama. She selected a memory of her each time to sit with. Playing them in her mind from beginning to end, some memories brought laughter, some made her cry hot, silent tears. The most revisited memory was the last one she shared with her mom.

On Friday, April 9th, 2005, at eight in the evening, the sun was ending its joy, disappearing for the day. Madera rode in the passenger seat of her mother's beige Toyota Corolla. Constance was playing "River Deep Mountain High" by Tina Turner. She was explaining to Madera about the branch of Buddhism that Tina Turner had turned to later in her life. Madera remembered her mother saying she really liked how Ms. Turner's new philosophy on life didn't deal with "blind faith." Madera recalled picturing a blind person at church, reading a Bible filled with braille. Whatever her mother was rambling about was a bit over her head at the time. Especially since Madera was occupied with learning how to cornrow and was busy trying to braid one to her scalp. It was the first time her arms ached at doing her own hair.

The car smelled like the BBQ brisket they just slammed at Famous Dave's, so the windows were down. Constance had a night out planned with her friends and was dropping Madera off to stay with Ms. Robyn, a substitute teacher at Madera's school who also lived on the first floor of their building.

Robyn was a young, soft spoken biracial woman who'd recently graduated college. She loved making friendship bracelets with Madera and could turn the most basic ramen noodles into a gourmet meal. Little did Madera know, Ms. Robyn would be holding her for hours the following morning in a soft rock, "God Bless you, baby. God bless you, baby. God bless you, baby," after hearing the tragic news about Constance.

Watching her daughter continue to struggle braiding her hair, Constance warned, "Don't hurt your scalp . . . or arms."

Aggravated and impatient, Madera said, "I suck at this!"

"You know it's going to be more difficult for you to do it on yourself."

Constance reached across the passenger seat to caress the front of her daughter's scalp with her left hand's index finger and thumb, her touch calming like aloe on a burn. To this day, Madera could channel the cool, balmy touch of her mother's hand on her scalp—she even smelled the scent of wet naps that lingered on her mother's hand from the brisket feast. This was the last touch she felt from her.

Aside from candles and pictures, Madera kept little words of devotion written on scraps of paper sprinkled in the folds of the altar's sarong. This was a practice Madera learned from her *Tia*. Amaryllis was Madera's spiritual staple for the most part, particularly in Madera's first three years living with her. Amaryllis taught Madera the importance of devoted altar time and care. She taught her that she could still be connected with her mother if she wanted. But recently, the shared altar Amaryllis kept in the living room was in dire need of a cleaning.

Madera added a new object in front of the middle candle that represented herself: the white coffee mug. Once again, she believed it held something special—that it somehow belonged there. Its handle grazed the picture of her father.

"What the hell is that?" Amaryllis called out from the doorway of her Madera's bedroom. She sounded slightly disturbed, even though the fat, black pocketbook in her hand proved she'd had a good bartending shift.

"Huh? A mug. Does it look like something else?" Madera rose, wishing she hadn't left her door open to her aunt's intrusion.

"Why's it there?" Amaryllis pulled out a cigarette, ignoring her niece's sarcasm.

"I like it there. Probably put one of your baby spider plants in it. Alchemy, right? That's that plant's name?"

Amaryllis smiled. "Ha! I told you many times to put one in your room. I'll cut you a little spider after dinner if you want. *Tienes hambre?* I brought some quesadillas home from work. Your favorite ones. *Quieres?*"

Amaryllis exhaled and spun around toward the kitchen.

"Yes, thanks!"

Madera touched her belly and realized she hadn't eaten anything since morning. The mystery blood flow had clearly snatched her appetite. Or was it the red eyes? It was after 7 p.m., and hunger knocked. She followed her aunt into the kitchen like an eager puppy.

"A good day at work, huh?"

Madera noted the two Sol beers on the kitchen table. Amaryllis had put a lime in hers and left a plain one for Madera. *If only Amaryllis could limit herself to one beer at dinner.*

"*Gracias A Dios,*" Amaryllis winked.

She put her cigarette out under running water, tossed it in the lidless trash can and quickly rinsed her hands. She sat the open carton of quesadillas with two paper plates on the round kitchen table, then added a mini bowl of sliced limes from the fridge and a bowl of homemade red salsa. She placed the paper plates on either side of the turquoise vase full of red and yellow harvest flowers.

Madera plopped down, anticipating the bite of heat from the quesadillas. Already, she felt in a better place.

"Good news. You have your first shift this Saturday at Hendricks! I told them you can work from noon until seven!" Amaryllis said as she bustled around for the napkins.

Humbled with a tinge of guilt, Madera responded, "Oh! Okay."

She knew the two of them couldn't get anywhere trying to live off Madera's shrinking savings and Amaryllis' day-to-day tips. She was ready to try a new job. Amaryllis was still pissed at her for leaving her last one without a backup "out of stupidity and pure hard youth." Madera was utterly bored and a bit depressed trying to enter data in a chiropractor's office. Sitting in front of a computer had resulted in listless legs and a mind shuffling through memories of her mama. Plus, the chiropractor had a bad case of halitosis.

Madera had been too ashamed and immobilized to look for work, so she'd left her job-hunting to Amaryllis, knowing it wouldn't be hard for her to find a place at the steakhouse. Madera didn't have the energy to hold this and judge herself; her mind was occupied today.

"Twelve an hour," Amaryllis said. "Easy host shift. All those *chicas* do is play on their phones, seat people, maybe file their nails. But there's tons of busy work to distract your mind. You're not the personable type, but you'll be working with Catalina. She talks to anybody and likes *everybody* so you'll be okay."

"You really think I'm strange?" Madera snorted.

"No, *pero*—yes, sometimes. Your hair's back!" Amaryllis chuckled, her gray eyes widening as she took a seat across from her niece.

"Oh, yes. I washed it earlier," Madera smiled, touching her full, wavy curls in a low ponytail.

Amaryllis lifted her beer, "*Salud.*" They clicked bottles. "Just wear something black and tight. You have a perfect figure, perky boobies, wide hips. So, you're good. You look like the evil young twin of Sade, so you might wanna soften your face up with a little makeup. Wouldn't hurt," Amaryllis said between chews.

Madera listened to her aunt's brutal critique without a response. Instead, she thought of the White Sox cap the Coffee Magician wore. She wondered if it was sitting in a big Ziploc bag in the police pound while he sat in a cold cell. *What was his dinner tonight?* She knew he didn't have a crisp beer or quesadillas filled with the best pepper jack cheese.

"How was school?"

"Oh. Fine. Well, blood came out of me and I'm not even on my period."

"Wait, what?" Amaryllis frowned, "When?"

Madera shared the bloody and the non-bloody details of the unusual flow. Amaryllis was already halfway through beer number two when Madera finished.

"What the fuck? That's weird. Get yourself a doctor appointment. That's not stress! I know stress and that's not it. Has this happened before?"

"No."

"Well, has this happened to your mom?" Amaryllis struggled to ask. "You know, some things are genetic."

"No. She talked to me about periods but you were the one here when I got mine."

"Oh, well then—holy shit!" The apartment buzzer startled Amaryllis. She called out as if she were by the intercom, "Who's that!"

Laughing, Madera rushed down the hall to find out. With food in her mouth, she pushed the button, "Who is it?"

With static, "Dewy."

Although Madera wasn't up for the conversation, she had to buzz him in. Dewy called and texted several times since she left school. Lost in her own heavy thoughts, she failed to answer or respond to his texts. His concern was expected.

"Dewy? What's he doing here, now? He thinks he can pop up whenever, since I smoked pot with him. *Ay Dios Mio*," Amaryllis said, rolling her eyes.

Madera giggled, wrapping her head around the bizarre details from the night when her aunt smoked pot with her and Dewy.

"We burned the stovetop popcorn—twice! And you made us watch *Boyz n the Hood* so you could fawn over that killer in the car. You rewound and paused that part like fifty times," Madera teased.

"Oh, shut up! I'm a sucker for captivating eyes! Ha, that's all I require! Remember, Dewy looked him up and found out that actor died the same year your mom did?"

Thrown off guard, Madera responded with a tight smirk.

"I'm sorry, Mad. Look, deal with your friend. He can stay but he has to be out by the time I say. No exceptions. We can't have bad habits. We want to be good people," Amaryllis said as she turned back toward the kitchen.

Amaryllis was infamous for adding herself to Madera's company. Her habit to serve and entertain, built over years of restaurant hospitality, was second nature. She never grasped the moment when her cool aunt persona was about to wear off.

Holding the door open, Madera heard Dewy scooting up the steps, two at a time.

Resisting the potential of a hovering *Tia*, Madera told him, "Imma grab my jacket. Let's go for a walk."

"Glad you're alive. You don't want to drive around the block?" Dewy scratched his head.

"No, I need fresh air."

It was almost eight o'clock when the autumn wind picked up its roar. The Chicago wind sliced at their eardrums and whipped around their foreheads. Dewy kept his head protected with his orange hoodie while Madera found herself enjoying the wind. All things cooling felt good. They walked slowly as the wind pecked them from the side. Half of the moon was exposed and the headlights of passing cars were dimmed as if covered with a murky film.

"You want some good news?" said Dewy.

"What's that?" Madera leaned into him.

"I like your curls. You should let them be."

"Quit playing! Tell me the good news. I need some."

"We didn't take the test today."

"Really? Why?" Madera cradled one remaining quesadilla half tucked in a soggy paper towel.

"He started reviewing and everyone was lost. Just reread chapter four about four times and you'll be ready on Thursday."

"So, he didn't put a bloody spell on me?" Madera joked.

"What?"

"Never mind."

"Listen, another thing. I've told you about my *Tia* Sofia and her dreams, right?" Dewy asked, his voice dropping into a pit of seriousness.

Madera hadn't met Dewy's Aunt Sofia. The couple times she was over his house, her presence pervaded all the rooms, but she was never seen. Madera knew she was an herbalist that had psychic dreams. One time, Dewy said something that made Madera think she was a *bruja* or a *curandera*, a healer.

"Doesn't she predict the future in her dreams?"

"Sort of. They work like this: if she dreams of a bird pooping on you, the next week you'll step in wet bird poop. Theme-related dreams, you know what I mean? But she said she dreamt blood was coming out of my mouth."

"She dreamt blood came out of *your* mouth?" Madera bit at the triangular slice.

"That's what she said last week. She said I had blood pouring out my mouth. I was sitting in a corner in a vacant house, rocking back and forth like I was drugged, with buckets of blood spilling out my mouth. I laughed because all I thought about was how perfect my teeth are. Right? I got a pretty-ass smile for a dude—always have and I got no shame in my truth." Dewy's smile spilled into laughter.

Madera joined in until her mind led her to picture her legs spread wide open with Dewy's mouth cupped over her womanhood. She chewed her quesadilla steadily and shook off the bizarre thought.

"You think that's related to what happened to me today? Somehow my blood is in your mouth?"

"I like to think we have some kind of connection," Dewy winked, then pressed, "Listen, my *Tia* didn't warn me. And she warns people by giving them a look if her dream means something to worry about, you know. So, I'm probably okay."

Leaning over, with his thumb Dewy brushed off a string of cheese that sat on the corner of Madera's mouth. At the same moment, Madera slid her tongue out to catch the cheese. Instead of spicy pepper jack she tasted marijuana and pencil shavings. This unexpected meeting was more of an embrace than a collision. Having caught the cheese, Dewy sucked it off his thumb.

"Dewy!" Madera's childish, gargle-like giggle flooded out.

Dewy tried to disguise his blush by shaking his head, "Mad, you got to know, I'm *here*. Whatever is going on. I don't care. My life hasn't been easy either."

"I have a question though . . . did my eyes really turn red?"

"I'm not sure. Maybe someone had one of those red laser lights in class and somehow it got in your eye? Listen, instead of you taking a train to your mom's gravesite, let me drive you. When do you think Diane will respond? Eh, did you leave her your number?"

Madera slowed her pace as they finished making their way around the block.

"No. No, I didn't. But I finally saved hers in my phone. She left it a couple years ago in one of her letters."

"All this time? Mad, why haven't you called Diane and talked to her?"

"I don't know. Makes me nervous. I haven't spoken to her in forever. Anyways, look, I'm finally doing it now. I should go."

Madera couldn't help wondering if her mother was behind her red eyes, her fever, or her bloody thighs. She wasn't sure if she was more confused or frustrated. It all made her angry.

"We gotta sketch and smoke soon," Dewy said.

"Yes, yes we do."

As she reached for the black iron gate, Madera gobbled the last of her quesadilla. The three-story greystone loomed above them like a haunted house in autumn.

"Let me know when. Now that it's getting colder, we should go to my house and save the forest preserves for spring," Dewy kicked his gym shoe against a crack in the sidewalk.

"Sure. Makes sense."

Where would so many sketch and smoke sessions at Dewy's house lead? Sometimes Madera was curious to find out, but she preferred Dewy in the friend zone. At times she found him attractive, but not worth wrecking their friendship for a fiddly moment in bed.

Under a streetlight, across the street, Madera saw her neighbor, Ms. Della. In her wheelchair, Ms. Della watched the pair of friends with a look of bewilderment. Her round eyes squinted, her brow wrinkled, and her hands lay folded against her belly.

"How you doing, Ms. Della?" Madera said as she waved.

Typically, Ms. Della responded with a mouthful of information. This time, she lifted her hand in a brief flick, almost shooing Madera away.

Madera knew Dewy was expecting an awkward embrace. She leaned in, surprising him with a tight hug and a tender, "Thank you for checking on me."

Pulling back, Madera noted a gleeful glint in Dewy's eyes. Turning to leave, he raised his hand to Ms. Della. She pretended not to see him. Entering his 2010 black Volvo, Dewy grinned and shook his head at the older lady. He drove off.

"You have a liking for that white boy, don't you?" Ms. Della shouted to Madera.

Making her way across the street to the old woman, Madera shrugged. "He's a good friend. You can wave back! He means well. And he's Colombian, or his mom is?"

"Well, whatever he is, he looks white and . . . he wants you!"

"Oh, Ms. Della! How are you? You're not your cheerful self today."

Ms. Della was a constructively nosy neighbor, rooted in the community since she was born. She was an ex-druggie turned what Amaryllis called "a stoop activist." She lived in the yellow apartment building across the street, a place some neighbors deemed sketchy. Ms. Della shared stories with anyone who'd listen, which included Madera. Her stories fed Madera hope that one could live a long, complete life, even if it began in chaos.

Madera stared down at Ms. Della's face lathered with Vaseline, shining under the streetlight. Her black patent leather jacket smelled like Dial soap and her coarse gray hair was gelled and severely slicked back into a stiff bun.

"Oh, I'm not doing too well. I don't think you know what happened at my building yesterday morning, do you?" Ms. Della's big, vibrant brown eyes looked almost as sweet as a child's. She batted her curly eyelashes at Madera, a signal of oncoming gossip.

"No, what?"

"Them mutha fuckin' CPDs, that's what. I can't stand them badge-ass fuckas! Busted through each and every one of our doors of the apartment building. I was on the damn stool and bam! My door got busted in by two pigs looking for somebody that don't *even* live in the building, don't *even* sleep in the building, and probably never *been* in the building! I almost had a heart attack, Mad. Mad, I was mad! Girl, my name could've been yours the way I cursed this evil-eyed one out when he came in the bathroom with his gun pointed right at my face! *Right* in my face like I was some target—right here!" Ms. Della raised her hand against Madera's face, her palm nearly touching her nose.

Madera inhaled the heat radiating from her neighbor's hand. How comfortable she was with this fiery wrath. Next up, Madera imagined her skin turning completely red. Maybe that was on tomorrow's agenda. At least this ardor that roared out of Ms. Della reassured Madera she wasn't alone. Many couldn't stomach the police and with plenty of reason.

"That pig caught the biggest spit cough I could pull outta me—right on his fucking leg!"

"Good for you!" Madera said.

"He looked at me like I was the ugliest thing he done ever seen, and with that, he spat at me right back. Oh, but he missed! God made sure of that! He missed my face. Got my naked thigh. He got my fuckin' thigh, and the other pig tore off my shower curtain as if this thug or criminal or whoever the fuck they were looking for was in the goddamn shower!"

"This sounds like madness."

"Man, Mad, if I didn't have to wipe my ass or have any sense of decency for my privacy, I would've gotten up and *fought*. If it was two decades ago, I wouldn't be here to tell you this because they would've taken my fucking life. Fuck them fuckas! And I'm sorry you got to hear about another story with them. I know your past. I know where you come from, and I pray things were different. I've prayed for years for things to change but shit has gotten bigger. Hell, shit has gotten worse. Fucking *nightmare!*"

Ms. Della shook her head and chewed on the inside of her cheek as they sat in momentary silence. The wind was gaining momentum, its cool gusts soothing Madera's balmy flesh. She gazed up at the skyline taking in the shapes of the Chicago buildings that lurked downtown.

"What if there was a way to exterminate these corrupt cops? A smart, outside-the-box way to rid them off the streets, for real?" Madera said.

Ms. Della laughed. "Wouldn't that be something? Hose them down until they disintegrate into the sewers, right?"

"I mean, sure, there's the occasional handful of decent ones out there. But many are . . . what's the word, compla—complacent?"

"Complicit. It's like a 'go along to get along' kind of thing."

"Exactly. That shit. How do we wake up that world? How does that get fixed?"

"Oh, I like you, Mad. You got a real heart, and it understands the grime. You ain't out here trying to impress anybody or follow the norm. Very smart for twenty. You know, a lot of these youth don't even return a 'good morning.' They're lost in their phones, competing with each other like fucking zombies. Sad, sad world."

"Yeah, you're not too bad yourself, Ms. Della. Really upset about what happened! Surprised my aunt didn't hear anything about it."

Ms. Della nodded. "Yeah, well, you be sure to let her know. We oughta have a wanted picture of his ass but all the cops look the same to me. Too bad we don't got the power to rid them out these streets. Pompous bitches."

"I liked what you said, 'disintegrate into sewers,'" Madera said laughing.

5

THE NEXT DAY, MADERA TREATED HERSELF WITH HER SEASONAL TRIP
down West Roosevelt Road. Amaryllis gave her the idea of taking such
trips when she turned eighteen: *Sometimes, we have to walk into the past
to center ourselves. If I were you, I'd walk down Roosevelt Road and ground
myself in my parents' memories. That's where they met and worked on the
same block.*

It gave Madera chills to creep along the busy road, mind buzzing
with imaginative memories while conjuring the ones she was told.
She wondered if her mother's foot stepped on the same sidewalk
cracks as her, or if her father had ever flicked his cigarette into that
dog's cemented footprint she passed.

Fresh off the bus, headphones in her ears, Madera strolled down
Roosevelt Road. Sometimes the weather was pleasing, other times it
sped up her pace. Today, the autumn draft was lukewarm and the sun
kissed her from the side. She passed the laundromat that was once a
mom-and-pop grocery store, Bella's Binge. Constance was a cashier
there, and a year before her untimely death, she made it to assistant
manager. Madera's nostrils revived the blended smell of cheap deli
meat and purple disinfectant that once clung to the walls of Bella's
Binge.

A few doors down, where an elaborate car wash stood, had been Louie's Garage. It was where Adan worked and died. Madera's eyes zeroed in on the car wash's sudsy cement. She wondered where her dad's drenched, heated body folded and collapsed. He passed away on the first day of summer, the longest day of the year.

Madera recounted her mom reflecting on first meeting her dad: *He had oil spots between his fingers and all over his palms like ink spills. They were shaped like the states on a map. Mad, your dad was a gorgeous tragedy. He had the most swagger I ever saw on a Latin man. He used to wear a cigarette behind his left ear and had a light bounce to his stride.*

Adan was fascinated with Constance. Whenever he went to Bella's Binge, he only went to her line to check out. After a few occasions of rejecting other cashiers' offers of, "You can step to this line, sir," everyone knew that Adan came to the store to entice the pretty *morena*, while buying a random soda.

A parade of funeral cars snailed west with Madera, aiming for one of the cemeteries in the suburbs. Madera couldn't help but focus on the people in the cars. Faces, arrayed in shades of brown, pained or stoic expressions, peering out their windows or staring straight ahead.

Madera wondered what her face looked like at her mother's funeral. She remembered Diane rubbing her shoulder and Gladys, a random second cousin on her mother's side, talking with her. Gladys had left Flint, Michigan, bound for New York at the same time Constance set out for Chicago. She was a fancy, selfish, type A personality who failed to communicate with Madera ever since.

Inspired by the funeral procession, Madera put on one of her mother's favorite rock and roll bands, Guns N' Roses, and flooded her eardrums with the gloomy song, "November Rain." She saw the video a couple times as a kid and remembered its funeral theme. Her mother pointed to Slash, the guitar player of the band and said, *When I was pregnant with you, this is what I thought your hair was going to be like. I'm glad it came out with more kink than this, though. You can do more with it when the hair is tighter. Don't have this world fool you.* Her mother was a rock lover. And while Madera's peers gravitated to whatever was hot, or pop, or some kind of hip hop, she enjoyed all decades of rock.

Stuck studying mourners through their car windows as she walked, Madera bumped into an elderly white woman carrying a dark oak cane. She must have been eighty, and smelled like fresh dollar bills, wearing a beige two-piece outfit: a long skirt and a silk blouse. The collision that felt dainty to Madera was clearly jarring for the old woman.

"Oh, I'm so sorry, ma'am!" Madera's sneakers squeaked to a halt. At least she hadn't lost her balance and toppled over the woman.

Using her cane, the old woman stepped back, her mouth opened in shock. She turned to her companion, a funky dressed, short haired fifty-something woman.

"Oh, dear god! Why do *they* move so fast?" The old woman questioned.

"Now, mother. I'm sure she didn't mean it," the short haired woman answered.

"They?" Madera, appalled, couldn't help but ask.

"You need to watch where you are going!" The old woman scorned. Her voice held a piercing weight.

"I didn't mean to frighten you," Madera muttered, caving into docility for the sake of the old woman.

Yes, this is what society stated was right to do; Why did it feel so wrong at this moment? Madera searched the daughter's face. They locked eyes.

"I'm so sorry," the daughter mouthed. She tugged her mother's shoulders lightly and guided the elder closer to the buildings. Madera slithered past them, hoping to leave the odd experience behind.

"She walked right into me!" Madera heard the old woman rattling off.

Madera figured someone from the funeral parade witnessed the pedestrian collision. How did the incident play out from their view? Maybe she had been careless, but she didn't walk into the woman deliberately. She swallowed the urge to turn and see where the white mother and daughter pair were headed. She assumed they were on their way into the podiatrist's office where she'd seen out-of-neighborhood people go. The older lady smelled too much like money to stroll these streets just for the scenery. Maybe she'd been going to that same podiatrist for years, from when the neighborhood was mostly Slavic and Italian.

The entire incident dropped out of Madera's consciousness as soon as she fixed her eyes on the local *elote* man, plying the street with his cart selling fresh corn on the cob and melons.

"*Hija de Adan?*" he called out to her boldly.

Madera removed her headphones and leaned toward the vendor, a round Mexican man with a narrow mustache. Sweat spots on his neck looked as if he'd encountered a sprinkler. He wore a dirty white apron over a bright yellow shirt that matched the color of a mustard bottle.

"What's that?" Madera responded in English, hoping he understood. Truth was, she knew what he said but considered her Spanish choppy and refrained from using it.

"You! You look like somebody I know. A long time ago," the man replied. His thick accent was watery and stretched, like it came from a southern state in Mexico.

"Did you say, Adan?" Madera asked.

"*Si*, Adan from Guerrero. He died—*como?*—twenty years ago."

Madera's skin warmed as if she snatched the vendor's heat. His sweat looked like it was evaporating while hers was beginning to form. This vendor knew her father.

"How? How do you know him?"

"I been here a long time, *senorita*. And I know he was with that *morena* from Bella's Binge. Was she your mother?"

Inhaling the smell of the warm, peppery corn, *If a god truly existed,* Madera thought, *he was making up for the incident with the old lady.* She craved good news, any news that would keep her body temperature from escalating. She experienced enough of that yesterday.

"Yes! Constance was my mom and . . ."

"I know, she died, too. Everybody was sad. The whole block." The vendor stretched his arms out wide as if anticipating a hug from another large person.

"You knew my mother, too?"

"She was *muy bonita*. And she didn't take no bullshit, but she smiled a lot. *Mis condolencias.*"

Madera glanced up at the sky before sighing. "Thank you," she said.

"I'm Tito. Adan visited me here. He gave me cigarettes, too. He was wild." Tito laughed, causing his entire belly to rumble.

Joining in on the laughter, Madera tried to organize her overflowing emotions. It was suffocating how sadness and happiness could comfortably share space with surprise.

"I'm Madera," was all she could say.

Tito simply nodded, distracting his own laughter by preparing Madera a cob.

"Nice to meet you. *Tus ojos*—your eyes are Adan's. You like chili?"

"Yes, please."

"One time, *esa vieja*—that old lady—you . . . you bumped." Tito cleared his throat.

"You saw that? I didn't mean to!" Madera slapped her forehead, annoyed.

"One time she got *elotes* and *este* . . . she thinks she's royalty," Tito said as he sprinkled *cotija* cheese on the cob. "Her daughter wanted her to try some. She held her cup like a princess." Tito managed to hold his fat fingers like the stereotypical little girl at a tea party, pinky up.

Madera giggled. Tito joined with his belly-led laugh. Madera was certain she just met someone with laughter as contagious as hers.

"Oh, I believe it," she said.

"She has foot problems and her daughter takes her there every week. He's a good podiatrist, but he's *expensive.*"

"*Gracias.*" Madera gleefully received her savory treat. As the steam of the hot corn tickled her nostrils, she honestly couldn't care less about the mother and daughter.

"What else do you know about my papa?" she questioned.

"*Muchacho Loco.* He was a hard worker at the garage. He did everything hard. He talked hard. He laughed hard. He joked hard. Everything. He loved your mom hard, too, *tu sabes*. He did too much—Cocaine! *Claro*, he did that hard, too."

Madera took a bite of the steamy corn cob. She appreciated Tito's honesty. She knew he had nothing to lose by telling her the truth. It wasn't hard to talk honestly about an associate who died two decades ago.

"*Una vez*—one time—your dad bought *elotes* for the whole block. He was so high. He said he'd feed every worker at Bella's, *tu sabes*, where your mom worked. He bought *elotes* for dry cleaners, the garage, even the podiatrist and the real estate office. Man, he was so high. Your dad felt bad because he knew I made no money for three days. The rain. Can't sell anything in the rain. We got so much rain that week, I couldn't pay my rent. He said he'd buy everyone *elotes* on the block. And he did. *Bien loco*—Very crazy. I made fifty cups of *elotes* that day, and melon, too. He was a good guy. Intense. Like you. I can see it in your eyes. They don't change. Just serious."

Wiping her chin with her napkin, Madera's heart sighed. "I never heard this story before."

"Your dad died a week later—or two? I think—two weeks. Horrible."

"Oh, that's why I didn't hear about it. My mom wasn't with him at that time."

"*Si, muy triste*—Very sad. I'm so sorry you didn't see him for all his passion. He had passion. Lots of it."

Madera smiled, taking another bite of her cob. This was her favorite trip down Roosevelt Road so far. She thought all that stored-up passion must have caused her dad's heart to explode. Sure, the drugs definitely messed it up—the way they messed up his relationship with her mother. But what kind of twenty-something-year-old buys *elotes* for an entire block to help someone else pay rent? There was a lot of passion in her father's heart. Her mother spoke of it before. Whenever Adan became invested in something, every inch of his being was invested.

"That's dope. What did people hear about my mama after she died? Anything?"

"They said she was friends with the anti-police people. I don't know what that is. A lot of people don't like the police. We knew she was killed by the police. Do you know who?"

Reluctantly Madera shrugged. "Do you?" Madera said.

Tito's eyes widened. "No," he said.

"What is anti-police anyway?"

Madera knew her mother was friends with community activists that talked about summer programs, urban gardens and rehabilitation for people. Those talks often led to analyzing the corrupt system. Madera also noticed the difference in interests between her mother and her Aunt Amaryllis. Constance read the local newspapers, while Amaryllis used them to wash her windows. Maybe all it took to be considered anti-police was simply being aware of neighborhood happenings.

"I don't know. I guess because she told people what she thought, *tu sabes*. She invited people to community stuff, and she was smart. Intimidating. Very strong voice. But your papa liked challenges. She was a big challenge to him. He was very proud when he got with her. *Pero*, too much drugs screwed that up—I think so."

Tito shook his head and continued. "*Mira*, you don't have to pay me for that, *tu sabes*. Adan already paid for it." Tito pointed to the sky.

Madera, gnawing on the last of her juicy cob, smiled brightly. A couple people lined up behind her, discussing whether to get either a cob or cup of street corn. Madera wondered if her next trip down the road would entail going in and talking to older businesses. Maybe someone could supply her with a cop's name in case Diane's details weren't enough? Madera's mind brewed with possible sources to assist her in figuring out who killed her mother. Perhaps it was a rookie. Easily, Madera could've cluttered her mind with possible cop identities, a slew of fictional characters to fish through. But today she needed a break, so she clung onto the sweet words Tito shared and stored them in her heart.

6

It was Madera's first day at Hendrick's Steakhouse, and Amaryllis was right. Catalina, the young woman training her, was indeed a chatterbox. Although she rattled off a lot, Madera found Catalina's hoarse Argentinian accent rather melodious. Madera abandoned her plan to take notes as she struggled to keep up with her trainer. It was best to follow Catalina's actions—this kind of work was in the moment; flexibility and efficiency were key. And *reading* guests was actually a thing.

In heels Catalina stood about five-eleven, Dewy's height. Her hair, dyed a strawberry blonde, swayed like a bundle of silk down her low-cut black blouse. She kept fluffing it up for added bounce. Madera hid her giggles, glad she didn't have to shake her head like a tornado to call forth volume. Today, Madera's hair laid in gelled two-strand twists an inch below her shoulders.

"Now, you have to over-quote guests on time by no more than ten minutes, but no less than five. Basically, tell them the wait is longer than it is. It's better to surprise them with an earlier seating time than later. Right now, it's super quiet here, but that's because our brunch isn't busy and other places still have their patios up. That will be ending soon. In about three weeks or less."

Catalina took a breath from her instruction. She smelled of sweet strawberries and cloves, and just about every other man that entered stared hungrily as if she were the perfect medium rare steak that drew them into the restaurant.

"Once their patios close, our business will skyrocket, like, big time and you'll wish for a quiet moment. So, enjoy this time to learn all you can before you're running on heels all day. Like, *por ejemplo*, the bar is dead now, but as soon as happy hour comes and tonight, whew! Your *tia* is going to be swamped! Actually, she's rarely swamped because she works the bar really well. Like, one day, I would love to bartend. She's, like, the best. I can't remember, do you live with Amaryllis?" Swiftly, Catalina nodded at Amaryllis who was setting up the bar.

Before Madera could answer, Catalina carried on. "That has to be fun to live with your aunt. She's so cool. Do you speak Spanish? I know your aunt and I kind of get on people's nerves because we talk in Spanish with each other and with the cooks, but you know, everyone likes to think we talk about them! Sometimes that's true but not most of the time. I don't think that'd be fair to do, right?" Catalina rolled her eyes in glamorous exaggeration.

"No. I understand a lot though," Madera replied. She clutched her bloodstone necklace that seemed suitable for her all-black outfit. Its coolness was satisfying.

"Oh, so you *do* speak Spanish, but you like to pretend you don't," Catalina tried correcting Madera.

Madera didn't respond, as a plump white middle-aged couple entered. The woman wore a pair of bifocals that gave her an old-lady caricature look, and the man's teeth had been long due for a pair of braces. Catalina took a step back, signaling to Madera to do the hosting.

"Um . . . Hello! Welcome to Hendrick's Steakhouse. How may I assist you two?" Madera cringed at the phoniness of her voice. She wished she could throw that moment away and do it all over again.

With a snarly whine, the man exclaimed like a little brat, "For two, please!"

"We have tables and booths available. Do you have a preference?" Madera remembered to push out a smile.

The man glanced at his wife who was staring at Catalina's cleavage.

"Booth," the woman said.

"Sure. Follow me."

Madera grabbed two of the leather-bound menus, along with a skinny wine booklet. She spun around and walked through the restaurant's charmingly lit room. Between the padded leather chairs, she led the couple toward the row of booths along the wall that she and Catalina had recently wiped down.

Madera could feel her aunt's eyes on her as she laid the menus down on the cherrywood table, one on each side.

"Your server will be Debbie. Our soup of the day is pumpkin squash. Please, enjoy," Madera said with clarity.

She removed two extra silverware setups from the table and turned to face the maze of tables. Awkwardly, she maneuvered around them to reach the host stand. The unfamiliarity of the space made her a tad dizzy.

"Great! One thing, you forgot to remove the wine glasses. I have to run to the ladies' room—I'll get them," Catalina said. Her heels smacked against the floor like bubble wrap popping over the light jazz that played overhead.

Madera had just sat the pair of silverware setups in their assigned brown wicker basket when a short, crew-cut man slivered through the revolving restaurant door. It wasn't the first or the second look that got Madera to recognize him. It was the third glance, followed by his aroma; the pungent scent of vinegar. His yellowish green eyes were borderline frightful. Madera lost the proper words to greet him. She simply stood there, hoping the words would find themselves in her mouth.

He wasn't in uniform, but his profession dripped over his demeanor: an overly erect posture, a sly smirk with his head cocked to the side. He looked like someone that would, with the slightest provocation, tell you just how much weight he could bench press. Sure enough, it was the cop that arrested the Coffee Magician. *Little girl, get up!* Madera recalled the cop's command. It reverberated in her head.

"Hi?" The man questioned.

Madera's stance mirrored that of a mannequin. She blinked her eyes, aiming them at the man's boots. She prayed her eyes wouldn't turn red; not here, not now, not on her first day of work.

In the form of a stutter, Madera responded, "Wel—welcome to Hendrick's Steakhouse. How may I assist you?"

"I'm not sure if you can help me. Are you okay, miss?"

Wow, now I'm a miss and not a little girl, Madera thought.

The cop looked toward the bar, so she numbly asked, "Would you like a seat at the bar?"

Madera was eager to keep him in her eye's vicinity. She didn't trust him and worried to see him eyeballing her aunt at the bar. She wondered if he could sense her disdain.

"Yes. Please," he spoke matter-of-factly.

Snatching a bar menu from in front of her, Madera nodded her head for the unwanted patron to follow. She walked slowly, holding a slight wish for him to remember her. After all, it had taken her a long time to obey the officer in getting up so he could arrest the Coffee Magician. Now, she sauntered as if his time simply didn't matter. If it was up to her, she'd seat him by the kitchen door, so he could be bombarded with the repetitive sounds of Mexican *canciones* and clattering dishes. She could only imagine how annoyed he'd be at such a table. But, of course, Madera wasn't going to perform poorly on her first day.

The cop sighed with impatience, his breath tickling her neck and sending an icy chill down her spine. With her empty hand, she swatted her neck as if to catch a mosquito before its bite. Madera hoped to have startled the officer, maybe even have him questioning his alertness. She stopped at an oval bar table and slapped the menu down at the table, forcing a peculiar smile.

"Here you are, sir. Please, enjoy your meal."

"Thank you," He gave a sly blink. "But I prefer to sit at the bar. Isn't that right, Amaryllis?"

"Hey, Officer Scott! How's it going?" Amaryllis smiled, revealing her dimples.

Officer Scott picked up the bar menu, handing it back to Madera. "You can take it back," he said. The cop had the nerve to chuckle, all while keeping his eye on her *tia.*

As if routine, Amaryllis reached for a bottle of gin and a rocks glass. She batted her gray eyes at the officer as he pulled out a barstool. He straddled the stool with forced swagger, rested his elbows on the bar and sat his chin upon his folded hands. He set himself up to stare directly at Amaryllis.

Feeling a heated lump emerge in the back of her throat, Madera could've split a bar table in half with a strike of the menu. That same hot discomfort returned; that pang of fever that had smothered her body before the blood came tumbling down in Psych class.

Amaryllis broadcasted her seductive vibes. She twirled around to replace the bottle of gin, gliding two fingers slightly down the neck of the bottle, caressing her hand along the bottom half and base as it made a soft slap against the glass shelf.

Madera wanted to clear her throat and get the lump out. Instead, she dutifully returned to the host stand. Back from the restroom, Catalina watched Amaryllis and the cop. The bar sat to the left, behind them, not quite close enough to spy on conversation.

"Officer Scott!" Catalina gossiped to Madera. "If he wasn't so old... Oh, my, his eyes are the purest of greens. They make me think of cat eyes—dreamy. Isn't he sexy? Look how he drinks like a man. Oh, Madera, here is where you'll get to know the best-looking men this city has to offer. He... "

"He stinks!" Madera said.

"What?" Catalina laughed out of shock, "Stinks? He smells like pine needles and the forest! That's a nice manly smell, don't you think?"

"No. Girl, he smells like vinegar or pickled pork."

Madera tried swallowing, but the lump was too big to remove. Its lodged presence kept her mouth ajar. She figured she looked stupid but that didn't matter.

"You're funny! What do you like your men to smell like?" Catalina giggled.

"Well? I do like men, so you got that one right." Madera shook her head to keep herself from turning her aggression onto the darling trainer beside her. "But I don't like cologne, and I don't think he smells like cologne. I think that's his natural odor."

"That's funny. Pickled pork. Oink! Oink, a *Puerco*! I get it."

"Does he have a thing for my aunt?" Madera questioned, holding onto the fact her *Tia* loved men with "startling eyes."

Catalina smiled. "He flirts and, of course, we know that she has to flirt. She's a bartender. I flirt and you will too if you don't already. That's how you get extra money but you gotta be careful how you flirt and with who."

"Does he like my aunt?" Madera demanded.

"You know, he does flirt with her the most. So, maybe? I think so. Why? I can tell you don't like Officer Scott. Some people don't. None of the cooks like him. They think he's a pig, too! And, they say he speaks rudely to them—and he does. Kind of sad. But he likes us ladies, so don't worry."

Madera didn't have the space to evaluate Catalina's words. She kept shifting her eyes to the bar where Officer Scott's back faced them.

Amaryllis' actions were completely exposed for her niece's critique. She stood with her lower back against the brass holding bar, resting her hands on its rim. One leg crossed over the other, she was long and limber. Open and spirited, her eyes gleamed and her smile showed often as she listened to the cop. She nodded playfully and bit her bottom lip from time to time. She glanced up, making sudden eye contact with Madera. Amaryllis didn't show any reaction: not a smile, a wink or a wave, just a short stare before she let her eyes rest again on Officer Scott.

What are they talking about? Madera desperately wished she could hear something: a few words, one word, a couple of syllables. Her aunt's focus on this unwanted patron was loud. If anyone insisted that it was only her years of hospitality expertise in play, Madera wouldn't buy it. She saw it in her *Tia's* eyes. They lowered into a tight squint, followed with a gentle smile that bled into a blush. Infuriated, Madera observed Amaryllis bestowing several of these looks, back-to-back, to Officer Scott throughout his lunch. Each time, Madera's fever spiked.

"Ay, Madera!" Catalina squealed. Her baby blue manicured fingernails sat below her eyes as she covered her cheeks. Her light brown eyes expanded as her eyelids flapped wildly as if something was in her eye. "Your eyes change colors! Wow! You're like my *prima*! Hers go from blue to green, not brown to red? I never saw anything like that."

"What? My eyes don't change colors. It's probably the reflection of that sign—I think it got in my eye."

Madera instinctively pointed to the crimson red light that emanated from the glowing restroom sign above the narrow hallway. Hopefully, Catalina was gullible enough to fall for it. Madera may not have been able to swallow that lump in her throat, but she swallowed her laughter, praying Catalina would buy her lie.

"You're probably right. I sound so crazy! Never mind. Don't think I'm *loca*!" Catalina shook her head gingerly, still holding her face with her hands.

"It's okay."

Madera clutched her bloodstone necklace, calming her like the tranquil buzz after deep breathing. Madera hadn't worn her bloodstone for several months, but she was drawn to put it on that morning. The bloodstone was a darker green jasper, and the red specks were more prominent than most bloodstones she'd seen. It was a gift from her *Tia* Amaryllis for her thirteenth birthday. Amaryllis gave her the bloodstone because not only was it Madera's traditional birthstone, but it also blessed warriors with strength for battles. Amaryllis claimed it would give her niece courage. That was the year Madera started high school and had a difficult time meeting friends. It was also the year Amaryllis taught Madera about crystals. Too bad she couldn't preserve her aunt's ways then. She missed that Amaryllis.

The sous chef stepped into the lobby through the office door. "Madera, why don't you follow me? Time to tour the kitchen."

What timing, Madera sighed. As much as she wanted to stay and stalk the sleazy details at the bar, stepping away may have prevented a more intense fever or even blood flow.

7

In the living room, cross-legged on the couch, Madera sat in knots. Her gaze was locked on the DVD's time, 12:39 a.m. Time was fading into the following early morning after her first shift. Her aunt wasn't home yet.

Rain was falling violently outside. The kind of rain that leads the exhausted to bed, that breeds worries in the anxious, and spoon-feeds tension to the stressed. The storm made the television's signal blink in and out, leaving Madera to face a bright blue screen. A lamp behind the couch cast a dull glow over her right shoulder.

Madera knew the restaurant's double shifts rarely went past ten thirty at night. The steakhouse was only three train stops east of them, but Amaryllis had driven them both to work in her little blue Honda. She was typically home around a little before eleven when she drove. It was now nearing one in the morning.

She'd called her aunt's cell a couple times with no answer. Madera was tempted to call Hendricks, but she didn't want to seem co-dependent to the people she worked with. However, Amaryllis was never this late—unless she had other plans. Leaving her first shift that evening, Madera recounted the strange look in her aunt's eyes. Madera told her aunt she was on her way home and Amaryllis responded with a stale stare as if she were a child doing something she repeatedly told her not to do. Madera took it as "bitch-work attitude" but could not help speculating further. What if this Officer Scott told Amaryllis about the incident on the train, if he indeed remembered her? So, what? She didn't do anything wrong. What was wrong was Amaryllis flirting with his dirty swine ass. It was over the top. And Madera didn't like how Catalina had said, *"You know, he flirts with her the most."*

The green-eyed officer was moving way too close for comfort, trespassing into Madera's personal space. Sure, it may have seemed lame to others for a twenty-year-old to be so plugged in to her aunt's business but, Amaryllis was all the kin Madera had. The thought of another man in a wicked uniform hanging on the edge of her family smothered and frightened her. It could ignite an untamable fire.

Standing up, Madera turned away from the TV. The plants stared down at her as if they were hiding a secret amongst themselves. They had to have felt the change in their mother, Amaryllis. Madera stretched her arms toward the ceiling, then flopped over like a rag doll, touching her toes. She headed into her bedroom to face her makeshift altar. An escape to the altar was always a good distraction.

Both blood and mind raced as she lit the three ivory candles on the altar. The flames sputtered as if the wicks, too, were irritable. Grabbing her mother's picture, Madera wished she could head to the cemetery right then. She knew Dewy was taking her in the morning but if she could teleport into the words Diane had hopefully already written to her, she would. Her body, still tight, felt the emergence of that lump in her throat again. She took a few of deep breaths. Clammy hand on her mother's framed photo, Madera escaped into a memory, following the buzzing sound of the bathroom light from her childhood apartment.

About one night every month, Constance advised Madera to stay in her bedroom when company came. Around 10 p.m., Madera would hear a variety of voices conversing in the kitchen. They'd laugh, they'd get loud, they'd fuss. Sometimes they'd start off in vibrant discussions, and then, in a chorus, their voices would dim as if to tuck away from spies. Then they would do it all over again.

A ten-year-old Madera lay in her bed, her sweaty feet tangled around her bed sheet. She had to use the bathroom, but she feared one of the visiting adults might say something as she wandered down the hall. Pulling back her damp covers, Madera set her sticky feet on the cold hardwood floor. She took a deep breath and tried to look invisible easing down the narrow hall. She'd have to pass the kitchen doorway to reach the bathroom where a shaky overhead lightbulb buzzed, flickered, and cast an alien glow.

She heard three voices earnestly debating.

A deep man's voice snarled, "You trying to tell me that everyone will know what really goes down on these streets with these pigs?"

"What I said was . . . by the time my daughter is my age, their dirt will be exposed. It has to," Madera heard her own mother say.

"Exposed is not enough. It won't get a police or politician to behave any different," a familiar woman's voice rang out followed by a dry laugh. It was Diane.

"Exactly! The shit will only change when we have the power. When unbiased people with conscious minds and good intent are in control," the man said.

"Even then, what kind of power would get one police officer, if they'd acted like a pig all their life, to behave differently?" Constance questioned.

"I get your point," Diane agreed.

"I doubt we'll be in a position of power that soon," Constance said. "Right now, I think we need guts. And we all know standing up to the system brings real repercussions on us. But where's our courage? What if we behaved as they did and struck back? Most of the time, our bad feelings about them are justified. Evil souls dressed in uniforms. Is it possible to re-train them? Does that mean we attack them? Would it be easier to kill the ignorant than to teach them? They already hate us. They're already killing us. They already made up their minds with what they want to do with us."

Madera had tiptoed about a foot from the kitchen door when she froze at the word, 'kill.' Her mind was replaying what her mother said, and she realized why she'd been told to stay in her room.

"Oh! Shit, you scared me!" Diane said, popping out of the kitchen and almost stumbling over Madera.

"Sorry," Madera rapidly responded as she heard her mother's feet march toward her.

"Mad? Whatcha doing up?"

"I have to use it." Madera said, cringing in wait for her mother's anger.

But Constance laughed a little and said, "Well, hurry up so Diane can use it, too."

Madera scurried to the bathroom and sat under the buzzing light. Outside the door she heard Diane's cackling echo permeate through the hall. It sounded like the cracking of thunder.

Madera stood listening to the thunder that shook the present night. Outside, the rain washed the stubborn remains of summer away, serving its duty of autumn's decay. It was now ten after one in the morning, and still no Amaryllis.

Madera heard her cell phone ringing and darted into the living room for it, answering without even bothering to look at who was calling.

"Hey!" said Dewy.

Madera's shoulders sank as she stretched herself across the couch, "Hey . . . what's up?"

"Glad I caught you up. Wanted to hear about your first day, you know, with the hosting gig?"

She could tell he was in the middle of smoking a bowl; his voice was low and murky. It would be nice to join him and get away from her weighty thoughts.

"It was okay. Not really my cup of tea but, what is? I'm not that personable, but I'd rather do this instead of office work," Madera tried to laugh.

"You should do some research work. Ever thought of that?"

"Hell, I wish I could research what's taking my aunt so long to come home. She had a double shift, and it never goes this late."

"She's not answering her phone?" he inhaled, "You tried texting her?" Dewey exhaled, coughed, "Right?"

"I called her. Twice. I probably . . . I guess I should text her."

"You're really bad with that shit, you know? Most people communicate like that, but you, my sweet, dear Madera, are an old soul. I love that shit," Dewy chuckled.

Madera's face went sour. She wasn't very fond of compliments, especially in the middle of misery. Maybe what she needed was a different feeling, anything. Her body soon reminded her that she hadn't eaten since sample tasting at work. With swiftness, the troubling internal flame grew into a hunger. "How about you let me go so I can text her?"

"That's cool. You still want me to pick you up in the morning for the cemetery, right?"

"Yes, of course."

"Amaryllis is probably having some grown woman fun. She needs that, too."

Madera's stomach churned as her hunger accelerated, suppressing any thought of her aunt having sex. "Bye, Dewy." Madera hung up.

She opened her phone's text window and pecked out the letters to Amaryllis: "Where are you? What time are you coming home?" She pressed send.

The hunger pangs mounted and Madera's body felt weaker than it was warm. She rubbed her right fist into her side; it rumbled.

Standing up, she slipped her phone into her back pocket. The television came back into view and ten o'clock news replay images jolted on the screen. A white news reporter, a police badge, caution tape, and a silhouette of the latest person shot by police. Never-ending images stalked Madera, dragging her mother's death front and center. This season was designed to make her confront it. Every stinky cop. Madera groped the remote control nestled between the couch cushions. She clicked the TV off. She needed to devour something.

In the center of the refrigerator, she spotted the plate of *Serrano* ham, *salchichón,* and dried *chorizo.* It was an appetizer she took from work that Amaryllis always raved about. The thinly sliced meat looked satisfying. She could smell the stank of the bloody colored flesh, stark and salty. The meat was tightly covered with a light pink plastic wrap with a child's handful of exotic olives in the center.

Madera grabbed the dish and slammed the refrigerator shut. She sat the dish at her usual spot on the kitchen table and unwrapped it like a giddy child opening the first gift in a Christmas stocking, expecting much more delight to come. Throbbing with hunger, she reached for the *salchichón* first. Rolling five slices into a ball, she took a huge bite, nearly inhaling the entire wad. She soon devoured every slice of *salchichón*, followed by the *Serrano*. Her eyes grew wild as if temporarily hypnotized, oblivious to her ravenous behavior. Before she went for the *chorizo*, she sucked each of her fingers that came across the salty, cured pig, scarfing down any leftover string of swine, all the greasy debris.

The aggressiveness of her tongue failed to satisfy her hunger. She soon led with the teeth, biting at her fingertips to pull every bit of stubborn pork residue. She wiped her tongue up at the speckle of pork oil that sat on the tip of her nose until she slurped it away.

A bellowing belch followed, then a buzz from her phone. Nearly in a stupor over this intoxicating dish, Madera had successfully forgotten about Amaryllis. But the buzz was only a text from Dewy: "Did she respond?"

Now, uncomfortably full as if a stack of bricks had mortared together in her stomach, Madera found herself on her bed in a doze. A click of the front door woke her up at a fuzzy, wee hour; her alarm clock read 3:37 a.m. She heard the springs of Amaryllis' bed squeak; her aunt had plopped herself down for the night. Finally.

8

Shortly after nine, before Amaryllis was out of her bed to be questioned, Dewy picked Madera up for the cemetery. His car smelled like fresh baked goods.

"Why does it smell like a bakery in here?" Madera said as she snapped her seatbelt.

"I had to drop off a few trays of cookies for my *Tia*."

"Huh? Does she make edibles?"

"Ah, it's not that at all." Dewy laughed.

"I don't know. I just know she's an herbalist, so . . . ?"

"Naw, I get it. But, what's up with Amaryllis? You talk?"

"Not yet. She's sleeping her drink off, I'm sure."

"Remind me, Mad? Amaryllis never wanted you to have a relationship with Diane?"

"Well, she's never said that. It just always felt that way. I mean, she likes to make sure I know every fucking time I get a letter from Diane that I don't have to respond. Up until now I never really wanted to write to her anyway," Madera said.

Diane, a woman with vibrant confidence, rubbed Amaryllis wrong when they had met after Constance's funeral. Diane was adamant that Madera stay at the school where Constance, with some effort, had enrolled her—an art school with an emphasis on community development. Due to the tragic circumstances, the school agreed to keep Madera's placement even though she was moving out of the community with her *Tia*. Diane's persistence forced Amaryllis to seek other employment in order to accommodate the school's schedule.

"*But she only has seven weeks left of fifth grade,*" Amaryllis pleaded to Diane.

"*I know you're not going against her mother's wishes, are you, Amaryllis?*" Diane responded curtly.

Madera recalled her aunt's tight-lipped glare as she chewed over Diane's persistence. Since then, when Diane's name was mentioned, that look reappeared on Amaryllis' face. With the help of the school counselor who dropped Madera off at a Deep Dish Pizza spot Amaryllis worked at a few times a week, Madera was able to finish fifth grade at her mother's chosen school. Feeling pressured, Amaryllis found employment at a Mexican restaurant located a few miles closer to Madera's school the summer before sixth grade. Even though Diane claimed the art school was Constance's wish, Madera recalled Amaryllis yelling about it in her car once, *How exactly is it your mother's wish when she clearly didn't know she was going to die? This is Diane's wish!* This was the first time Madera felt like an inconvenience to her *Tia*. Madera wished her aunt would have just asked her how she felt about the school because she really didn't care where she went.

"What's really pissing me off right now is that my aunt may have a thing for the cop that arrested the Coffee Magician! That same cop, I can't even . . . ugh, imagine!"

Dewy peeked over at Madera. "Yo, when you texted me that this morning, I was like, whoa! Are you sure he's the same guy from the train?"

Madera stared back, her mouth curled in disgust, as last night's cured pig feast lingered on her tongue. How bizarre was that? Not even the cap of Listerine she gargled that morning rid her mouth of swine.

"Trust me. I remembered that smell," she said.

Madera adjusted her white t-shirt under her maroon jacket so it didn't wrinkle against the seatbelt. Madera had adopted her mother's habit of adjusting her attire in cars. Constance was a stickler about wrinkled clothing; she owned three irons and a shelf full of starch sprays. The neighborhood dry cleaners knew her well; each year she sent them Christmas cards. Fifteen-year-old Madera was appalled when Amaryllis failed to replace her broken iron for three whole weeks. Disrespect.

Madera took a hard look at Dewy. His sandy brown bed head smelled like weed and wildflowers, and the heavy bags below his eyes were pearly gray. He reminded her of a hazel-eyed Johnny Depp in *What's Eating Gilbert Grape*—one of Amaryllis' favorite depressive movies.

At a red light, Dewy lifted his disheveled khakis over his backside. "Sorry I look this rough. I hurried to get you."

"You rushed out of bed, huh?"

"Those are the things I do for you," he winked.

"Well, you had to drop that stuff off for your aunt, too. But, yes, I'm grateful for your help." Madera swallowed any complaint of Dewy's messiness and faced the cloudy day out the window. She wondered what Diane's letter would say. Did her mother's killer have a rare or generic name? How long had he been in the police force? Was he still a cop? Did he flirt with bartenders like the green-eyed snake? Was he even a he? He was white, right?

"Oh, fuck!" A thought struck her.

"What's up?"

"Why didn't I think of the rain? What if she wrote it and . . . "

"She leaves laminated notes, Mad. Remember?"

"Yeah, but I didn't, and what if she just wrote it out when she got there and, like, now it's wet?"

"Only one way to find out."

Madera anxiously hoped for a response from Diane. A wave of heat swelled from her gut, flowed up to her head, then flooded out as sweat between her toes.

Pulling into the cemetery, Dewy shifted down to five miles per hour.

"Dude, just make a right at the second stop sign and park. Hurry up, grandpa!" said Madera.

"Give me a sec. Shit." said Dewy laughing. "I don't know this place and we gotta be quiet or . . . "

"Or we'll wake the dead?"

"Mad, let me respect the cemetery, okay?"

Dewy's snail-driving turned Madera's anticipation into uncertainty. If she really learned exactly what happened to her mother, would it bring more trauma or healing? Acceptance or maybe something else? Was she welcoming a natural disaster? Regardless, day by day, the older Madera grew, the more necessary it felt to know everything.

Dewy found a parking space. Madera's hands felt clammy as she got out and closed the car door. Her fingertips left a sweaty residue on the door handle. The cemetery grass was damp from last night's storm.

"Where to?" Dewy stared at the collection of headstones as Madera ignored the place's guaranteed eeriness.

"This way," she muttered.

Reaching Constance's gravesite, Madera spotted the bouquet of sunflowers she left earlier that week, their weathered, golden leaves shriveled and curled from the rainstorm. Madera spotted three small balloons on hard plastic stems, the kind you buy in the drugstore line. Each read "Happy Birthday." Diane had been there. She always left balloons. And behind them, she left half a dozen white roses. Unlike the sunflowers, they were sturdy, as if built for the brutal rain.

Madera stopped at her mother's dark slate headstone. Dewy stood a respectful two feet behind her. She spotted the teardrop shaped rock that Diane left her letters under. Sure enough, a green, see-through laminated envelope stuck out from underneath. Madera snatched the envelope so fast that the rock waddled. Bending over, Madera caressed her mother's headstone. Constance Maria Miller. Born September 28th, 1975. Died April 10th, 2005.

"Miss you, mama. Love you so, so, so much. I hope you're proud of me—maybe? I'll see you at my altar," Madera said.

Back inside the car, Madera pulled out Diane's letter. The pages shook in her hands.

"Dear Madera," she cleared her throat.

"Should I drive?" asked Dewy.

"Um, yeah. Let's not stay parked here like a bunch of weirdos."

"A couple of weirdos."

"What the fuck ever. Okay," Madera sighed, "Dear Madera—"

"Do you want to read it to yourself . . . or—"

"Shush. No. It's okay. Okay . . . Dear Madera, I got so excited to see your letter that I tossed the one I was going to leave and wrote this one. I'm so happy you are well. I'm thrilled to know that you keep my letters and read them often. Sharing good memories of your mother brings me so much joy, I can only imagine how it feels for you when you read them. Maybe we can connect sometime in person? I'll always respect all the time you may need. As you know, your mother was extra special."

"I have revisited the ninth of April 2005 over and over." Diane's new paragraph began a story. "To start, your mother and I were at Andy's Bar on the West Side with a couple of friends. It had to have been a quarter after midnight when we called it a night. We split and said our goodbyes in the parking lot. Your mom pulled out a couple slices of Wrigley's Doublemint gum and stuffed them in her mouth." Madera paused her reading to add, "Sounds just like her."

"I asked for one. She gave me three," Diane's story went on. "I lit a cigarette, and she took a drag. We gave each other a peace sign and went our own ways. And damn! I saw her left taillight was still out. I should've been harder on her about it. I told her a couple times before to get it fixed and she'd shrugged it off like it was nothing. Within ten minutes, that cop pulled her over for that same taillight. It was even in the stupid police report. Your mother was pulled over on Kostner, north of Roosevelt. She was heading northwest, back home to you."

Madera paused to release a long breath before carrying on.

"You want to know the cop's name? Phillip Hughes. He worked

over twenty years with the CPD and was a known piece of shit. Ruthless. People in K-Town called him Mr. Piggy Hughes. He was so foul, Madera. He routinely gave grown men wedgies and oinked in their faces before arresting them. And he used to compare women's legs to drumsticks. If they had flappy legs, he called them fried chicken drumsticks. If they were light-skinned, he'd call them undercooked. If they were dark skinned, he called them burnt legs."

"Talk about a cannibalistic creep. What the fuck?" Dewy said.

Madera furrowed her brows as she cleared her throat and continued, "Piggy Hughes killed a twenty-two-year old deaf kid, a bagger at Jewel's by the name of Simon Spears, a year before he killed your mother. According to two people in the neighborhood, your mother argued with him. He wanted her to get out of the car but she found no reason to. She eventually got out. Does this sound familiar to you?" Madera paused in Diane's narrative.

"Are you asking me?" Dewy asked as he slowed toward a stop sign.

Madera shook her head and said, "Remember Sandra Bland, the woman arrested this summer in Texas? Arrested for nothing and then she died in custody? That's gotta be what Diane means."

"Oh, shit. That's right," Dewy said.

Madera continued reading. "Yes, it's still happening, Madera! The witnesses said they had an exchange of words. They were loud. Your mama called out Piggy about injustices, how certain cops had mistreated people on the West Side. She said, 'Y'all aren't here to keep the peace. You're here to pick on us!' Seems that Piggy didn't want to listen or answer. He just laughed and cut her off, saying, 'Are you done? Are you done? Are you done?' or was it, 'That's enough? That's enough?' Over and over like a damned broken record! Both witnesses said they heard him say this."

Diane's words were blowing out of Madera's mouth like wild tumbleweed. Reading the letter was invigorating. She paused for a breath.

"Mad, you don't have to read it out loud if—"

"—Now, according to the police report—basically, according to Mr. Piggy—your mama reached for his gun and tried to shoot him!

Now God knows that wasn't even close to the truth. Not a soul could picture your mother doing such a thing. Hardly a fool in this city would try to grab a cop's gun, least of all Constance. She was ballsy all right, but never, never would she try to hurt someone unless they tried to hurt her or you. But both witnesses saw Officer Phillip Hughes pull his gun on her and yell, 'Enough!' Then he shot her twice in her stomach. They said she fell instantly."

Madera grabbed her abdomen and held it firmly. She kept reading.

"How do I know? I went to the exact neighborhood two days later and knocked on every single door. There were two people that saw what happened, from two different families, on two different sides of the street. And I asked them, I begged them, to tell the police what really happened. One was with me and the other didn't want to get involved at all. So, a couple of friends and I wrote it all up and took it to the detectives. But it just brought us more trauma. They didn't care what we had to say. They blocked us like we were complaining about a stolen hubcap, a murdered dog, or something."

Madera released her flesh when she finally felt the pain she was causing herself, but didn't stop reading.

"By that time we felt like we did all we could, and we were mad! We prayed for you so hard, too! You have got to understand and know this. Please hold this fact. Hold it dear to you, and please reach out to me. What I know now is that Phillip Hughes is retired and lives in Florida. He retired about five years ago. I want to say he's settled in the Keys, but I'm not certain. Maybe knowing this will help your healing journey. Love you dearly, Diane with the big feet."

Madera placed the letter back in the green envelope.

"My mommy was pulled over because her left tail light was out!" she said. "A piggy cop shot my mama in her stomach. He fucking *killed her* for yelling at him?"

Dewy shook his head, for once at a loss for words. Madera's question lingered in the car like trapped smoke. In silence, young minds held grave matters.

9

"YOU ATE ALL THE CURED MEAT?!" WERE AMARYLLIS' FIRST WORDS WHEN Madera returned from the cemetery.

Stretched out across the gray couch with an open magazine on her lap, Amaryllis held a clear cocktail in a highball glass. Her hair was up in its comfy, sloppy bun, and eye makeup from last night still clung to her face. It had been over twenty-four hours since she started her double shift at Hendricks.

Amaryllis had taken to drinking early on Sundays, her day off. By 9 p.m. she'd be on her seventh round of drinks; a wild-eyed giddy that led to lavish baths she'd forget to drain before sitting at her altar. Even then, it never failed—she'd doze off and forget to blow out a candle or two. Madera would complain, "*Tia*, you're going to waste your candles if you keep them lit through the night—if you don't burn the building down first." And a hungover Amaryllis would retort, "Too bad it can't burn out your sass!"

But this Sunday, there were other issues to contend with. Along the roof of her mouth Madera could still taste the salt of the pig that she'd maxed. Weird. Especially since she just had a bite to eat with Dewy.

"Oh. Yeah. Sorry," Madera said.

Standing in the living room doorway, she unwound the gray scarf from around her neck and tossed her maroon leather jacket across the arm of the lime green rocking chair, where she sat down to unlace her faded boots.

"It's okay. I just noticed the meat so that's why I said it. Where the hell have you been all day?" Amaryllis cocked her head to the left, bugging her eyes out like a bat.

"Me?"

"Naw, the idiot behind you. Where you been all day?"

"What about you last night?"

"Have you gone mad, Mad?!" Amaryllis took a swig.

"Honestly, *Tia*, I was worried. I called and texted you."

"Oh! Now, I see—I get it. That's why you didn't return my calls or texts today? To get even? Where were you?" Amaryllis eyed Madera's white t-shirt and ripped jeans, as if looking for proof of something.

"I grabbed a *jibarito* with Dewy." Madera cleared her throat. What she said was only half true. After the letter reading, the friends sat down at a little industrial restaurant on Division and California in Humboldt Park. They smashed their *comida* while struggling to talk about school or art. Instead, they kept revisiting parts of the letter between mouthfuls of their steak and fried plantain sandwiches.

"*Mentirosa!* Liar. You two sleeping with each other?" Amaryllis spat out the question with ease as if it sat at the tip of her lips.

Madera's steady eyes found her aunt's. She wanted to laugh but instead she frowned and answered, "No."

Maybe Amaryllis wanted to be updated on her sexual activity. Ever since Madera's first experience with Stanley, her Haitian boyfriend from high school—an experience that Amaryllis had caught in the act —*Tia* had mentioned many drunken times that she could confide in her about bedroom matters. She gave Madera all the locations of local Planned Parenthood clinics and left her a sandwich bag of condoms on her nightstand.

"Really? Because I swear you two should be fucking if you aren't! But . . . safely, of course. Want to be good people," Amaryllis squinted, jokingly.

"What? Are you serious, *Tia*?" Madera's heart started to race.

Madera wished she could vent to Amaryllis—share the letter Diane wrote, have her feel the fever that spread through her limbs whenever a cop was involved. Madera wanted to share everything, but all that came out were tears.

"Yes, I'm serious. A little. Look. Why? Why are you crying? A girl has to get off from time to time and—"

"—That's what you were doing last night, huh?" Madera interrupted. Her eyes grew weary.

"Da fuck? Really, Mad? Last night I was at the police station filing a report! Some drunk idiot threw a martini glass at my head! I'm so sorry I didn't call my worried niece and explain to her why a grown-ass *mujer* wasn't home in time for my curfew! I had a drink with my friend, Officer Scott, who made things *much* better for me, thank you very much! Okay? Now have some fucking respect!"

Madera wondered exactly where the glass struck Amaryllis. There was no marking on her face, not a scratch or a bruise. And, why in the hell would she need to file a report at the police station? Wasn't her friend good enough to report to? Madera chewed over these thoughts and blurted out, "I don't see any scar!"

Amaryllis tossed the magazine off her lap and let it tumble onto the wooden floor. Slamming her highball glass onto the coffee table, she rose like a hawk, glowering over her niece. Madera knew what was to come next; her aunt's anger was ignited hot enough to hit somebody. Instead of throwing fists, Amaryllis' long body burst into a frenzy of jerks, reminding Madera of the spiraling Taz from Looney Toons. This was a classic angry reaction of her aunt's, and something Madera saw her do more and more when she drank. Spitting, dancing fists, hissing mouth, and alternating knee-high jumps in a fruitless, childish, but entertaining display. But this time, her dancing fists lost control and with an erratic swing she accidentally punched Madera in the face.

Madera's hand covered her right cheek and chin as if to flatten the pain. She held it and rocked back in the chair, mentally extracting the soreness from her face to hold the burn in her palm. Her tears grew fast and steamy, but her mouth and eyes remained closed. Still hovering above Madera, Amaryllis' breath and body reeked of liquor as she huffed and pivoted to pick up her magazine.

Gradually, Madera opened her eyes. The sting from the sloppy drunk punch fainted in her palm. It gathered itself and crept up around her face like a rapid rash. She wondered if her mother had witnessed this from the world of the dead or wherever she was. What were her thoughts on this woman that had picked up where she left off?

In their own state of shock, both aunt and niece sat in silence until Madera announced, "I don't like that guy."

The ice in Amaryllis' drink jiggled and clanged as she picked it up from the wooden coffee table. "What's that?"

"I don't like that pig you were talking to yesterday," Madera said as she released her hand from her face.

Amaryllis smirked and folded her arms across her chest, stretching the smiley face print of her pajama coat smooth against her body. "What? That's what you have to say to me? Not: 'Oh, poor *Tia*, are you okay?' But, you tell me that you don't like Officer Scott? Really? Did you get high with Dewy?"

"No, I didn't fuck Dewy and I didn't get high with him. He took me to the cemetery before we ate. And from here on out, you don't need to take me there anymore. I don't need you at my mama's grave. I also got another letter from Diane—the letter I wanted. A letter that I asked for! She told me all about my mother's death."

Amaryllis arched her neck back to stare at the ceiling. Her eyes followed the ceiling fan fins as they attempted to circulate the thick air around and around as she pursed her lips. Madera tried to guess where the anger and drunkenness would take her next.

The answer was a rather calm question: "Why did you ask for details?"

"Taking care of my trauma, and there's nothing wrong with that. It's about my mother," Madera said monotone, direct, and unashamed.

As if recklessly retrieving a weapon, Amaryllis yanked out a cigarette from her left pajama coat pocket. Her gray eyes still watching the fan, she coughed and pulled out the lighter from the other pocket. The cigarette hung limp and loose as she lit it.

Madera knew Amaryllis, deep down inside, felt discarded. No longer was Madera relying on her for things they used to do together —praying at their altars, talking about the properties of crystals, decorating her mother's grave. Things Madera knew Amaryllis felt proud and satisfied to do with her niece—moments that made Amaryllis feel confident wearing the guardian's cloak.

"Did you find out what you needed?" Amaryllis spoke lightly.

"Yes, I did."

"Good. Now you can leave it alone. Let your mama rest, for her sake. *Ay Dios Mio*! I don't know what you are trying to do digging up the past. Just do this—live your life. Your mother had no problem living her life. You could respect what she would want from you: to live your life," Amaryllis said.

"I don't know what that means," Madera countered. "Live your life? What about direction or purpose? There has to be something worth living for. My mama believed that! That's why she was engaged in the community."

"Oh, fuck. You're such a college student. Leave it alone. Just live. Nothing philosophical about it. Or you know what? You should pull out your journals and write some poems or sketch something. Have you tried that lately? That's a good way to deal with your trauma, too!"

Madera didn't feel like arguing. Amaryllis might have a point about poems and sketches, but she was only talking to hold space.

"I want to know one thing," Amaryllis said in a smoky exhale. "Why don't you like Officer Scott? You're not that shallow to say it's just because he's a cop, are you?"

In the rocking chair, Madera folded her legs, finding an odd, angular comfort sitting cross-legged against the wooden seat. The sting from Amaryllis' unexpected punch had dissolved into a memory.

"Because," Madera answered, "he stinks—like burnt vinegar."

For days after Amaryllis punched Madera, they found it best to keep their distance. The lingering tension between them was as useless as a dull razor. So, after biology class, Madera insisted on a sketch and smoke session with Dewy. A blushing Dewy took them back to his bedroom in his aunt's bungalow to draw their versions of autumn scenes: Dewy sketched a thriving apple tree, Madera opted for a self-portrait wearing a version of her knotty gray scarf made out of thorns. Thanks to Dewy's red paint pen, blood freckled her neck's flesh in the sketch. Staring at it made her neck tingle, like something was keeping her from using her voice. She cleared her throat and stared around Dewy's room. She'd been there twice before. One time to smoke with him on a rainy day, and another to watch a class-assigned video on his laptop.

Dewy's bedroom walls were painted a shimmery, bright olive, like the garnish on a martini, and a psychedelic aura permeated his room. Smoking a fat joint, Madera sat at the foot of the queen size bed. Elbows on her knees, she faced the slightly opened window behind his rouge window shade. Madera stared at a framed profile of Bob Marley in spray paint and chalk—one of Dewy's mixed medium creations. Madera loved how he made Bob Marley's chin pointy like an old man's cane handle.

Dewy sat beside her, tablet in his lap, slumped over like an old man who could no longer control his alignment or the squint of his near-sighted eyes.

"You're finally ready for this?" Dewy asked.

Madera suggested searching for Phillip Hughes. She didn't want to do it alone.

Under the Friend Finder in Facebook, Dewy typed in the name "Phillip Hughes." Nearly five pages of results appeared. He studied only the faces that made sense: old, white, and male. Even while focused on the screen, he managed to pull the joint out of Madera's right hand and take a puff.

"This guy? It says Florida but he doesn't look like a cop. I'ma check out his page likes."

"I feel so old . . . maybe dumb is the right word. Shit!" Madera giggled and said, "People like *that guy* have a facebook, but here I am, twenty and I have no clue what you're doing."

"Social media's overrated, Mad. It keeps us from looking at real life. Anyhow, this guy ain't him. Likes too many puppy pages. Looks like he was in a plumbing union?" Dewy inhaled the smoldering joint. On his exhale, he asked, "What happens after we find him?"

"Oh, I have to see what happens when we do. I don't know."

She hadn't allowed herself to think that far. Everything that needed attention was being paid its respects in due order. She was still combing through the details of her mother's murder. She wondered how her mother's stomach felt when it was shot. Over the last few days when she thought of this, her own abdomen quivered.

Madera recalled all too easily what it felt like to rest her head on her mother's strong yet soft tummy during lazy Saturday mornings. She'd curl herself under her mama's warm cotton bedsheets, pulling them halfway off her mother's body. In every season, Constance's pajamas were nothing more than halter tops and sweat shorts. Madera found great pleasure both in staring at and finger-tracing the stretch marks on her mother's stomach. *The map of your making*, as Constance called it.

"They look like tree roots," Madera noted.

"You extend from me, baby girl," Constance remarked, stroking her daughter's messy ponytail. *"Your roots lie right here, with me."*

Dewy pointed to the screen again. "None of these guys seem to be him but, I'll look again. Phil Hughes. Phil Hughes. Phil Hughes," His voice tumbled into a deeper octave. "Want another hit?"

"I'm good."

Dewy finished the joint off, killing the flame inside a beer bottle cap. He ran his smoky right hand through his wavy hair before typing "Phil Hughes" into the Facebook search box. Once again, a number of pages appeared, and he began his scrolling search.

"Wait. Click on that one!" Madera pointed to a picture of a blue-eyed baby boy.

The location of this male's residence read Chicago. There was no cover photo to the private account. The three profile pictures in public view showed this Phil Hughes to be a bearded, young college student. "Didn't know so many people have this name but . . . it is kind of generic."

Dewy then clicked on a picture of a half-bald, gray haired man. His name: Phil J. Hughes. His residence: Tamarac, Florida. His friend count: 439. His occupation: retired. His hometown: River Forest, IL. His Liked Pages: NRA, Golf Extraordinaires, Super Foods for Super People, The Eagles, Red-Winged Blackbird fans, and the CPD. His profile picture showed an informal headshot. Gray stripes above his long, wide ears and a thin strip of silver mustache. He wore a tight smirk, and his small deep-set eyes shone a weathered, stone blue.

"He looks like a pedophile," Dewy said.

"That's him. CPD. Florida. It has to be. Worthless animal. I've seen enough old, white men today. Fuck him."

A rapid roll of hard knocks sounded against Dewy's closed bedroom door. They exchanged stares as if they were being spied upon.

"Yeah?" Dewy called out, setting his tablet on his bed.

A rusty voice answered, *"Tu Tia."*

Madera stood up and moved to one of the rickety yellow stools that sat beneath Dewy's windows. Madera preferred Dewy's aunt not see her so comfortably close on his bed.

"Come in," Dewy said, his English signaling to his aunt that he had company.

Sofia was a petite woman, skin the color of copper with dyed blue-black hair. She wore a burgundy shawl and tight dark blue jeans and held a steaming black mug. As Dewy rose from his bed, Sofia's nostrils flared at the marijuana stench. Her eyes eagerly took in Madera's coy presence.

"Your bedroom felt like fire," Sofia said. "A very hot feeling—like blood boiling."

Perched on the wobbly, splintered stool, Madera began to feel the warmth Sofia was talking about. She knew she was its source.

"This is Madera—" Dewy started.

"—Of course!" his aunt responded gleefully, "I'm Sofia. Nice to meet you."

"Nice to finally meet you, too," Madera said blushing.

Unlike Amaryllis, Sofia didn't congest her nephew's space. The couple of times Madera had been there, she found herself a bit curious about her kitchen, where flowery, herbal aromas emanated, and of the back sunroom, which resonated with meditative music and chimes.

"Your bedroom door was a big, throbbing red light. You have to air out your room," *Tia* Sofia said to Dewy as she playfully slapped his chest. "Be good to your lungs, children. There's much smoke in your souls. Do not need smoke in your lungs, too," she said, this time with her eyes on Madera.

"Yes, *Tia*." Dewy gave a half smile.

"I'm serious."

Aunt Sofia downed another gulp of tea. Madera didn't know how she did it; the mug looked piping hot, and she sought coolness in herself with deep breaths in.

"Dinner will be ready shortly." Sofia locked eyes with her nephew and then wafted out the door.

"Gracias," Dewy responded.

"It's time for me to leave. There's a storm coming too, right? You know, your aunt knows everything. She looked right at me when she said we have smoke in our souls? What's that about?" Madera said giggling.

"Doesn't take a genius or a psychic to notice there's something going on with you. But don't let her scare you. These are just signs that I really need my own place."

"First, a job."

"Man, Mad, wait until this spring. I'll probably have about five graphic design gigs. Better yet, I'll be an apprentice at a tattoo parlor."

Madera tried to cling to any pocket of coolness inside her. Her jacket and scarf laid across her arm, damp and heavy like soggy life jackets. She didn't like that she was high when she met Dewy's aunt. Shrugging it off was easy as Phillip Piggy Hughes' brittle blue eyes flashed in her mind.

Dewy parked in the driveway; they had to use the kitchen side door to exit. In the kitchen, the aroma of garlic and fresh oregano was overwhelming enough, especially since it was settling into a pan of sizzling hot butter. Madera realized it wasn't Sofia in the kitchen, but someone else—A woman, the color of her mother, stood over a ceramic bowl. Her thick hair was an amethyst purple and she winced with intrigue at Madera. She wore a professional white apron and looked about forty years old. She greeted Dewy warmly.

"Hey Romi, this is Madera, my friend. And, Mad, this is Romi, my *Tia's* friend." Still buzzed, Dewy laughed at his own words.

They exchanged greetings. Madera cleared her throat and cinched her jacket. She became instantly intimidated and curious if Romi had something special about her like Sofia. The air in the kitchen was fluid like there was a fan somewhere spinning energies around the room. Surprisingly, it wasn't chaotic but managed. *Maybe this Romi woman is doing this, or maybe I'm just blazed?*

Madera took note of the small clay pots that cluttered the wooden island, herbs spilling out of them. Romi was concocting something delicious. She rotated a little Cornish hen in the ceramic bowl filled with spices and oil. Raising her eyes, she gave Madera a frisky, closed smile, then said, "Get her home safely, Dewy. There's a storm a-brewin.'"

Madera trailed out the kitchen side door eager to take in a deep breath of the promising rain.

11

THE CAR RIDE TO MADERA'S WAS HEAVY. AFTER SHE WON THE COIN TOSS for music—Led Zeppelin over Mobb Deep—Madera stared out the window as the waves of moody rock and roll silenced Dewy. The face of the murderer—Piggy—the last living person her mother saw, raced through her mind, settling the fever into her bones. Sweaty puddles formed inside her boots. *Mama, what should I do with this news? I want to go after him if I'm honest. He took you from me. He took you from this world.*

"Look at Ms. Della!" Dewy broke Madera's thoughts as he pulled up to her building.

Reigning from her wheelchair, Della docked herself three feet from Madera's building. She lifted her head up toward the sky, which hung like an old gray slate, thunderclouds stretched out like streaks of angry chalk.

"Damn, why does she look pissed all the time? Was her life really that hard?" Dewy asked.

Ms. Della looked at the pair still sitting in the car with scattered eyes. Madera knew something was on her mind.

"Yes, a hard life. Too much to get into now. You know your white-looking ass won't understand anyway."

"Stop, Mad."

Dewy never embraced his privilege; he wore it awkwardly. If anything, he was disappointed he didn't get much melanin, certainly not like his aunt. Madera never saw a picture of his mom to know what she looked like and Dewy always avoided the topic.

"Well, we found out who the beast is. Finally put a face to him. You let me know how that's all coming along? I prefer you sit with it before doing anything too crazy," Dewy said.

"Whatever I decide to do will be for the best . . . but, you have dinner waiting for you!" Madera said.

"Yes, I do." Dewy forced a smile before they said goodbye.

The first thunderclap came as Madera closed the car door. She inhaled the forthcoming rain intertwined with the diesel clouds from Dewy's Volvo as he crept off.

"Good Evening, Ms. Della," Madera said as she waved.

"Looks like your aunt is getting busy with the pig that stormed my place! You know that?" Ms. Della's big deer eyes widened.

Madera flinched. "Did you just say the same pig that stormed your place?"

"I sure did. She left outta here with him about an hour ago. All dolled up like he's taking her to some fancy restaurant. That same pig that had the nerve to spit on me after invading my bathroom! I really like your aunt, you know, but shit like that makes me want to punch the wall—if not her ass. I been waiting for her to come back just to let her know what that muthafucka did, but it's finna storm, and you know what? *You* should let her know. She's your aunt! Your blood! Let her know she's lying with the devil. It really ain't for me to tell her. That's your family, Madera. Good Evening!" Ms. Della spun her wheelchair to the right and rolled down the block to the crosswalk that would lead her home.

Madera watched the growing collection of raindrops darken the pavement. Finding a rhythm of breathing to settle on, she yanked her keys from her jacket pocket. She tried to swallow the now familiar lump of anger pinching her throat. It was too stubborn and powerful, like the rain that pounded on her jacket, on her backpack, and on her head. But, just like that volcanic drink Aunt Sofia was sipping, Madera's head was hot with rising steam. The pit of her, somewhere between her small intestines and stomach, began to churn, warming like an oven set for broil.

Dense as it was intense, the rain arrived in angry claps. The thunderstorm mirrored the blood that started to flow between Madera's legs, darkening her light blue jeans as she made her way up the stairs. A raindrop. A blood drop. An announcement of change, of replenishing, of becoming.

As she entered the apartment, Madera's temperature rose higher. She craved a way back out into the rain and its promising havoc. After removing her backpack and tossing her scarf in the hallway, she squeezed her wet arms into her leather jacket and headed out the kitchen door. Rain pellets, hard as hail, thudded against the plastic chairs on the back deck.

Madera followed the rain's discordance up the back stairs to the rooftop. Their chipped, pale blue paint cracked and crumbled at each step, exposing their corroded wooden underbelly. No other foot, no other rainy day, had ever caused such damage.

Madera reached the final step to the expansive metal rooftop. Rain pounded her eardrums, skirting along her brow. Rain slid down her scalp and neck and even found peace inside her navel. Chicago's wind seemed to take a backseat to the rain, at least in Madera's presence.

She strode to the center of the rooftop and lifted her face toward the clouds. She felt the madness of her life streak blood farther down her legs. Each rumbling cloud shook out more blood to lather the glimmering ground. Dancing bloody puddles circled her boots like little hurricanes. Receiving what the universe called upon her, Madera held out her arms and stood strong, smiling and solid. Her drenched hair hung limp, heavy, and curdled, stuck like a soaked towel to her upper back.

With each raindrop that struck her face, a curl of smoke rose. This must be the smoke from her soul. A fire determined to flare up, to chase her blood from her body and direct her to her destiny. She stayed planted in that position until half past two in the morning.

1 2

RETURNING TO THE APARTMENT IN A WEE-HOUR, RAINWATER DAZE, Madera met her reflection in the kitchen's storm door. Something looked different—something was happening to her. Her eyes were changing color. Rich brown faded to almond, to russet, to a flicker between maroon and muddy red. After she blinked one too many times, the changes stopped and her eyes reverted to their natural dark brown. She finally saw what others had.

In the kitchen, Madera noticed her backpack, ransacked. Her journals laid haphazardly on the kitchen table, a couple of sketch pads sprawled open on the floor. Her body lotion, tampons, an empty one-hitter, three lighters, a nail file, and three random crystals: lapis lazuli, carnelian and clear quartz lay about the table. Her phone sat in the middle of the kitchen counter with only 8 percent of the battery left. The red battery bar glowed sharper and brighter than Madera remembered. She picked up her phone and realized someone had used it. Clearly, Amaryllis.

Her aunt had exchanged several texts with Dewy:

"Hey this Amaryllis. Is Mad with you?"

"No. Everything ok?"

"Her stuff is here. Her bag and everything but no sign of her."

"Maybe she went for a walk? Can you let me know when she's back."

"In the rain?!"

"Just trying to be helpful."

"Keep me posted on your end. She may turn up at your place."

"Ok."

And then an incoming text from Dewy at eleven at night: "Anything? Mad? You there?"

Amaryllis (an hour later, fifteen minutes after midnight): "It's Amaryllis. Still nothing."

Dewy wasn't the only person that Amaryllis reached out to. She contacted Diane:

"Hi. This is Madera's Aunt Amaryllis. You wouldn't happen to know where she is? Do you?"

"Hi. No, I am sorry. I do not. I hope all is well."

"No. All is not well. I don't know where my niece is. If you happen to find out, please let me know."

"Absolutely. I can't help but be concerned, too. Can you have her contact me when she's back at home?"

Amaryllis didn't respond to that text. Perhaps she got too boozed up, or she still held contempt for Diane.

The thunderstorm gave Madera a breath of certainty, a divine mettle that assured a particular calling. She didn't know the details of her assignment, but she knew it was serious and had to be done: put an end to Piggy Hughes.

Madera's wet skin felt like leather. She imagined tiny ants racing along the winding roads that lined the palms of her hands. Her hair was one knotted, wet lump. It would take a mighty long shower to comb through it all. Madera peeled off her leather jacket, loosened her boots and kicked them off in the middle of the floor. A layer of sullenness, murky and cold, settled in the kitchen. It clung to the walls and hung in beads on any exposed metal; a faucet, a spoon, a key, the paper towel holder. A chill brushed over Madera's shoulders as she walked down the narrow hallway.

Amaryllis' bedroom door was ajar. Her small amber antique lamp was left on, underneath which lay scattered, balled-up tissues and a pair of handcuffs. Madera giggled, as if the thought of her aunt with the vinegar cop was truly funny. She knew if she didn't laugh she would crack or burn or sever something— or someone.

In her smiley face housecoat, Amaryllis lay on her stomach, sprawled diagonally across her bed, asleep. The backs of her feet showed a gray-tawny color from dirt, and her callouses held their usual glazed flakiness. Jimi Hendrix' "Little Wing" played softly through her phone speaker, which lay on her pillow above her messy bun. Amaryllis' bedroom, just like the kitchen, adopted the new cold, morose feeling. Everywhere Madera went, it spread. Whatever was washed out in the rainstorm, or burnt by her blood wrath, crept between her living walls to mourn. Maybe it was some kind of innocence, something sweet and kind.

Standing like a spirit herself against the bedroom door frame, Madera spotted the kneeling prayer pillow that Amaryllis crocheted for her to mark her guardianship. Intricate and detailed, the weave shone blood red with traces of gray, silver, and ivory and lay beside Amaryllis next to the mini figurine of the *La Virgen De Guadalupe*, the one Amaryllis painted just for Madera when she moved in. Madera remembered when she saw her *Tia* dip a small paintbrush into a tiny saucer filled with brown paint. Amaryllis had caught her eye and explained, "If Jesus' feet were like bronze and his hair kinky like wool, like the Bible says, and since most men resemble their mothers, then *La Virgen* looked more like you than me." Like a ghost, Madera watched her sleeping aunt. She wondered why she had those items in her bed. It was as if she were mourning her niece, as if Madera had died.

The Jimi Hendrix song played on repeat. The opening strums of the guitar chord of "Little Wing" sailed up and over Amaryllis' head. By the sound of the first chime, Amaryllis' entire body shifted onto its back, as if pulled by an unseen force. On the second chime, her head turned, facing the door where Madera stood. And when the third chime dinged, her upper body lifted, sitting straight up. Opening her eyes, she stared directly at her niece and asked, "Who are you?" Then gracefully, as if guided by the beauty of sleep, Amaryllis shut her eyes and laid back down.

LATER IN THE MORNING, WHEN AMARYLLIS WAS SOBER AND MADERA had showered, they met in the kitchen. Madera's hair was wet and combed out when she took a seat across from Amaryllis. Both aunt and niece held their cups of piping hot coffee. Before them, on paper towels, they each had a plain bagel, smothered in cream cheese and sprinkled with Valentina hot sauce.

"I had to text Diane and Dewy to let them know I'm okay. You really had to get them involved?"

Amaryllis sighed before responding. "You see, *I* pay the bills here. I am your guardian, *me entiendes*? It is important for you to communicate with me about where you are at one in the morning. I shouldn't be chasing you down in that freakish thunderstorm we had last night. *Ay Dios Mio!* I swear there was blood falling with those raindrops!" Amaryllis bit into her bagel.

"Sorry," Madera said mechanically.

"I'm . . . I'm not sure that you are." Amaryllis' eyes, the color of a deeply overcast sky, focused her eyes just behind Madera.

"Well, guardianship really doesn't exist anymore. But since I can't contribute financially, I understand your point. But I am no longer your quote-unquote-child."

Madera cradled her mug and randomly thought of Sofia sipping that piping hot tea, then of the trained coffee on the L train. The thoughts faded as Amaryllis added, "You've changed. Like literally changed since the last time I saw you. Did you make an appointment to get that blood checked out?"

"No. I've learned to embrace it."

"Whatever the hell that means. Listen, I know I am not your parent, but I've been here for you since you were ten. Give me the fucking respect I deserve while you are still in this home. You got it? Can you get that?"

"I respect you."

"You better."

"But I do have a question for you."

"What?" Amaryllis wiped a bit of cream cheese from the corner of her mouth.

"Do you know that Officer Scott was the same man that busted into Ms. Della's apartment . . . into her bathroom when she was taking a shit and spat on her? Do you know *that*?"

Amaryllis' eyes widened above her coffee mug. She slurped the hot drink down and asked, "And how would you know?"

"Della told me she saw the man that spat in her face pick you up on a date yesterday. She did tell you about the police busting in on her, right?"

"No, you told me about it . . . but Della exaggerates a lot. She's a master storyteller—she can't help it. That's not the Officer Scott I know. I know his zone or whatever it's called is near here, but I would never guess he'd do something like that."

"Wow! You really believe that?"

Amaryllis shrugged. "Were either of us there to see what happened? Huh?"

"But you're defending him."

"No. Not at all. I just happen to know a very different Officer Scott than what Ms. Della claims! Was she even close enough to know it was him? Because I didn't even see Ms. Della yesterday. And how did you see her if you were out? Oh, but I get it. Your mom was murdered by a piece of shit of a cop. Doesn't mean we can paint all cops like . . . "

"We're not talking about all cops. We're talking about one. Why would Della exaggerate about an officer who spat in her face?"

"I see you keep pressing this. What the hell should I do about it? Want me to ask him if it's true? Want me to—"

"—I want you to know who you're sleeping with. I saw those handcuffs." Madera snickered.

"Damn it, Madera! Didn't you just tell me you respect me? Huh? Did you forget what you said a minute ago? Where were you last night? Huh? That's what really needs to be dealt with. Where were *you* last night?"

"On the rooftop."

"You were on the rooftop? In that deadly storm? You were on the rooftop, *really?*"

"Yes. I was turning the rain red." Madera smiled.

She knew her aunt wasn't ready to embrace her truth. Amaryllis may have admired the mystical, but her spirit was too alcohol-clouded to see it when it was right in front of her.

"By the way, *Tia* . . . does Officer Scott even know my mother was killed by a police officer?"

"Um . . . no, that's not his business." Amaryllis let out a small belch.

Madera wasn't sure how she felt about that. Amaryllis was separating things into easy compartments—a mental trick that allowed her to ignore her niece's life story to get some action. She'd much rather Amaryllis be dating Fabian again, the wannabe Nicaraguan thug. He was so thirsty to be cool, but much better than this pig.

Amaryllis' hair, damp and wavy, danced an inch below her shoulders as her eyes narrowed with intensity.

"Are you taking drugs?" she demanded. "I'm not talking about weed. You look like your *father*. Just like him whenever he was high, so fucking high. It's like this entire building needs to be saged! Adan has returned!" Amaryllis yelled.

Standing up, Madera finished her coffee. She wiped her mouth with a paper towel and clanged her mug down on the counter.

"*Ay Dios Mio!* Mad, your eyes, again!" Amaryllis shrieked, cupping her mouth with her hand.

"Huh?"

"They look like they're red . . . wait, not anymore. Maroon? What the fuck? Listen, I'm fucking exhausted—so exhausted that I'm seeing things! That's what real stress does to you. It makes you see all kinds of crazy shit. And do yourself a favor, at work today, please, ditch the witch act!"

13

MADERA AND CATALINA SAT AT AN OVAL BAR TABLE AT THE WHISTLER'S Room, a small bar a couple doors down from Hendricks Steakhouse. With gray, cold walls, drab colors, and low lighting, the decor strived to recreate a 1920s speakeasy. Shabby vintage gray and white picture frames held photographs showing barrels of alcohol, white women in feathered headbands and painted dark lips, and grimacing crowds rocking anti-prohibition protest signs. Like a cigar tavern, the bar smelled like burnt matches, but the husky aroma here came from air diffusers that sat high on corner shelves to combat the smell of mold growing in the bar's walls.

Madera was surprised when she agreed to go to a bar after work. Usually, she'd take comfort in meeting up with Dewy for a sketch and smoke. But last night's thunderstorm shed all of her meekness, heightening her impulsivity. Stepping into a new scene felt not only refreshing but required.

Earlier, Catalina arrived at work showing off her new hair color, a deep, dark brown with caramel highlights. A few inches were cut off, but her hair was still long, kissing her bra straps. Madera and several other women coworkers complimented Catalina's new hairdo, saying it gave her an edge of mature sophistication.

Eddie, the Whistler Room bartender who served them, said, "Darling, you made one of the best decisions of your life. Yes!" He snapped his fingers, circled their bar table, and delivered two dark cocktails using his left hand like a shelf.

"You're the first guy to tell her that," Madera blurted.

Catalina's eyes widened with concern. "Really?"

"I'm not *those* guys, now." Eddie placed the drinks at their tables.

"Very true," Catalina said laughing.

"This is on the house, beauties," Eddie said and strutted off.

The cherries in the cocktails captivated Madera. For whatever reason, hues of red held her attention. During their host shift earlier, she found her focus on Catalina's burgundy fingernails. Then her eyes kept drifting to the mean glare of the exit sign above the door, and even the restroom sign.

"You come here a lot, huh? Is he your usual bartender?" Madera took a large gulp of the free rum cocktail, the cherries circling the glass's bottom.

"Yes. I'm always here on Thursdays," Catalina said. "I sit at the bar and scroll through models' instagrams with Eddie— we always end up mocking their poses. It's fucking hilarious, Madera. Give me three drinks, and bam, I'm a model."

"Ha! Well, you could be one," Madera said.

"Why, thank you," Catalina said, batting her eyes. "So . . . do you know what this bar once was?"

Madera shrugged. She scanned the walls and gathered a mellow sadness from the place. It was like someone had had a really good cry, and the energy in the room rang damp from it.

"There's like mildew or mold in the walls, I think?" Madera sipped her drink. It was strong.

"It was a 7-Eleven."

"You mean where that murder happened?" Madera tried to recall the horror of the story Amaryllis told her years ago. She took another sip, savoring the coconut flavor.

"Some crazed woman came here and killed her husband and his mistress." Catalina recounted. "They were having an affair at work, and I think it was like a night shift, no? And the wife came in with a knife and—"

"—It was a garden knife! A soil knife. I remember Amaryllis telling me this!" Madera roared remembering the newspaper picture of the man with his family. They had kids. Twins."

"That's right! She killed them both, the mistress and him, stabbed them right in their heads, right?"

"All the ways you can kill someone, she chose a garden knife?" Madera rolled her eyes. She wanted to think more on the choice of murder weapon, but Catalina was already off to the next subject.

"Isn't it cool that Eddie didn't even ask for your ID? You should go out more. At least you should go out more than your aunt! She has a good time, so why not you? Your *Tia* knows how to—how to say it? —'put it in,' something like that—when you can drink like a fish? That's Amaryllis."

"When have you been out with my aunt?"

"Oh. Several times. She has a high tolerance, and her Spanish gets super fast when she's drunk."

Madera knew this all too well. Now it dawned on her how alcoholism can be a way of life in the hospitality industry. Every day that she worked at Hendricks, Madera heard coworkers argue about the correct way to take a shot, or which energy boost was the best to get them through the next day. Some swore it was cocaine, others were Red Bull addicts, and Amaryllis chugged her Baileys and coffee. The coworkers only agreed on drinking copious amounts of spirits after work.

"Yeah, by the way, I've been meaning to ask you about something that happened like a week or so ago," said Madera.

"*Que?*"

"Were you around when my aunt got hit with a glass in her face?"

"I heard about it." Catalina's gaze shifted back and forth.

"What did you hear?"

"There was some drunk lady at the bar at the end of her shift. It was your first shift, actually! And *este* . . . the woman said that your aunt was ignoring her because she was too busy talking to Officer

Scott. I guess he came back to the bar that night after his shift. He was in uniform. I can't believe someone would throw a glass at a bartender in front of a cop, *verdad?* But people do all kinds of crazy shit. Why? Why'd you ask?"

"I just wanted to know if you were there, if you saw it happen." Madera shrugged, figuring that was a good enough excuse. She didn't want Catalina sniffing out her distrust for her aunt.

"Yeah, well, I probably should be honest with you. Officer Scott definitely has the hots for your *Tia.* He calls her his hot tamale," Catalina said with a laugh.

Madera's nostrils flared. What was up with cops or men or men cops referring to women as food? Drumsticks from killer Piggy Hughes and calling a Mexican woman a hot tamale from Officer vinegar? And, of course, Catalina thought it was funny.

"In front of her?" Madera sipped her cocktail.

Catalina suppressed a nervous smile, "It's kind of racist what he says, right?"

Before Madera could release her frustrations, she locked eyes with a patron walking into the bar—a woman with a vivid red bob and familiar light brown, maybe hazel, eyes. Maybe a white woman, maybe not. Her mouth was a little round, her nose a little wide, and she looked so familiar. Was she one of her mother's old friends, or maybe Madera greeted her at Hendricks? Madera didn't want to stare, but the woman's blood red hair color is what did it. It was magnetizing. She was accompanied by a Black man in a tan trench coat.

Catalina peered over her shoulder to see what snagged Madera's attention.

"She's beautiful," Catalina said. And then, like a toddler, she spun around in the bar's rotary black stool. "Maybe I should dye my hair red."

Dismissing Catalina's call for attention, Madera studied the pair as the man took a bag of carryout from Eddie's hands. He turned gradually toward the redhead just as she relocked eyes with Madera. The woman's eyes seemed to glitch with a haywire program, and they held a tender yearning. It was as if she wanted to tell Madera a secret.

The woman dropped her gaze when the man nudged her with his elbow. The redhead spun around as if inebriated, stood on her tiptoes and whispered into the man's ear. Led by spirit, the duo locked their arms like little toy soldiers; they were on a mission, rather than a romantic interlude. Madera tried to get a look at the man's face, but it was shaded beneath a wide-brimmed fedora. Could he be the Coffee Magician, or did he just look like him? With the bag clenched tightly in his other hand, the pair exited the restaurant.

Bolting from her stool, Madera hurried after them. Swinging the door open, autumn's wind flocked to tickle her ear drums. The couple dipped across the street in bounding strides, neither looking back over their shoulders. Madera was left in the dark to realize the sky was missing a moon tonight. She coughed and retreated inside the bar.

Catalina waved Madera over. "Come on, you have to get in this pic!" The brunette hostess held her phone high with her right arm, camera facing in selfie position, and pulled Madera into the stool next to her. She clicked away madly, hollering out photo captions. "Hashtag drunk and pretty. Hashtag hostess with the mostess. Hashtag white girl and Black girl. Hashtag Latinas. Hashtag brunettes do it better. Hashtag threesome dreams. Hashtag bar. Hashtag Chicago nightlife. Hashtag Hendricks Steakhouse. Hashtag Argentina gems. Hashtag Dama de Argentina. Hashtag Latinas do it better. Hashtag party girls. Hashtag What you see is what you get. Hashtag—"

"—Girl, enough!" Eddie broke the photoshoot and placed another round of drinks before them. Catalina immediately started scrolling through the images on her phone. Sighing, Madera settled back onto her stool. The bar cherries sat in their cocktails like blood clots. Grudgingly, she chugged her new cocktail and thought of the couple she'd chased after. If that was the Coffee Magician he certainly knew how to clean himself up. And the woman—how did she know her?

"Did you seriously run after that woman?" Catalina snickered, face still in her phone.

"I thought I knew that man. And her, too." Madera belched. "Oh, excuse me. They were already across the street when I got out there."

The rum gave Madera a warm, rising feeling, like she was perched on a cloud. The rooftop experience left her feeling like she could be anything she wanted. This sensation mirrored what Amaryllis described as the feeling cocaine gave her father. *Maybe this is how alcohol feels the day after a life-altering thunderstorm?*

Bold and capable, Madera recognized the urge to leave Catalina to her hashtags and go see Dewy. She ordered an uber.

At a quarter past midnight, Madera stepped out of the Uber facing Sofia's brown bungalow. Her thighs were spongy. During the car ride, the alcohol settled, and her tipsiness found new height.

Madera's plan wasn't to surprise Dewy, she just didn't feel the need to prepare him. Rather than calling him when she arrived, she tapped at his bedroom window. At the twelfth tap, Dewy opened his curtains and lifted his window as far as it could go.

"Yo! Everything alright? How you get here?"

"Uber, Uber, Uber," Madera said, climbing in. She jumped down to Dewy's bedroom floor and spun around. "I have to pee real bad!" She didn't recognize the volume of her voice until Dewy pressed his index finger to her mouth.

"You're wasted!"

Dewy stuck his tongue out, repulsed. Interlacing his fingers with hers, Dewy quietly led Madera into the hall toward the bathroom. There were voices through the home. Someone was humming an old-fashioned tune. Something smelled strong, like the burning of garden herbs or just hot, fragrant oil. Whatever the smell, it gave Madera ritual vibes and sunk into her pores as if to either cleanse her out or cast her out. She felt intrusive, but excited.

"It's just my aunt and her friends." Dewy explained as a man emerged from the bathroom.

Sporting eyes like an intense villain, the older man's hair was black and luscious with just the right amount of facial hair. He wore a button-up cobalt blue shirt and a pair of light blue jeans. Madera blushed.

"Excuse me," he said as Madera slithered past him. Their auras grazed each other.

"This is my friend, Madera." Dewy said, standing back a bit.

Out came one of Madera's gargle-like giggles as she hurriedly closed the bathroom door before hearing the man's name.

Back down the hall, settling into his smoke haven of a room, Dewy snickered. "What the fuck Mad, why are you so drunk?"

"Is that your aunt's boyfriend or something?" Madera changed the subject.

"No, that's Oscar. My aunt entertains a lot. Not like that—She has a lot of different people here. All of them are good, trust me. Anyways, where'd you drink?"

"Catalina took me to that Whistler's Room next door. Then I saw the Coffee Magician with some redhead lady that looked—"

Dewy flinched at the mention of the woman.

"—Nevermind! I'm, yes, tipsy. I guess I could be drunk."

Madera sat at the edge of her friend's bed and carelessly took off her boots. Dewy was wearing silver gym shorts and a teal t-shirt with a hole in the right shoulder. He scratched his head.

"I kind of want to doodle on you but probably not when you're like this."

"Where'd you want to doodle on me, Dewy? It may turn you on, huh?"

"Oh, I'm always turned on . . . " Dewy laughed before saying, "You wanna smoke?"

"Sure. Um, any idea how much a ticket to Florida is?"

"Oh, shit. You found out what you want to do, huh?"

"I just want to know."

"Google it, Mad. But what's your plan?"

"Ugh. Not exactly sure but I think he needs to die," Madera stated matter-of-factly.

"Sleep on it. You're drunk. One time I got drunk and I thought I was going to turn the world into vegans."

"That don't make sense. You're not even vegan."

"My point."

"Well, that sounds like some high shit, not drunk shit."

"I still think you should sleep on it." Dewy packed marijuana into his turquoise bowl. His ounce of weed sat beside him in a yellow-tint mason jar that he stored under his bed, as if he really needed to hide it.

Madera, dressed in all black as her uniform called for, leaned back. She rested her elbows on Dewy's squishy bed. His mattress had random lumpy spots, like a waterbed. She struggled to get comfortable and then plopped back onto it.

"My point, again," Dewy said laughing.

"So what! I think he needs to die. That simple! An eye for a motherfuckin' eye. Like, why not? He shot my mom in her stomach like some kind of rag doll. But I—I won't do it with a gun. Maybe poison. I have to think that through. There's so many ways to kill someone."

"Well, you definitely have intent." Dewy lit the bowl, raising it to his mouth. He drew a long inhale.

Madera, staring up at the ceiling, pondered, *How?* She knew that saving up for a ticket could take up to Christmastime, especially factoring in how much of her money she was going to give her *Tia* to help at home. She didn't want to wait until next year, but that was starting to look like the best thing to do. It would be perfect to go in the middle of Chicago's winter anyway. Perhaps February, if she had enough patience.

"Would you come with me?"

"To Florida? You're serious about this?"

"You think I'm not?"

"This is some serious shit." Dewy laid beside his friend and passed her the bowl.

Accepting it, Madera sat up to properly hit it. She crossed her legs first, settling her eyes on *The Wounded Deer* replica of Frida Kahlo mounted on the back of his bedroom door. The red blood coming out of the Frida deer stole her eyes.

"I know. I know it's serious. I also know it's possible to do without getting caught. I think drugging him is the best way to go."

"You need some real strategic plotting—after some real ass praying. But something tells me praying may tell you what you don't wanna hear."

"Yeah, I know you like to think so. He needs to die. And the only thing that will stop me is if he dies before *I* get to him. But it needs to be painful. I'm not sure how you can make it painful without leaving evidence. What kind of poison is slow and painful?"

"You know this won't bring your mother back and—"

"—Blah . . . blah. Enter the school counselor's talk."

She felt a little queasy. The combination of rum and weed didn't pair well in her unfledged system. Declining the next offering of marijuana, Madera settled for the bit of relief she found on Dewy's one long pillow.

"Your fucking pillow needs air in it," she laughed.

"Let's just talk about it tomorrow. We can fall asleep watching Woodstock if you want?"

"You're obsessed with that documentary," Madera groaned.

"It's the best! People getting lost in the crowds and shit. Days before you could google how to poison someone. And, Mad, don't throw up on my bed."

"Ha, ha. Don't tease me," Madera said and belched. "I'll gladly poison someone! It was, you know, last night I was on the fucking rooftop drenched in the rainstorm, blood gushing out of me like I was some kind of monster."

Standing up to put his weed away, Dewy nearly yelled, "What the fuck is going on with that?"

"I don't know."

"You're not dying, are you?"

"I kind of feel like I am right now. "

"No, you're just drunk, but you do need to take your ass to the doctor!"

"You sound like my *Tia*. Oh shit, let me text her." Madera reached for her little black purse that sat between her heeled black boots.

"If you're bleeding for no reason, you need to see a doctor, Mad."

"I think it's a sign. A sign to kill that motherfucker!" Madera texted Amaryllis: *Don't worry, I'm at Dewy's.*

"You don't need to kill that man. You just need to write him a letter. Let it all out and—"

"—Write him a letter? Are you fucking kidding me right now? Why would I write someone who killed my mother a letter? Go ahead and send my feelings off? Stamp it and drop it in the mailbox? That pig has no soul! He got away with it. He got away with it, Dewy. He killed my mother. He took her *away from me.* Why would I write him a letter?"

"Okay, maybe that was some dumb shit I just said but . . . " Setting his laptop on the yellow stool, Dewy turned, alarmed at the sound of Madera heaving.

"Come on. Come on. Come on." Dewy nearly chanted in a rushed tone. He leaped to Madera, tugging at her arms to lift her up.

She swayed, "Damn, Dewy. I can manage."

The bathroom door was open. A young, curvy dark-skinned Black woman, wearing an oversized green hoodie, stood at the sink wringing out a soggy hand towel. She stared with large, gentle eyes, yet she was puzzled by Dewy and Madera's appearance. Of course, Madera noticed the young woman's painted red mouth. And there was Romi, with her amethyst hair, sitting on the closed-lid toilet with a curious face.

"Oh, shit! She's gotta puke!" Dewy said as he approached the bathroom door.

Romi hopped off the toilet seat and said, "Then bring her in, Dewy. You know we don't bite!"

Madera noticed a slight Spanish accent from Romi as she lifted the lid.

"I'm just dizzy, Dewy! And . . . who is she?" Madera mumbled, kneeling down in front of the toilet but staring at the girl in the hoodie.

"I'm Adora," said the woman. Her velvety red lips looked like the inside of a rose petal. Her hands moved in a pattern as she twisted the dripping towel. "Good thing your hair's in a ponytail."

"A *lot* of hair—and Mars energy. Never mind us. You focus on getting *that* out," Romi advised.

Like a toddler eager for sensory play, Madera grew an unexpected urge to grab Adora's red lips to feel their texture. Madera closed her eyes and clutched the toilet seat instead. Her mind raced, *What does Mars energy mean?*

"Why don't you go to the kitchen to get her some water, Dewy?" Romi suggested.

"Yeah, or I can." Adora folded the white washcloth into fours.

Then Madera vomited. The sugary bar cherries tumbled out almost completely whole, orbiting the inside of the toilet bowl like little planets. The remains of the alcohol scorched its way passed Madera's throat, trickled and splashed into the bowl. Wiping drool from her bottom lip before it could graze her chin, Madera lifted her gaze to Adora. Although young, Adora had a wide, generous face that shined a calm wisdom. Adora and Romi stood on either side of the open bathroom door; a pair of pillars at the gate. With focused eyes and closed mouths, both observed the ruddy blush spreading across Madera's face.

"You should talk to Sofia soon," Adora advised. Madera wasn't sure if she was addressing her or Romi.

Dewy reappeared with a glass of water. "Thank you," Madera and Dewy said simultaneously; Madera to Dewy, Dewy to the women.

"You're a good friend, Dewy." Romi said before she turned to leave the bathroom.

Adora, gripping her folded towel, peered over her shoulder one more time to nod at Madera before leaving down the hall. Her eyes were soothing, reminding Madera of her mother's last touch, her hands on her scalp when she was trying to braid cornrows in her hair. That calm feeling, like soothing aloe.

Reaching for the glass of water, Madera stood up, one leg at a time. "Your aunt hangs out with that young one?"

"Drink up," Dewy said, rubbing Madera's back.

After chugging the full glass of water, Madera began quizzing him. "What the fuck is Mars energy? And Adora said I should talk to your aunt?"

"I have no idea, but do you feel better?" Dewy shrugged, taking the glass from her hands.

Madera turned to look in the mirror. Her face was burning. Like vomit, words tumbled out her mouth. "Wrath. Wrath is Mars. Violence. Aggression. Action. Drive. Passion. That's Mars." Answers to her own question.

Leaning against the door frame, Dewy winced and ran his hand through his hair. "Do you feel better?" he asked again.

"Yes, but I think I need to sleep."

Sagging and depleted, Madera latched onto Dewy's arm.

"Come, let me take you home."

14

The season of Amaryllis' festivities arrived: first her birthday, then Halloween, and lastly, Day of the Dead. The wind was kind, the air was crisp, and store windows were blooming with pumpkins, gourds, and cinnamon brooms when Madera traveled to a flower shop downtown on Amaryllis' birthday. Even though nights were getting longer, Madera favored the fall season. Still not ready to pack up her maroon jacket, she layered herself with a thermal undershirt and an extra scarf.

She found the perfect slender glass vase of red amaryllis flowers to match all the red hues of autumn that were competing for her gaze. As the L train rattled back west, she watched the reflection of the rich red blooms in the train window. Beside the vase, a paper bag from the deli leaked the aroma of cured meats. She looked forward to watching Amaryllis carefully roll the pork slices into cigarettes before washing them down with a hefty glass of red wine. Sure, they may have been on each other's last nerves lately, but Madera always held onto what her mother said, *Never been much of a champion for killing people with kindness, because that just makes you phony. But you gotta treat people nice on their birthdays. That's just a given. Celebrate the life that gets on your nerves if you have to. Just about everyone deserves love on their birthday.*

As she walked up the three floors and entered the flat, Madera felt the steam from the radiators sizzling hotter than usual. She slid her boots off and placed the vase of flowers on the kitchen table. They were lovely, strong, and pretty—all the words she, as a ten-year-old, labeled her aunt. After setting the cured meats in a circular pattern on a gold and red colored plate, Madera watered the plants. A bubbly pop song she heard blaring from a pre-teen's cell phone on the L train found a home in her head. She hummed the tune while watering and removing dead leaves—even the ones on the floor she usually ignored. Severus, the snake plant, stood three feet tall. He hadn't really grown since she blessed him last time. His waxy leaves were lackluster like ashy knees. Madera cupped her hands around Severus and, rubbing the dust off his leaves, she prayed for his shine to restore.

Sweeping up the fallen leaves of the Boston fern, Madera caught a whiff of vinegar. Typically, around the first of the month, Amaryllis would clean the hardwood floors with a touch of apple cider vinegar mixed with olive oil. It was something she read in a witch book. She even had a particular pattern of sweeping the floor to release negative energy. But today would be a tad early for that chore. Plus, who the hell wanted to clean on their birthday?

Knowing her aunt was sleeping in from her late shift at Hendricks last night, Madera hummed quietly until she heard Amaryllis' bedroom door open. She spotted a flash of her aunt walking down the long hallway and into the bathroom, closing its door lightly. Madera thought to seize the moment and make her *Tia's* bed—Amaryllis had a bad habit of not making it. Bashfully, Madera tiptoed toward the half-open bedroom door. She felt like a nervous five-year-old with a pounding heart. As she reached the doorway, she picked up a smell from Amaryllis' room—a stench she was never fond of—when she saw something move. Someone was sitting on the bed. A gray and black flannel shirt was being buttoned up by none other than Officer Scott. And, just like an officer, he sensed her and turned his head over his shoulder.

"Good Morning," he said with something that looked like a wink— Madera wasn't sure; Maybe her presence irritated his eyes.

"You're that nervous hostess. Don't you have a pretty mouth," he said standing up.

"Excuse me?" Madera flashed her response like lightning on a mission.

She spotted the pair of handcuffs, this time resting on top of her aunt's comforter next to a whip with feathers at the tip. The room reeked of sex.

"You're Amaryllis' niece. I see some resemblance. Do you two have a lot in common?"

Madera sniffed a rank odor in his question, a seedy and toxic suggestion. Nauseated, Madera gripped the door frame.

Amaryllis reappeared in a pearly satin robe. She smelled of peppermint Listerine.

"Happy birthday," Madera mumbled, knowing she would never use that same mouthwash again.

"Thank you," said Amaryllis shakily.

Under the satin, her aunt's bosom perked, held firm in a tight brassiere.

"There's swine on the kitchen table," Madera announced. "I know how much you like pig. So, I got you some, and I don't know what you had planned for the day but—"

"—He's taking me to a play," Amaryllis answered, unblinking.

Her straightforward ease pinched Madera to the core. "Oh," Madera mumbled.

"Join us at Hendricks afterwards? They're giving anyone cele-brating with me an hour of open bar. You should come out. I think Catalina is going."

"Okay. Maybe."

"Bring Dewy if you want. Open bar at nine. Maybe I'll see you there." Amaryllis nodded before closing her bedroom door.

All things do change when the police show up.

Biting her bottom lip, Madera took out her sketchpad and strug-gled to find solace in her room. That pig called her mouth pretty! She wanted to snatch it off her face, seal it with some duct tape, put a mask over it. As she formed flowing women's bodies on paper, she heard soft music playing. Both women had a habit of blasting their music through the day, hollering over the sounds to hear each other, and irritating Mr. Glass who lived below them. Only at night did they lower the volume. Now, the radio played so low that Madera could hear Amaryllis' laughter through the closed bedroom door. Loud laughter and exaggerated footsteps, like a live stage play, intertwined with Officer Scott's voice; pompous and edgy, playing the part of the school bully no one wanted to fight. Madera wouldn't be surprised to see them galloping together down the hallway, arms interlaced like Irish folk dancers. She wished Dewy was there to witness the performance. Actually, she wished she was at Dewy's house. Maybe she could spy on his aunt and her friends. What an odd bunch—and Adora with the red lips had to be in her twenties. Madera found herself pondering two competing thoughts: calling Dewy to vent and opening the door so she could scream. She had the idea to grab the white mug from her altar and shove it in Officer Scott's face, reminding him he had dropped something.

Instead, she turned to her mother's picture on her altar with the fact that the happy glints in Constance's eyes were wiped out by a man who oinked in people's faces. Officer Piggy Hughes' frigid blue eyes were etched in her mind. *And this lowlife took my mother away from me?*

Resting in her feelings, blood erupted from between Madera's legs. Hot and scratchy, it trickled down her legs like lava. The blood wrapped around her bare feet, filling the spaces between her toes, cushioning her heels and calluses. It itched. She didn't want to stand in it any longer and watch the bloodbath expand across her bedroom floor—But it did, and the pool of blood seeped right under her door.

Down the hall, Madera heard the stereo turn off. An excited anxiety latched onto her. Did the bloody fountain reach Amaryllis' room? Would she and her pig freak out? She heard only a man's cough, then the clicks and locks of the front door.

Without a word, they were leaving.

Did they not see the blood out in the hallway? Didn't it chase them out?

"Hello?" Madera hollered, sweaty palm slowly turning her door-knob. The long hardwood hallway lay bare, clean. Nothing. Not a drop of blood. She turned around. Nothing on her bedroom floor either. Glancing down at her legs, the scarlet stream had disappeared. The blood had come; The blood had gone.

"It happened again. I am fucking magic!" Madera shrieked.

15

AT THE OPEN BAR CELEBRATION OF AMARYLLIS' THIRTY-SEVENTH birthday, little silver skulls holding fake marigolds were aesthetically placed between liquor bottles. Orange-flamed, black votive candles decorated the bar top for Halloween and *Dia De Los Muertos* just days away.

Madera, in an indigo turtleneck dress, arrived early. Her hair slicked back in a high bun so tight it tugged at the skin around eyes. Her pout was glossy. She had to convince herself to adore her mouth while getting ready. She wasn't going to allow some funky cop to have so much power over her body. Madera also wore the bloodstone that Amaryllis gifted her years ago. More and more she gravitated to the precious stone. It bounced against her chest as she walked.

The solemn sounds of Radiohead played softly overhead, lyrics audible only to those who loved such music. Taking a seat facing the brown liquors, Madera mumbled the words to the song, "Black Star."

Dewy placed his phone in his leather jacket, slid his hand through his ruffled hair, and cringed at himself in the mirror at the bar's back-splash. Madera could tell he hadn't a clue what to wear. His wrinkled burgundy tie sat sloppily against a black button-up shirt. Nonetheless, Madera was overjoyed that he was able to accompany her—even if he could only stay thirty minutes. He was due at another birthday party in the west suburb of Elmhurst. His father's birthday. Another quiet story. Madera knew very little about him. She knew he had money— money Dewy didn't like to accept for whatever reason. On the car ride over, he said he wasn't too thrilled about going but it was something he felt he had to do.

"Better soak up the time with me now," he told Madera.

Across the room, Catalina laughed hysterically with a patron. Of course, the hostess had gone back blonde. Too blonde, like a dollar store Barbie doll, wearing a sleek, black jersey wrap dress. Her lips were painted a burgundy matte. She bounced over and laid her hand on the top of Dewy's chair.

"Hey, lady!" Madera tapped Catalina's hand.

"Your tie matches my lips. You must be the infamous Dewy! So very pleased to meet you!" Catalina said, batting her lashes.

"Oh. Nice to meet you, too. You have to be Catalina, no?"

"Of course! Your family is from Columbia, right?" Catalina blushed. Her breath smelled of coffee and wine and chocolate. She flirted because she never knew what else to do.

"Yes," said Dewy as he cleared his throat and adjusted his tie.

Madera eyed Dewy and whispered, "It's okay. I know, she's poisonous. She can't help it. Just let her flirt. Your time here may just go faster." Then she moved her gaze to Marvin.

Like Amaryllis, Marvin was a senior bartender. He was Filipino and in his early forties with a beer belly and a hipster beard that contrasted his hairless head. He wore thick dark eyeglasses, and his left wrist was adorned with threaded bracelets from his worldly travels.

"Madera, you made it out! Where's Amaryllis?"

Madera shrugged.

"Yeah, well if she's not here in twenty minutes, no more free booze. So, what's your deal? You drinking something tonight?"

"I'll have vodka and soda with lime. What about you, Dewy?" Madera nudged her friend, who was trying out his awkward Spanish with Catalina.

"Gotta drive, remember?" Dewy answered, still facing Catalina.

"Ugh. Do you really have to go? Can you get him a coffee, Please?"

"Black?" Marvin asked.

"Sure. Whatever."

Madera straightened her posture, scanning the gradually growing crowd of Amaryllis' regular patrons as Marvin brought their drinks.

"Thank you."

"Mad, why don't you bring out this *guapo* more often? You have to get him together and then show him off. I'll be back. I forgot to clock out—shush!" Catalina said and then sauntered away.

"She's a handful. Did she really just side roast my attire? She told you to get me together," Dewy said.

"No shit. I told you. Did she flirt hard with you? She's not your type, is she?"

"Nah. She kept rambling about her hometown and everything she misses about it."

"Did you pretend to understand her?" Madera teased.

"Now you already know, I *know* my Spanish." Dewy's eyes landed on the cup of coffee in front of him. "This mine?" he asked.

Before Madera could answer, the birthday lady arrived in the short, snug black dress and spiked-heel boots Madera found for her last summer in a consignment shop. Amaryllis carefully worked up her look for the occasion: her large, almond eyes popped under the marriage of mascara and eyeliner. She'd painted her lips an electric ruby red and done her hair in two layers—a bun up top and loose, wavy curls on the bottom.

Amaryllis' gaze was sultry. She must've been a few drinks in already. She and Officer Scott walked arm in arm toward the bar, nodding to all from an invisible red carpet. Madera wanted to gag.

"There you are!" Marvin announced. He acknowledged Officer Scott with a, "Richard! Of course."

"Richard, huh?" Dewy muttered, sipping his hot coffee. In the bar mirror he locked eyes with Madera. "Never knew his first name."

"That makes sense since you've never met him. His first name should be asshole. But I guess it's Dick," Madera said, sucking in her laughter.

Madera felt her aunt's warm beating heart against her shoulder and cleared her throat, "Ahem."

"Gracias, *sobrina*. So glad you came out," Amaryllis said through puckered red lips against her niece's cheek.

"And, Dewy! Richard, I'd like you to meet Dewy, Madera's best friend," Amaryllis nodded between the two parties.

Dewy stood up and the two men shook hands. Richard's handshake looked mighty, but his eyes flinched. He straightened his posture as if to outrank Dewy in height, succeeding by only half an inch.

Dewy released his hand when Marvin sat Richard's gin on the bar.

"Cheers," Richard said, picking up his drink eagerly and raising it in mock toast to no one in particular.

"Looks like you brought the stone out," Amaryllis said to Madera as she placed her fingers on her own chest.

"Ya, I did," she answered.

"I loved the flowers. And the pig. Of course, the *pig*." Amaryllis mocked, pulling on Richard's suit pocket.

"Oink, oink," Richard responded.

Madera held back a sneeze before turning it into a deep exhalation. Madera had seen enough of these two today. They were so frisky and annoying—as if they've been together for years and were trying to embarrass their children or something. She really wasn't feeling Amaryllis' forced demeanor either. And it wasn't the alcohol. Who waits until they're inebriated and in public view to thank someone for their birthday gifts? It's gotta be the same person okay with being called a hot tamale.

Then the drinking started. Back-to-back cocktails were served and as the crowd grew, the music got louder. Amaryllis' birthday crew took over the left side of the bar, overflowing into a couple of bar tables behind them. Amaryllis hopped from table to table, juggling conversations and people as if she were on the clock.

Standing up from his stool, Dewy swallowed his last bit of coffee.

"You gotta go, huh?" Madera said.

"I don't wanna go. Shit, to be honest, I'm afraid you're going to hurt Dick—I mean Richard. Call me later," Dewy said. His mouth was so close to Madera's ear that his lips glided along her cartilage. Her ear tingled as she felt the beginnings of her inhibition leave with him.

As if claiming the last spot of musical chairs, Richard pounced onto Dewy's old stool. Madera tasted the word "repulsion" on her tongue. Amaryllis was bantering about politics to a couple of coworkers and swinging her curls over her shoulder.

Bravely, Madera turned toward Richard as he finished off his gin and placed it on the bar. She sneezed. *Why am I the only one to smell the vinegar on this man?*

"Madera? Interesting name," he said. "Never heard of anything like it. What does it mean?"

"My mother was a rebel is all I can really say."

"Oh, now what does that mean?" He poked, unimpressed.

"Mad. Like, M-A-D. You know, the feeling. Like, *angry*. And the 'era' end of my name. So, I'm an era that is mad."

The officer gave a peculiar frown, his bottom lip curled up over his top lip. "Would you say your name is fitting?"

"I guess it's as fitting as your smell." Madera reached for her cocktail she'd been nursing as Marvin gave the officer another gin.

Richard smiled playfully. "You are definitely your aunt's niece."

"Is that a compliment?"

"You tell me, Mad-*era*. Let me guess, I smell like a pig?" he snorted.

"Ugh, like pickled bologna."

"I witnessed these immature interactions between you and your aunt today. I don't know if you are like fifteen or—or what? Should you even be drinking? Hope you're legal or I'll have to shut this place down."

"I'm twenty-two, officer." With this lie, Madera finished her drink. She wondered if he thought she was as young as fifteen when he commented about her mouth earlier.

Madera cradled her cold glass between her hands. She yearned for something more to cool her down, the heft of her turtleneck dress weighing against her skin.

"Good to know. Are you in school?"

"Harold Washington."

"That downtown community college? Always swarms of people hanging out front—no one appears to be studying."

"Well, I am." She ignored his slur on the entire student body, mostly Black and Brown, and perhaps on the man the college was named for—Chicago's first Black mayor.

"What's your plan?" Richard asked, his eyes lingering on Catalina's backside as she passed by.

"Not really sure. I'm only taking two classes this semester. Thinking psychology or maybe social work. Did you always know you wanted to be a cop?"

"Yes. Actually, yes. Since I was about three years old. I used to play good guys and bad guys until sunset every damn night. I have three cousins in the force, too. I thought about being a fisherman but that didn't last long. I'm now a cop that loves to fish," he said.

"Fish for what? Women?" Madera wasn't holding back as her stomach heated up. She waved at Marvin. He gave her a simple nod and made her another cocktail.

"Not so much anymore. Just bad guys. Bad guys and sailfish, tarpons, trout. Why? You fish?"

"Are all the guys you catch bad?"

"You're funny. Let me see. My biggest catch was a loudmouth Black." He released the words slyly, eager to revel in her response.

Did he just say a loudmouth Black? Madera's head throbbed. Marvin slid Madera her cocktail and hurried to a patron at the other end of the bar.

"Black bass fishing, that is," Richard joked.

In hopes of cooling down, Madera chugged her drink. The cocktail's crushed ice slid sharply down her throat, but it went down smoother than Richard's words. Sure enough, she felt blood flowing. "That shit's not funny," she said.

"I'm talking about fishing . . . *Mad* . . . *era*. I knew you wouldn't like my humor. Just a wild guess on my part," Richard snickered. "I go fishing every April. A couple of officers and I go to Florida for black bass game fishing. One of my favorite things to—" he began coughing.

Madera struggled to examine herself while holding still. The last thing she wanted was blood oozing from her dress, but shockingly, nothing flowed. Her blood was quite well behaved. Richard, though, grew more intense in his short, sharp, angry coughs. Madera's flesh steamed as she spotted little dots of blood on the cherrywood floor.

Amaryllis' jaw dropped, "Richard! You okay?"

With a racing heart and a hot chest like rocks under a July sun, Madera was too nervous to move. The blood wasn't coming from her. The blood was coming out of Richard's mouth. Frantically, he snatched a pile of beverage napkins from their holder and slapped them over his face. He rose like a trained dog as Amaryllis led him back into the narrow hall toward the bathrooms.

Madera didn't understand how the flow of her blood between her legs stopped, dried up or—was just placed somewhere else? She'd felt the same instant fever, the red knot in her core, and imagined the fountain flowing between her legs. But where did the blood go? It must have gone to Officer Scott.

Catalina placed her hand on her own forehead as if a Barbie doll manipulated by a child. A biker couple, regular fans of Amaryllis, aimed matching looks of puzzlement at Madera, who responded with an instinctual shrug. She realized her lack of words made her vulnerable, but what could she say?

"What was that about?" Marvin's whisper made Madera flinch. She spun her stool around, grabbing the cold bar for a touch of security.

"I have no idea," Madera lied.

"That was serious. Ugh. You see the other half of my bar? Don't look now, though. Disgusting! This better not be contagious," Marvin said in a low voice. He sprayed a damp, white bar towel with diluted bleach spray. Skeptically, but wearing kitchen gloves, he cleaned Richard's area then asked Madera, "Want another one?"

"No. No, thank you."

"Mad? Mad!" A distressed Amaryllis called out from the hallway.

Her calls stung Madera like a swarm of bees. Madera nervously pulled herself from the stool and checked it one more time to make sure there was no blood. Richard was nowhere in sight. With an impatient eye roll, Amaryllis motioned her niece toward the restrooms.

"He's in the bathroom?" Madera asked as she followed her aunt, the bar crowd behind them picking up their stifled conversations again.

"Where else would he be? Look—what happened?"

"I don't know. I heard him cough, looked up, and there was blood coming out his mouth. I didn't see it before you did." Madera folded her arms around her chest. Her left hand clutched her bloodstone.

"Fuck, Madera. His blood is on your stone." Amaryllis yanked her niece's hand from the crystal, pulled her into the restroom, and unhooked the necklace.

"Are you serious? Ew!" Madera stuck her hands under the automatic faucet and water sprayed carelessly against the white porcelain sink and onto her turtleneck dress. None of the blood from the bloodstone stained her dress.

"There's *a lot* of blood coming from his mouth like a . . . like a fucking *volcano*," Amaryllis said as she washed the bloodstone she'd given her niece years ago. "He doesn't want to go to the hospital which doesn't make any sense to me, but . . . fuck, I'm not his wife. I'm not his mom—"

"—He has *a wife?*" Madera scowled.

"No! He better fucking not. No. No. He doesn't. I mean, I can't demand he go anywhere." Amaryllis patted the stone with paper towels and clasped it around her niece's neck. "Let me just say good-night to everyone out there, and let's go home. You and me. Just the two of us. We can watch something or play something or just go to bed. But I'm not spending the night with a sick man. We should clean up our altars and wash our crystals. Just because—well, it's my birthday."

"Whatever you want," Madera said, smiling. "I still don't have to like your friend."

"Did he give you another reason tonight? Too many negative tally marks, huh? We can talk later."

They walked out to have one last round at the bar. Amaryllis clung to Richard as he exited the bathroom. Madera proudly watched her aunt give Richard a rather pathetic kiss on his cheek as he decided to make his way on home.

1 6

"What did the doctor say?" Dewy asked as soon as Madera sat down in the passenger's seat.

With an apple between her teeth, Madera struggled to fasten her belt. "She doesn't know. It made no sense to her. Well, she told me to document it and reach back if anything."

Truthfully, her doctor's visit was foggy, already sort of a fleeting memory like trying to capture nature scenes from a moving vehicle. Pressured no less than five times by Amaryllis to make an appointment since Richard's bloody spillage at the bar, Madera lucked out and snagged a time later that week. Nothing came out of it—except for the apple Madera plucked from an overflowing basket brought by one of her doctor's patients.

"Never seen ruby red apples like this before. I couldn't keep my eyes off 'em," Madera said as she crunched.

"An apple a day keeps the doctor away, right?" Dewy said with a little chuckle. "But seriously though, Mad. I'm glad she didn't find anything wrong with you. Let's go back to my place. We can have a good smoke, clear your head."

"Sure. Thanks for taking me here. Glad you didn't have to wait too long," Madera softened, watching Dewy shift into reverse.

Madera's lips felt a bit dry. The day was nippy. Channel 7 forecast a high of 47 degrees, but Chicago's wind made it feel like 39. Madera swapped her maroon jacket for her black bubble down which was longer and grazed her hips. With her right leg over her knee, she leaned toward Dewy for warmth.

"Remember that dream your aunt had about blood pouring from your mouth?" she asked.

"Yeah. Why?"

"That dick cop had blood coming out his mouth and Amaryllis said his doctor had no clue why." Madera took the last bite of the apple.

"Blood is in the air! Oh, shit. We about to die. A bloody massacre is upon us. Look out, everybody! Blood will be in your dreams! In your nightmares!" Dewy hollered as if searching for a laugh.

Less than amused, Madera lifted both eyebrows in exaggerated judgment. Her stare disappeared when Dewy honked several times at a truck that cut them off, "What the fuck, man!"

"What if my blood came out of Richard's mouth?" Madera blurted, hoping Dewy could accept this possibility. Living in a house with a *Tia* like Sofia, he shouldn't be shocked.

Slowing to a stop sign, Dewy kept his eyes straight forward. "Maybe," he replied softly, almost like a child. He lifted the lid from his coffee to finish the drink off.

"Is your aunt at home?" Madera asked as she put her apple core into the empty cup.

"Ought to be. Let's see." Dewy placed the lid back on the cup.

ALMOST AS EXPECTED, SOFIA WAS SIPPING OUT OF A BIG BLACK MUG. Instead of tea this time, she was treating herself to steamed apple cider. A handful of cinnamon sticks rested like miniature logs across her drink. She sat cross legged on a burgundy chaise in the living room. Her bare feet poked out under her knees, and her blue-black curls hung big and loose. A thick book lay on her lap, opened to one of the last pages. She held it open with her left elbow.

"*Tia?*" Dewy sat his backpack on the couch and unzipped his jacket.

"Hmmm?" Sofia glanced up, her polished brown eyes moving from her nephew to Madera.

"Hi," Madera stated, suddenly overwhelmed.

"Hi. Do you need something or are you just here to visit my nephew?"

"It smells like cider. Strong cider." Dewy hung his jacket on the coat hook, defusing his aunt's tactless question.

"Both," Madera replied.

"Something is making me hot. Dewy, hang your friend's coat up," Sofia politely ordered, closing her book. "Help yourself to some cider, Dewy. Bring Madera one, too. Come here, Madera. Sit with me!" Sofia patted the ottoman.

Flattered that Sofia remembered her name, Madera passed her coat to her friend. She then felt she was walking on a shifting plank as she edged toward the *Bruja*.

"Sit down, please." Sofia gave a closed smile. "My nephew cares about you. A lot. I can feel it."

Sofia quickly rubbed the top of Madera's right hand, then rested her own hand there. Her hand was warm, a little worn, but heavily moisturized. She was probably older than Madera expected. Amaryllis had told her that you can tell the age of a woman by looking at her hands.

"You . . . you need to work your magic," Sofia declared. "I see it in your eyes. In your face. Through your whole body. That's why you are here with me. What do you need help with?"

"Um . . . wow? How do you know what I have is magic?"

"Magic isn't uncommon! Honestly, I hate the word magic." Sofia gasped and then continued, "But magic is everywhere. Magic is in everyone. Every one of us has magic. You don't know this?"

Madera shrugged and said, "I keep bleeding. And one time . . . "

"Shush!" Sofia released her hand from Madera's and waved as if to shoo her off. "Everyone has magic, but you have a very special degree. A very powerful magic. Now, you may speak."

"Oh. I keep bleeding between my legs like . . . "

"A period?"

"Yes! And one night I bled for hours on the rooftop . . . in the rain. A thunderstorm. I don't know why. And then the other day, I thought I was bleeding at my aunt's birthday celebration, but I wasn't. See, what happens is that I get this really hot fever throughout my body. I mean really hot and—"

"—Oh, dear" Sofia said as she sat up sharply. "Where did your blood go if it didn't come out? Do you know? It went somewhere."

"Funny you ask that."

"Really? Is it really funny?" Sofia waved Dewy in and asked him to leave Madera's hot cider drink.

"Okay. Now, tell me, what is so funny?" Sofia asked again.

"Well, not really funny. That was the wrong word. Look, I just think that this guy that I don't like for . . . many reasons. Maybe he coughed up my blood?"

"Why do you think *he* coughed up *your* blood?"

"Well, he did it right after I got this fever. We were talking at the bar on my aunt's birthday. He said a few things that really upset me. All of a sudden, I felt like I was about to start bleeding. Then I saw blood on the floor, but it wasn't mine. He was coughing up blood— lots and lots of blood. He had to grab bar napkins to—"

"—I see. You gave it to him."

"Really?"

"Don't act like you're surprised! You got so upset that the blood went directly to the person you were upset with. That was his blood. Not yours. You caused his blood to come out. You have a form of blood magic, Madera. Let me ask you this: Do you feel sick after you bleed? *Tu sabes*, tired or maybe even dizzy?"

Madera sipped on her cider. Dewy must've poured half a bottle of caramel syrup in it. "Um. No."

"Good, you bleed when you feel deeply or intuitively. Does that make sense to you? All the other times you've bled, were you emotional? Just think about it. I'll be right back." Sofia got up, taking her mug with her.

Madera knew the answer was yes, absolutely. The Coffee Magician started it all on the L train. True, it didn't happen right there, but once her emotions built up in Psych class, her first blood tumbled out. There was the bloodstorm night when Della identified Officer Scott as the cop who burst in on her. Come to think of it, that Romi lady said that "a storm was a brewin'!" And, of course, Amaryllis' birthday bash and earlier that day after she saw the Dick cop in her *Tia's* room.

Madera was perplexed though. Why hadn't it come out on her first day at Hendricks? Her eyes did go red, but there was no blood. Hm, maybe it had something to do with all that surrounding activity with Catalina, or maybe the sous chef stole Madera away before it had a chance to start. When she devoured the cured pig meat, there was no blood there either. *Sofia only asked if she was emotional whenever the blood appeared. Nothing to do with all the times I've been emotional since the first blood flow.*

The velvet chaise she sat on felt richer than it looked. She'd never taken a good look around the house outside of Dewy's bedroom. Now she noted that the color of the living room walls were an opaque ivory, with bronze lamps, and burgundy curtains detailed with golden dragonflies. Each color held a vibrancy, and every detail made her smile and wish for her sketchbook. She realized she didn't know what Dewy's aunt did for a living. Come to think of it, Dewy kept a lot of his family business private.

"Drink your cider up before it's cold." Sofia said upon her return, holding two mason jars. The larger one looked like it was filled with marijuana, and the smaller one was only half-full with gray-red tinsel.

"Dewy put too much syrup in it," Madera said.

"That boy! He loves everything so sweet—too sweet. Except his ladies. He likes his ladies bold." Sofia gave Madera another closed smile.

"Oh," Madera coyly acknowledged, even if she didn't consider herself Dewy's lady.

"What happened the day you went out in the thunderstorm?" Sofia asked.

As Madera told of the thunderstorm, Constance's death and even the Coffee Magician, Sofia kept her eyes on an herbal concoction she was mixing. Not once did she look up at Madera. She tossed each herb in separately, even when two were of the same kind. She caressed the plants, broke several in half. She braided a few. She rolled some between her palms. She smelled them. She chewed on one. She opened up Madera's hands and placed a few herbs at a time between them. She took them out of her hand, gathered all the others, and placed them into the smaller jar that contained the grayish red specks of tinsel. She yawned, and then she prayed over them. Finally, she said, "Amen" as Madera finished her stories.

"You possess magic of the blood. Powerful magic. Blood can be used for many great spells, potions, healing salves, everything. But, at this time, Madera, you need to find out why you have this and what to do with it. It's useful. It's for you to use!" Sofia caught herself. She took a deep breath and began whispering. "I'm sorry for yelling. But people with this type of magic have been called. Sometimes they are called from the other side to finish business. The other side *can* be bad with malicious and angry ancestors, or not. Don't hurt anyone else until you're certain you've mastered it. Pray and look in your dreams. I won't say any more right now. But I have been instructed to give you this."

She put the small jar in Madera's hands.

"Uh. What do I do with it?" Madera asked. The jar buzzed with energy. The mixed herbs formed a community and were talking to each other between the glass.

"You take this home and you boil three cups of water. You take what's in this jar and pour it in as it boils. When it is all in, turn off the water and put a lid on the pot. Let it sit for an hour, nothing less and nothing more. Time it. Then take off the lid and pour yourself mug after mug and drink and drink until it is gone. Drink it up within thirty minutes and then go to bed."

Sofia went on: "Don't open it until it's ready to be boiled. Don't ask me what's in it because I won't tell you. It won't hurt you. It will lead you. You can go now. I also wrote the instructions on the lid for you. Dewy's impatience is at our backs."

Sure enough, Dewy opened his bedroom door as if anticipating a runaway. His brows frowned. He bit his bottom lip and pulled Madera into his room.

"What is that?" he asked.

"I don't know. I was told to just take it." Madera backed away from Dewy and gently placed the jar on one of his yellow stools.

"Oh, I rolled a fatty." He showed her the thick joint.

"Your aunt is the real deal, huh?" Madera looked up at the poster of Frida Kahlo's *The Wounded Deer* painting and could almost feel the arrows piercing Frida's deer body.

"You can say that. I just stay out of it," Dewy said on an inhale.

"Does your mom have *bruja* powers, too? Where is your mom, anyway?" Madera took a seat on the other yellow stool.

"Shit's complicated. I don't want to get into all that."

"Yeah, well. Like the way you're here for me, I'm here for you too." Madera smiled, pulling her thick shoulder-length curls up into a ponytail. She stared at the exotic plant life in the jar, almost positive that each herb was named something she could not pronounce.

"I really just want to kiss you," he said.

Dewy's hazel eyes brightened behind the flame of his lighter.

"Dewy!" Madera rolled her eyes. "Way to change the subject!"

"Only stating facts."

Dewy took a deep drag of the joint and then pulled out his box of sketch pencils.

17

April 3, 2005

Ten-year-old Madera notices the missing letter "I" in the Michaels craft store sign at the outdoor mall. The sun sets on the row of stores, they glimmer as if sprinkled with bronze glitter. Madera believes the stores will be closing soon since her mom is tugging at her hand, pulling her in a desperate hurry as if she were a three-year-old toddler.

"Keep up. Don't lose track!" Constance's command is stern.

The store is filled with large marked-down Easter baskets and frizzy plastic grass for nestling chocolate eggs. A long aisle of fake flowers smells like plastic and fresh-sanded wood. But Constance's destination is the row of white canvases and the wire pyramid of paint brushes.

"Wow. This is the stuff artists in museums use," Madera beams. Is her mother going to take up painting pictures? Why? The idea of an artsy mom makes her smile.

Constance grabs three of the 20'x 29' canvases.

"Wow, mama. Those are big. What are you going to do with them?"

Constance scrutinizes the brackets of paintbrushes, grimacing like Riley from the cartoon show "The Boondocks" and making Madera laugh. Then *she plucks a few brushes from their bases, pretending she knows which types to pick. Fat, skinny, long ones, short ones. One here, one there, as if to recite, "Eenie, meeny, miny, moe"—a nursery rhyme which, Constance once explained to Madera, was rooted in racism. Clutching five or six brushes, Constance moves to another aisle looking for the paint.*

Nodding at the acrylic paints, Constance orders, "Grab that dark gray one!"

Madera obeys.

"Get the black and a white. Not ivory. White. And grab that sienna brown. And that mahogany."

Madera's hands start to fill up. She grabs a green shopping basket on the floor holding old issues of Michaels sales flyers. A couple of paint bottles shaped like toilet paper tubes miss the basket and roll down the aisle as if resisting being purchased. Feeling her mother's agitation nip at her back, Madera leaps to capture them.

But Constance isn't done. Again, she sends Madera down the aisle, small sneakers squeaking on the glossy linoleum floor.

"Red. I need the apple red, the ruby red, that light red, and that deep maroon."

"What's all this for?" Madera asks as they maneuver the canvases, paints, and brushes through the checkout line.

"I dreamt something last night. I have to paint it."

Madera watches her mother's eyes soften. "I didn't know you painted pictures, mom."

"I did in high school. Abstract stuff though. But my dream told me to paint this." Constance holds the canvases close to her body like a shield.

"What do you have to paint?" Madera is curious—curious what abstract means, curious about what her mother plans to paint.

"That's my business." Constance winks.

Madera knows she'll find out when ready. Her mom doesn't hoard secrets.

As she awoke Halloween morning, Madera felt like her ten-year-old self again, rushing down the aisle of Michaels craft store.

Rising hazily from her bed, she felt the residue of last night's bitter apple-flavored concoction still coating her tongue. It was heavy, like stubborn tomato paste stuck to a wooden spoon. In the bathroom mirror Madera expected to see a rather pulpy tongue, but to her surprise, it looked normal. It didn't feel normal, though. When she slid her tongue against the bottom of her upper teeth, Sofia's concoction felt like a layer sewn to her gums. The invisible bumpy texture made her want to gag. And every time she wanted to gag, a vision of a paint bottle from Michaels settled in her mind's eye. Madera concluded the craft store memory of her mother must have repeated itself in a dream. What did it mean though?

"Boo! Boo! Boo!" Amaryllis screeched, banging on the other side of the bathroom door like a belligerent ghost.

Startled, Madera swung the door open to return the startling vibes back to her *Tia*.

"Happy Halloween!" Madera screeched.

Amaryllis was wearing a half-face masquerade mask and a pair of purple satin wings over a long, black witch dress. A traditional hodge-podge costume that she always built for herself. This past week, Amaryllis decked out the apartment with both plastic and sugar skulls, marigolds, masks, spiderwebs strung from plant pot to plant pot and nasty candy corn in an open jar on the coffee table.

Madera was pleased to see her aunt in her usual skin: excited, accessible, wild. Since her birthday bash a week ago, Amaryllis hadn't spoken of Officer Dick Scott. There was no sighting of him at the bar either. Madera didn't want to ask and risk a conflict with her *Tia*. She could only rely on faith that Amaryllis left his foul guts behind after learning of the crude Hendricks bar conversation. Amaryllis was horrified over Richard's racist fishing joke while she and Madera blessed their crystals and slammed late night tacos on her birthday.

"What the hell did you make last night? It smells like rotten food in the kitchen!" Amaryllis slid her mask on top of her head, exposing her full face.

Heading to the kitchen, Madera mumbled, "A concoction Dewy's *Tia* Sofia told me to drink."

"*Como? Por que?*" Amaryllis asked, appalled.

Madera heard the clumping of her aunt's *house chanclas* following her.

"She really is a witch, like for real," Madera said.

She took the sauce pot she used to boil the concoction and drizzled dish soap inside.

"What? When did you start taking advice from his *Tia*? And, for what? How old is she?"

"Um, maybe in her fifties, I think. I can't tell," Madera said, shrugging.

"Well . . . what makes her a *bruja*? Do you even know?" Amaryllis cleared her throat, resting her long body against the kitchen counter.

"I mean. She's an herbalist for sure. And, she's kind of moody like a witch." Madera laughed lightly.

"She's from the jungles of Colombia, no? She probably is well versed in that wicked stuff!"

"See, that's the kind of stuff you say that is questionable to me. I mean, you're generalizing. I don't know Sofia's story, but she is from Columbia. It's like sometimes you'll do stuff like paint *La virgen de Guadalupe* my color, but then you complain about this neighborhood like you don't like Black people and . . . "

"Hold up! I'm not racist so don't even go there."

"Trust me, I am not trying to go there." Madera rolled her eyes as she scrubbed the pot.

"Good, now, why did—"

"—Wait, *Tia*. Why were you sleeping with my prayer pillow and the virgin figurine that time anyway?"

"Oh, the night of the thunderstorm? I wasn't sure where my niece was at...and I was scared. You usually keep me involved and when you didn't answer and you weren't with Dewy, I got scared. But don't change the subject. Did you talk to Sofia about that blood?"

"I guess."

"You guess? Why did she tell you to drink that nasty stuff? I'm not leaving you until you tell me everything you know!"

Madera wasn't going to spill the beans about manipulating

Richard's blood. She needed details of a serious breakup for that snake to be released. But she did share her Michaels Craft Store dream that she was told to tap into.

"Sounds intense. So, what happened after your mom bought the paints?"

"We went home. No, wait . . . I stayed with the neighbor that night." Madera's memory unraveled gradually like the foil on a chocolate egg. "Mom dropped me off at Ms. Robyn's with one of those Healthy Cuisine dinners, a lasagna one."

"And? Where did your mom go then?"

"Those frozen dinners are horrible! Then Ms. Robyn made me some doctored-up ramen noodles. Oh, my god, they were so good! But I remember my mom almost brought the paint bags in with her. She was excited but then impatient, I guess." Sifting through the details, it finally dawned on her. "Diane's! She said she was going to Diane's." Madera's eyes stretched as wide as they could go.

Expecting to see the tight-lipped look that stole over Amaryllis at the mention of Diane, Madera was surprised to see her aunt's warm eyes. Maybe Sofia's potion was having some kind of effect on her too.

"You sure?"

Madera nodded, still feeling the bitter apple taste of the concoction on her tongue. "You . . . you talked it out of me, I guess."

"You guess?" Amaryllis laughed and said, "I love you, Mad."

"Even though I want to go to Diane's? Like, right now?" Madera teased.

Rolling her eyes playfully Amaryllis said, "Oh, you're funny." Cool as a cucumber. "Listen, you're becoming a woman, Mad. This is all natural, right? You want to understand who you are and your past. And I know I haven't been open about you pursuing that stuff because I was afraid it would make you sad and depressed and shit, *tu sabes*, but I get it. As much as I can, I get it. Sometimes, I remember how sad you were when you first came to live with me. You were like a little ghost, mute. Poor little girl lost her mom. And I tried, as hard as I could, to get you out of that feeling. I didn't want to see you that way again. And, sometimes when I think about your past, I want to keep you from feeling so sad and . . . I know it's not about me."

Reaching for her cocoa butter, Madera nodded. "I never saw it like that."

"Well, that's because you're not me!" Amaryllis joked. She pulled her masquerade mask down and said, "It's Halloween and we've gotta look through different eyes."

18

MADERA WASN'T SURPRISED WHEN DIANE ANSWERED "YES, OF COURSE I'M FREE FOR YOU!" to a text asking if they could meet up last minute on Halloween afternoon. She even agreed to drive Madera to work after. Madera only had a couple hours to spend with Diane before her night shift started at Hendricks. She felt impelled to call her shift off to stay longer with Diane and catch a haunted house with Dewy. But after witnessing her *Tia* actively showing her *we want to be good people* by being honest and open about her feelings, Madera swallowed the temptation.

Diane didn't live far from where Constance was killed; two blocks east and five blocks south. She resided on the first floor of a two-flat she owned. A light drizzle and misty vision accompanied Madera's walk from her aunt's car. Madera asked to be dropped off at the corner. Not only was Amaryllis dressed as a full-fledged wicked spider, she was already a bit late for work.

Wilted old wildflowers cradled the walkway of Diane's two-flat building. Beside the front door, a lonesome jack-o-lantern stared at Madera as she strolled up the pathway. Madera noted the jack-o-lantern's silly face and joined the sweet laughter of giddy, costumed children across the street. Wouldn't it be nice to have her own home someday, just to hand out treats on Halloween?

She rang the doorbell that read, "D. Howard."

Diane wasn't as big as Madera remembered, a sort of looming giant with great intimidation and a big sense of humor to match.

"Ahhh! It's not a trick or treater! It is Madera!" Diane sang out, unlocking her screen door. She pulled Madera inside with an enormous hug. They swayed back and forth. She smelled like a fresh linen —a comfortable, clean scent.

"Come. Come in. Let me . . . let me just do this." Diane reached down for a chalkboard sign by her feet, which, again, weren't as large as Madera remembered. Perhaps a size ten shoe for a five-foot-eight lady. Madera tried not to stare as she watched Diane place a Victorian-style frame chalkboard on a small hook outside her door that read: "All Candy Gone! See you next year! Brush your teeth well!"

"I like your sign," Madera said, happy to have words to say.

Diane closed the door. "I still do have some candy, but now that *you* are here, I am not answering the door and I won't leave candy out because there is always some little knucklehead that will take it all. Come on in! Look at you! Just as stunning as God intended you to be! Wow! Little Connie. Oh my!" Diane waved her hands over her eyes to keep herself from tearing up.

Madera swallowed her own tears. She gulped so much she worried Diane would think she had a sore throat or something.

"First things first: we gather in the kitchen."

Diane grabbed Madera's hand. The smell of chili permeated the room. The blond wood cabinetry seemed too modest for Diane's personality, but a collection of mini pumpkins and squash and apples glowed in a red ceramic bowl by the sink. To the right were two mugs the color of copper.

"It smells great in here." Madera smiled, trying not to fixate on the red bowl.

"Thank you! I made apple ginger tea, also chili—it's vegetarian. I don't do meat, but I will have a bit of cheese. Care for either?" Her hair was pulled up in a natural hair bun. She wore a gray shawl over her cream blouse.

Having successfully rid her tongue of last night's drink, Madera wasn't looking to taste anything apple. But it all smelled so good. She unzipped her coat and said, "I'll take a little of each. Thank you."

"I guess I should've offered you some candy too, the way I always did when you were a girl. Your mama used to roll her eyes every time I pulled out some Now and Laters or Jolly Ranchers. 'Member that? She did not like you eating candy," Diane said laughing.

Madera agreed, "Dentist-approved teeth. That's what she always wanted."

"Definitely. And, what a smile your mother had. Listen, I know you don't have a lot of time but when I got your text, I was really, really beside myself."

Diane dished out two bowls of chili.

"I've really been wanting to see you, just nervous about it all. Thank you for all the letters. I keep them all."

"Oh, yes. I love letter writing! It's therapy for me. Now that you're grown, I know you got some questions for me, huh?" Diane spoke over her shoulder.

"Yes, ma'am," Madera said.

"Oh, please, spare me with the ma'ams." Diane spun around, "You care for hot sauce?"

"Oh, yes, please." Madera cleared her throat.

"You are your mother's daughter. Plus, you're half Mexican. You gots to be a champion for spice. No offense."

"None taken."

Any doubts Madera had about Diane were evaporating as she slurped up the chili. Women like Diane were women Constance chose to be around. Women that made her feel brilliant being just who she was. Women engaged and eager to improve themselves and their community. This took energy, love, and dedication. Madera gathered that maybe, sometimes, Amaryllis didn't know how to handle the power of Constance's old friends. Some people rather pretend such women don't exist. Deep down, Madera started to believe that her *Tia* was probably afraid of her own potential since she often shunned the power in others. She wished there was a way for her *Tia* to get unstuck. Madera knew it would take Amaryllis letting the booze go. *Whatever, it's not time to judge Tia. This is time to spend with Diane.*

Madera's gulped the last of her chili. Her body responded to the food as if it were a gallon of water awaiting a long-distance marathon runner. Her limbs craved this kind of nutrition—warm, earthy, and healing. She stood up to rinse her hands at the sink.

Diane placed a warm towel on Madera's hands and dried them for her. The towel felt like a small, fluffy pet or a baby—it almost had a heartbeat like one too. It throbbed softly.

"You ready to come to the basement? Your mom used to spend a lot of time there. She'd say my basement was like a mother's loving womb. She loved it down there. A lot of people still do. They come here because it's an oasis! So many of us used to gather at your mom's apartment to talk politics and laugh and debate. But people come here for refuge, and rest, for creation. We need a space to release our frustrations. A place to vent, scream if we want to! Everyone's invited here to cry. Sometimes I leave some fruit or a bowl of soup for them, water. Come, let me show you."

Diane smiled playfully. Taking the towel off Madera's hands, she returned it to its place on the rail of the stove. She turned the heat off the chili pot and waved at Madera to follow her. The door to the basement was just off the kitchen. It creaked ever so longingly, like a baby taking its first breath-turned-cry into the world. Madera giggled, reflecting on how her mother would sometimes use poetic words: *a mother's loving womb.*

"You still have that laugh," Diane said.

"Yeah, I guess I can't help it."

"Don't ever try. You keep it the way it is."

Each wooden step welcomed Madera with its own small hug into the wide-open space below. The basement was a finished piece of beauty. Natural light flooded in from the row of high basement windows lining the eastern wall, tiled in teal like a Caribbean bathroom. Multicolored hallway rugs lined the floors. A functioning claw foot bathtub with a silver shower liner sat next to a full wooden dining table with chairs. An opened treasure trunk overflowed with candles and mason jars and empty wine bottles-turned-tissue-paper-stained-glass art that the neighborhood kids made. Near the bathtub, a toilet sat in a corner behind a flowery Chinese room divider. A stereo and a record player stood ready to broadcast sounds from the center of the room, with plenty of space to dance or roll or stretch or pray.

Diane pointed to something flat and colorful leaning against an interior wall half-covered by a black trash bag. It looked like an amateur painting on a large canvas. At the bottom, the painting exposed a miniature town composed of ivory and gray buildings saturated by red rain. These homes and buildings looked like Monopoly houses and hotels. Then it hit Madera: that's how Constance drew her homes. When little Madera would ask, "Can you draw me a house please?" Her mother always sketched one of those boxlike houses and added a door. Madera would color in grass and flowers and a big sun on the upper right corner of the page. Then, she'd draw herself and her mother holding hands.

"Your mother made that painting a week before she died. She worked on it right here in my basement. She didn't tell me anything about its meaning. She just said it had a great purpose, it was in her dream, and she needed to paint it. I respected that and left her to do her thing."

Diane slid the trash bag up and off the painting so gracefully that it felt like she was revealing a fragile masterpiece. The top of the painting showed a naked woman the color of burnt sienna. Her dark hair was curly, loose, and big. Her eyes were closed tight, and her mouth was open. The woman was spreading her legs in a wide squat like a fertility goddess, her hands pressed down on her knees. Blood poured from her legs, spilling onto the miniature Monopoly town.

"I believe you may know what it means," Diane said.

Madera began to shake. She didn't want to spill the blood story to Diane; instead, vital questions poured into her head. *Mama, is it you telling me to do this? Huh? I thought you'd just let me know. Did you know this would happen to me? Is that woman supposed to be me?* Madera tried her best to prevent her body from shaking. She had to pay attention to Diane's words.

"That night, your mama found joy at the table. She dumped out her tubes of paint and pulled out her canvas as soon as she got down here. She said she heard herself in her own ear the night before. She said it was herself talking because, you know, your mama didn't believe spirits could talk to her. We had many debates about this. I'm more fluid in my belief, but your mama associated spirit talk with either gifted people who deal with spirits their entire lives or those who are fragile-minded and latch onto any and everything. But this, right here, is what she wrote down before she made that painting."

From a plastic cubby, Diane pulled out a heavy stack of long, multi-colored envelopes bound by a fat old rubber band. She handed Madera the bottom envelope. Of course, it was red. She opened the letter. Her mother's handwriting in a dark blue pen, written quickly on lined paper in a blend of cursive and print.

Blood taken. Blood giveth back. Bloodshed to bloodshed, Out from the legs, the pain will be theirs instead. Blood taken. Blood giveth back. Blood taken. Blood giveth back. Bloodshed to bloodshed. Out from the legs, the pain will be theirs instead. Paint the city red. Paint it red from blood. Blood out between the legs. Let the pain be theirs instead.

Madera lifted her eyes from the page, damp with the desire to cry. She released a whistle of a sigh. Her mom heard a message from somewhere to paint that picture. Somehow she knew of her fate and maybe even what must be done.

"Listen, this painting is yours. I wanted to give this to you when you turned eighteen, but I had no real way of reaching you. I only prayed that it was you taking the letters from your mama's grave. I had real faith that it was, but you never really know."

"Thank you for not giving up on me." Madera felt overwhelmed but still not full. Diane had more to tell her.

"After your mama wrote this, she wanted some space. So, I let her at it. She painted for about two hours or so. Then she started hollering that some man was peering in from one of those windows."

Diane nodded toward the east wall. "She was pissed. Like, really pissed. I felt bad, so I put shades up there after that, so that people can protect themselves from the alley's view."

"Good. That sounds creepy," said Madera.

"But later I found out who was peeking in. Everett, just a brilliant friend of mine. He saw the basement light on and happened to look at the painting. He was moved by it. Knew it meant something. Come on, darling. We have hot tea waiting for us before work."

Madera, cradling the lined paper with her mother's words, took one last long look around *the mother's loving womb* and headed upstairs.

THE LAST FEW HOURS OF HALLOWEEN SPED BY AT HENDRICKS. DIANE drove Madera home to drop off the painting in her room, but she had no time or inspiration to put together a costume there. At work, she wore a cat ear headband that Diane gave her. Catalina drew whiskers on Madera's face with her eyeliner. Throughout the shift, Madera's cheeks itched. She assumed she shouldn't be wearing someone else's makeup.

"Are you okay?" Amaryllis questioned her niece during her shift. "How'd it go with Diane?"

"Very good. Felt like old times in a way."

It was hard to read Amaryllis' expression underneath the copious amount of makeup. She batted her eyes and nodded her head gently as she spoke. Madera made sure not to mention the painting, at least not yet. Amaryllis would only hover over her in wild speculation about her own opinion of what everything may mean.

Instead, Madera found herself juggling the mundane duties of work and how she wished she could jump into her mother's dream of the squatting woman to piece everything together.

19

Madera first heard about the Day of the Dead when her grade-school class visited the Museum of Mexican Art in Pilsen, not far from Roosevelt Road. She was fascinated with the little candy skulls, the bright orange marigolds, and the idea that the dead could come back to mingle with their living relatives for just one day out of the year. When she asked her mother if they could celebrate Day of the Dead, Constance merely smiled, understanding that her daughter would be interested in the holiday by the sole fact that her dad was Mexican. She advised Madera to look into the holiday for next year.

Constance had no idea that next year, her own picture would appear on Madera and Amaryllis' *ofrenda* as they celebrated their first Day of the Dead together.

"Traditions say that the dead have to go on a long journey to get to their final resting place. So, we leave them food and their favorite things on the ofrenda," Amaryllis explained. "What is something your mom liked to eat?"

Madera decided to put out some sunflower seeds, Constance's favorite snack. Together she and her Tia cut squares of cloth and paper to string a holiday banner over the ofrenda. *Then they set out to make sugar skulls.*

Amaryllis never claimed to stand out in the kitchen, so she didn't fuss at the mess that followed. Half the skulls fell apart before they finished molding them. Small tangerine and teal beads lay scattered about like black pepper. Globs of fallen icing hardened along the rim of a kitchen chair.

As Madera grew older, she and Amaryllis made it a tradition to stuff their faces with *Pan de Muertos* while watching horror movies, laughing as they criticized the foolish characters and the mistakes of film directors. Then Amaryllis would plunge into her own drama, donning plum or black mini veils and creating her own meticulous layers of extra eye makeup inspired by the traditional *calavera* designs. On the radio, she'd play the infamous "La Llorona" as well as other popular Mexican songs that dealt with death. She'd dance and spin in circles, cry and curse in whispers, maybe leaving behind an empty bottle of Sol beer with a yellowed lime.

As an embarrassed young teenager, Madera wondered if her aunt had succumbed to the overzealous stereotype of the grieving Mexican woman. But she also began to ask Amaryllis to tell her more about her father Adan. All she knew about him seemed to be sitting on the ofrenda: the old black and white picture of him at the garage and the white powdered sugar her aunt would leave for him as an offering in a small ceramic box.

At age fourteen, Madera accidentally knocked over the little ceramic box. It cracked and the powder spilled out.

"I'm sorry! *Lo siento.* I'll clean it up and find something else to put the sugar in," called Madera, grabbing the broom and dustpan.

"The fuck!"

"What's wrong? I said I'd clean it up!" Madera cried, embarrassed.

"It's not sugar," Amaryllis said, frozen.

"Huh? What—What is it?"

"*Sobrina.* I'm so sorry. I should . . . I should've just told you. Shame on me for even bringing the stuff in here, but it is what it is. Your *Apa'* loved his cocaine. It's the truth and . . . yes, it's a drug. *Peligroso.* It's how he died, but I leave it for him anyway because . . . well, it's one thing I know he truly loved in his life." Amaryllis wiped her brow and laughed while Madera stared at her in shock.

The white powder tradition would continue. This year, Amaryllis placed the cocaine in a thin line on its designated pedestal, a small rectangular mirror the size of a matchbook. A candle decorated as a dollar bill stood behind it. Adan's youthful picture watched over it, with his squinty eyes and tight-lipped smile, the naughty vignette of the *ofrenda* display. All the other family spirits, including grandmother Hilda, had their offerings: a shot of tequila, cookies, even a leg of chicken.

Since the holiday fell on a Sunday, Amaryllis was fortunate to have it off. When Madera arrived home from a slow shift from Hendricks around 2 p.m., she kicked off her boots and sat to admire the *ofrenda* in all its glory. Amaryllis was in her bedroom at the time with her television's volume set up high. Madera found it rather odd but wasn't inclined to ask why. She soaked up the Amaryllis-less moment by spending a good thirty minutes in front of the *ofrenda*.

She was curious if her mother was standing over her shoulder. Had she nibbled on the sunflower seeds Madera left for her? Had her mother and father danced together or shared a flirtatious moment? Madera doubted they'd ignored each other. Did Adan know about Constance's painting? What were his thoughts about it? Was it truly her mother that was behind all this blood magic? That wasn't quite Constance's style. She was more of a realist; Diane even confirmed that a bit. What if her mother blocked her own connection with her daughter after her death because of her limited human beliefs, and now she was trying to burst through? If so, today was the day to let her know, with the veil between the living and the dead so thin. Madera sighed with weighty thoughts as she gathered a deep appreciation for Amaryllis. She guided her in embracing and honoring the dead.

Exhausted, Madera went to lie down. In her bed she folded her hands against abdomen, mimicking her mother's look in her casket. She thought hard about murder, so hard that she imagined Romi showing her the ropes. She was the one that mentioned Madera's "Mars Energy"—maybe that means she's familiar with it? Perhaps she could make her a "kill the piggy" concoction.

Madera heard Amaryllis's television set turn off, her bedroom door squeal open.

"Hi *Tia!*" Madera called out.

Amaryllis didn't answer, but she knew she wasn't alone. Sliding up into a seated position on her bed, Madera felt her muscles lock up into knots as she heard the rugged scuff of Officer Richard Scott's shoes on the floor. He coughed. Madera's comfort vanished.

What the fuck is he doing here? Why the hell are his shoes on? Why did Amaryllis, once again, invite the man who had not only busted into her neighbor's apartment but also insulted her niece, into their home, again? That's why the television volume was so loud. They were in the room fucking the entire time. Madera's tummy rumbled. It was disrespectful to the spirits on such a precious day. By now, they'd probably all left. Madera was surprised that not one of them warned her.

She gazed across the room at her mother's painting, still in its black plastic bag, leaning against her closet door. *No way am I showing that painting to Amaryllis.* To think she believed her aunt was using this time after her birthday to focus on her spiritual practice. It was official now: her *Tia* was a genuine disappointment. One who cast her pearls before swine, something someone who had no problem being called a "hot tamale" would do.

Madera heard her aunt in the living room showing the Dick the *ofrenda:* "*Mi Hermano.* My brother. Mad's Dad."

Madera's curiosity piqued at her tipsy aunt's slurring, 'Mad's Dad' to a police officer. Oh, shit! Officer Scott was probably standing over her dad's drugs. *Dia de los Muertos* or not, why the fuck would Amaryllis leave drugs out in front of a cop?

"He liked blow, huh?" Richard laughed, cocky and sinister. "You are truly something special. How darling of a little sister to leave her big brother cocaine."

Richard continued roughly, "Well, how 'bout you be a good lover, huh? How about you give me that bump? Your brother has definitely enjoyed his imaginary share, right?"

Madera lifted herself off her bed to slam her door. She didn't want to hear her aunt say yes to this vinegar-scented pig. Heat enveloped her body. As if she were full of life, Madera rubbed her abdomen as the fever brewed. She unveiled her mother's painting. With her back against the foot of her bed, she closed her eyes, took a deep breath, and mirrored the woman's squat. She focused on Officer Richard Scott. *Bloodshed to bloodshed. Out from the legs, the pain will be theirs instead.*

Over and over, she visualized her fever onto Richard in the other room. She saw a stream of blood, sailing up his gin-tainted throat, hurling out in chunky little bloody balls. An insatiable excitement nipped at Madera.

"Again! He's bleeding again!" Amaryllis dashed into Madera's room, shouting, bullet-sized tears scorching her face and smearing her eyeliner. Standing up and out of her squat, Madera grabbed her painting and turned it to the wall as her aunt stared hopeless at the floor.

"Really? So, what do we do?" Madera pretended to be concerned.

She really didn't want anything terribly bad to happen to Richard, she was practicing. Well, kind of. He did spit on Ms. Della. Who spits on a woman? And complimented her mouth after sex with her aunt. The list went on—He was the villain, no doubt. Plus, the blood was always better out than in, right? In two months, she'd have enough experience and money to book that trip to Florida.

"I don't want to call for help because . . . come!" Amaryllis pulled her niece's hand, leading her out into the living room.

The living room was still lit by the group of candles around the altar. Flames danced and flickered, teased by a small draft coming in from a cracked window. Madera wasn't sure how she missed all the busy activity bestowed upon the coffee table when she was honoring the dead. There were a few wine bottles scattered about, balled-up tissues, lighters and incense sticks. Though the smoky fragrance of long-burning incense drifted, a pungent smell of sour vinegar pulled on Madera's nerves.

Wearing his uniform, Richard sat hunched on the edge of the green rocking chair, head between his legs. He upchucked blood into the pot holding Severus, the ailing snake plant.

"Why's he not in the bathroom?" Madera questioned, feeling

miserably sorry for Severus—how did her prayers result in him being watered by Richard's blood?

Richard vomited blood clots, vibrant red as if lightened by his bile. In the pot they connected to form a tiny bloody pool of phlegm. It sparkled as the muted setting sunrays streamed between the half-closed blinds, landing on Severus' bloody soil.

"*Tengo miedo*! I'm scared. He's a cop. He just did a line of coke! What if he gets in trouble?" Amaryllis said as she paced.

"Really? You gave him my papa's cocaine?" Madera's body heated up again as if she were locked in a steam room for an hour. She clapped her hands over her ears. If she heard anymore, would her blood boil over and kill the man?

"Rich? Rich?! You okay? Come! Come to the bathroom," Amaryllis pleaded.

Richard lifted his face, his sea green eyes turned foamy. "Why are you floating?" he asked Amaryllis. He coughed; more blood plummeted out his mouth.

Madera glanced at her aunt. Amaryllis was not floating. There was no doubt the lost blood was making Richard's mind foggy. As he braced his hands on the rocking chair arms, blood drizzled down his chin. Amaryllis supported him as he tried to get up.

"Give him some fucking water! Something!" Madera shouted, heading back to her room.

Stuck between deep frustration and an itch to hit something, Madera blew out the three candles on the altar in her room. Her head throbbed. Salty tears, heavy and confused, fell sturdy like rain drops down her face and slid into her mouth.

Should I take a train ride to the end of the line? Call Dewy or Diane? Or just stay in and pray? She couldn't find it in herself to deal with Amaryllis and her drug-cop drunk-woman drama.

A standing lamp hovered over her bedroom mirror and offered a calming glow. Why had she been given this unusual magic? If only this gift was her mother's, Constance would've been slaying the streets clean of evil. Piggy Hughes would've folded over into a pool of blood as the sight of his flashing lights would've triggered Constance's internal brew.

Madera retrieved her bloodstone necklace out of the Coffee Magician's mug. She pulled it over her head and watched it rest above her breasts. Her black v-neck top hung loose over the black ripped jeans that snuggled her hips. She reached for her maroon jacket, even though it was too thin for the weather. She brushed her hair with extra gel, pulled it up into a messy bun and headed out to the front door. As she slipped one of her big black military boots on, Amaryllis appeared, arms folded against her chest, a freshly lit cigarette lobbing from her mouth. Her face wore drying tears and smeared black mascara. With each smoky exhale, a rich whiskey aroma fluttered out.

"He's sleeping," she reported, as if Officer Richard Scott was a baby that finally went down.

"And?" Madera slid on her other boot.

"What's up with you, Mad?" Amaryllis was clearly sobering up. She moved her hands to her hips. "Wait, where are you going?"

"Anywhere but here."

"Severus is saturated with Richard's blood! I diluted it with water but still."

"Wait, didn't you say blood can be good for plants?" Madera suddenly recalled, trusting there was hope for Severus.

"Yes. Well, I prefer my own menstrual blood if any. But you can't just leave me here like this, Mad! There's blood on the bathroom floor, too."

"That's your problem, you brought Richard back into our home! I'm the ass, *Tia*! I'm the ass because I actually believed you let that one go. He said some racist shit about a black bass to your Black niece and now he's sleeping in your bed? That's your business, I guess. Just like where I go right now is mine!"

With her keys in a tight grip, her phone secured in her back pocket, Madera stormed out.

20

THE FIRST WEEK OF NOVEMBER, MADERA CONCLUDED SHE NEEDED TO practice her gift. And not strictly on Officer Richard Scott. She understood very well that there were plenty of rotten apples in the police department to crush into disposable cider. And, she had time to do so as she sat a portion of her check aside for the Florida flight and hotel.

Whenever Madera spotted the excited jumpy lights of red, blue, and white blazing down the street, she'd wondered: would their actions add steam to an issue or simmer it down? Regardless, each time Madera saw a Chicago Police car light up, she couldn't help imagine what her mother must've thought or felt when she saw Piggy in her rearview mirror. The sicko that took such a radiant mother away from her. Sometimes, Madera wondered how much more of a person she would be if her mother hadn't died.

With this fervor, Madera became determined to learn to control her body and her blood. Like a mischievous toddler discovering the boundaries of their own wee power, Madera steered hers. If she wanted, she'd get mad. Such madness stirred havoc in her belly almost like a bad meal. The fever would follow. Then the blood would flow. She learned she had a choice where the blood could go. If she wrapped herself up in her own sadness or anger, the blood came from her, the way it did in Psych class the first time. If she focused her anger on the person inflicting pain—any member of the CPD that she deemed vile—the blood came from them.

One morning, for fun, Madera ventured west of her usual train stop. She recalled her mother always complaining about the cops having ill intent around Pulaski Road and Lake Street. Constance had a way of sniffing out misbehavior. Her instincts for bullshit were spot on. Sure enough, walking down the metal stairs of the raised train stop Madera spotted a pair of sketchy cops; a man and a woman, standing at the corner across the street. They weren't being violent, but Madera observed them sneering at random pedestrians that probably fit their sewn-in stereotypes of criminals. The cops' presence alone intimidated many people of color strolling by. They stood like plastic toy soldiers.

Madera planted herself across from them, as if waiting on a bus. The pair of cops with toothpicks dangling from their mouths went from studying faces to shooting dirty looks at an already disgruntled homeless man.

"Street wouldn't be so bad if you got yourself a job," the woman cop joked. She raised her eyebrows like a mother warning her child in public. The male cop chuckled so hard it vibrated through the cement to rattle right under Madera's own two feet.

Madera's piercing eyes lasered across the street. She was certain her eyes were red. With this energy, her thermostat rose and the fever fell over her. It was time, and she decided to give the pair of cops something lighthearted, just to annoy the—ruffle their feathers a bit. The madness was an organic emotion, but when the moment came to release the blood, Madera tapped into her mind. She decided to give them a pair of bloody noses.

"Cokehead ass cops!" The disgruntled homeless man retorted.

The cops' noses were bleeding. Bystanders cringed, stared, and tried swallowing their laughter. After a droplet of blood found itself between her lips, the woman cop caught the rest of her bloody nose with her sleeve. The male cop turned to his partner and flinched. He swatted his own face and looked up toward the sky as if something sprinkled blood onto them. They ducked and headed for their patrol cruiser. A stream of blood reached the male officer's mouth before he nearly yanked off the cruiser's door handle, startling a couple of senior citizens trying to get into the L station entrance. A group of shaking heads glared as the cops slithered north down Pulaski in search of tissues, siren roaring.

Moments like this tickled Madera.

After each random episode of blood flow, she'd squeeze the bloodstone necklace around her neck. A trickle of blood would appear on her index finger and thumb. Then she'd heave a deep breath, alerting the blood to begin its fade. Madera believed it was the bloodstone necklace that prevented her own blood flow on her first day at Hendricks Steakhouse.

Madera also noted the blood would come either out of the cops' noses or mouths. She hadn't sent it out of their eyes, ears or between their legs; she never went that far with it. She wasn't sure she could even do all of that without maybe hurting herself. Plus, blood flowing from their noses or mouths was always enough to stop the situations she encountered. But there was that time Madera got so mad at her target she sent blood out through his nose and mouth.

This happened on Madera's own block one day at sunset. A cop was picking on a young man jaywalking. The young man's hands were pushed deep down into his jeans that sagged from his body, hampering his walk across the street. He wound up sauntering like a snail. His red-tinted eyes shone a stereotypical haziness and he must've been wrapped in his thoughts. Arriving at the sidewalk, he was startled by the broad-shouldered cop, who brandished his two hundred pounds, pencil-thin porno mustache, and nasty sneer. Madera knew of this cop. She saw him multiple times coming in and out of the corner store by the L tracks. It was as if he had some side business going on with the Lebanese owner. Amaryllis called it fishy once, and if Amaryllis thought it was fishy, then it was really bad.

The young man tried to smile at the cop and keep going. The cop could have let him pass but instead took a stand to block him. Madera slowly strolled on the sidewalk across the street. Her black jeans clung dirty, heavy, and clammy against her skin. She had a messy day at work which entailed a raspberry smoothie spilling on her. Wearing her maroon jacket wide open, exposing her black v-neck top and her gold-chained bloodstone, Madera watched. She took baby steps as the young man tried to walk by the chain-link fence outside a nearby two-flat.

As if programmed in a video game, the cop pushed the young man against the fence and whacked the side of his head with the back of his hand.

Madera's belly tightened, warming and spinning in its anger.

"Pull up your fuckin' pants! No one wants to see your Black ass. We have—ooof!" The cop began coughing, almost gagging.

The young man bounced off the fence and sparingly bent over like a struggling flower, attempting to raise his hands in a "don't shoot" position. Then he dared to look behind him as the cop coughed and yacked. Once his eyes caught sight of the ruby red blood, beaming as bright as a coca cola can on a sunny day, he opened his mouth to say, "You cool? You good?" as if checking on the welfare of a regular human.

Madera centered the energy inside the cop's nose and mouth. Since it was coming out of two places, her body became hotter than usual. She imagined if her tummy was exposed, it would probably show red like flaming timbers.

The cop continued to yack up. His face, the hue of a sucked Fireball candy, showed alarm at the blood spraying from his face. Each spurt caused him to step back, little by little. He painted half a sidewalk block a crimson red.

The young man released his grip from the cold gray fence, hiked up his pants, and moved toward safety. As if in a hopscotch game, he took multiple awkward steps to avoid stepping into bloody vomit. He then walked backwards, surveying the entire scene in awe. He shot a glance across the street and may have glimpsed Madera's dark eyes peering at him. She felt strong in her stare and unworldly.

Madera gently rubbed her bloodstone as if it were the head of an infant child. She caught the eyes of the young man, who was more or less her age, and mouthed the words, "Go. Slow." He nodded and made his way back down the block. Madera continued to rub her bloodstone, mentally cooling the heat from her abdomen with deep breaths.

The cop hovered over the ground like a drunkard's head looming over a toilet. He stared in disbelief at his creation.

Behind him, a woman in her forties holding a toddler on her hip called out, "Officer? You okay? Do you need help?"

Madera was unsure where this woman came from. She wasn't a resident of her block as far as she knew. The little boy buried his face into the woman's gold-colored jacket. The officer shook his head as he turned to face the concerned woman. Blood stained the corners of his mouth like Kool-Aid and his breath reeked of iron. His dark marine haircut and beady brown eyes caught the light of the dim sun. The sun's dying rays seemed to burn him as if his flesh was raw and open.

"Excuse me, miss? Do you know what's wrong with him? Huh? Do you know what happened to this policeman?" The woman hollered across the street at Madera.

"I don't know. Something. I don't know," Madera said, voice sweet like a lullaby. "Don't worry. I'd leave him alone."

Madera gave the woman a bit of a smile before continuing her slow stroll. Oh, how bad she wished Ms. Della was on the street right now to witness this.

The officer waved his hand at the woman and child, shooing them away. The woman carried on. The little boy lifted his head to watch Madera walk away across the street. He pointed his chubby brown little finger at her and asked, "Who's that? Who's that? Who's that?"

The woman struggled to find the words, "Someone. I don't know. Probably a ghost."

21

Madera watched Sofia's new Russian blue cat, Lamb's Ear, race up and down the kitchen, paws landing compact and tight, thudding like a drum. He chased something inside the walls, a mouse or a withering spirit.

Dewy opened the refrigerator door. Madera wished she could wear his gray hoodie; it looked comfy and warm. With the exception of her maroon jacket, she was dressed in her usual black.

Sofia stood above the small cutting board island, her hand on a jade cast iron tea kettle. She slurped on a red chili sucker and penetrated Madera with unusually grave eyes.

"You shouldn't play so much with your power," said Sofia.

"How?" Madera grew a sudden urge to head to Dewy's bedroom rather than face a lecture.

"What?" asked Dewy, trying to show concern while staying aloof from witch business. He pulled a bunch of black grapes from the refrigerator and headed for the sink to wash them.

"When you do what you've been doing," Sofia explained as if to a first grader, "your powers can give way, right when you need them the most."

"How would you know what I did?" Madera lowered her voice.

"It's written all over you." Sofia raised her eyebrows, biting into the chili sucker. It crunched like a rumble of tiny rocks.

Madera scanned her own body up and down, eyes rolling in sarcasm, dramatically hunting for invisible writing.

"Oh, it's there, my dear!" Sofia huffed, tossing the lollipop stick into the trash can.

"How so?" Since her rooftop blood bath, Madera's tongue had grown more nervy.

"You can control your power. You definitely know how to punish, right? Save some energy for the big one. Those little punishments will be much easier after that. Trust me."

Sofia grabbed her mug of hot tea from the cutting board island. Joyfully, she twirled around and spun out of the room like a preteen. The cat followed, its fuzzy tail pointed high in the air.

"Lamb's Ear? Interesting name for a cat," Madera said. "Damn, she got him trained like a dog."

"Crazy, huh?" Dewy tried to slice the still-heavy air with laughter. "Is she right though? Did you figure things out with your blood? Are you doing better?"

Steam rose from the tap water over the grapes. A foggy mist diluted Dewy's hazel eyes into a milky hue.

"You're washing the grapes with hot water." Madera said.

"Oh, shit!"

As Dewy switched the taps, Adora, the young, gentle-eyed Black woman who'd stood guard in the bathroom the night Madera vomited, glided into the kitchen like a ghost. Not one shuffle of a footstep. She was shorter than Madera remembered, maybe just five feet on the dot. Dressed in black yoga pants and a snug green t-shirt, her hair pulled back, Adora was barefoot, almost as if she was in the comfort of her own home. She carried a silver dinner tray that held a pair of matching pearly white teapots. Along with them sat about five tiny clay sake cups.

"Good afternoon." She spoke softly like a preschool teacher focused on Madera.

"Hello," Madera mustered. She glanced at Dewy to see if he noticed Adora's ample coke bottle silhouette.

"What's up, Adora," Dewy said swiftly. He stepped away from the sink, and the colander of grapes drizzled little water onto the floor.

"Oh, spreading love, you know," Adora responded. The heat from Sofia's boiling tea water still stretched like a blanket throughout the kitchen. Madera leaned against the side of the stove and watched Adora move around like a roommate with sweet familiarity. Like Madera, she exuded a quiet, intricate web of mystery. But unlike Madera, she also broadcasted an energy of harmony and loving kindness. Madera felt much more comfortable around women with grit, like Sofia or even her *Tia*.

Dewy was taking sandwich bags out of a kitchen drawer while Adora stood at the sink. With the rhythm of dripping honey, Adora washed the cups.

"Are you Sofia's friend?" Madera questioned, suspicion on her tongue.

Adora turned, resting her gentle eyes on Madera, "Yes."

"Oh, where did you meet her?"

Madera felt Adora rubbing her sweetness into the spicy kitchen. Perhaps, deep down inside her there was grit?

"I'm leaving these for later." Gesturing to the teapots, Adora announced to no one in particular.

Raising his bagged grapes in a cheesy salute, Dewy tried to derail Madera's attention from Adora.

"I asked where did you meet her?" Madera repeated, crossing her arms and extending a foot, proposing to trip anyone getting too close to her.

Adora, drying her hands on the dish towel, "At a farmer's market."

"Are you an herbalist?" Madera dug.

"I have a relationship with herbs, but I'm not an herbalist. Hey, it was nice to see you again, Madera." Almost as fast as she appeared, she left the kitchen. The calm rosy feeling scurried out with her.

The two teapots sat abandoned on the silver dinner tray. Madera rushed to lift the lids off the teapots and probe whatever was inside.

The tea smelled like sulfur and sage; the odor drove her back. *Why are there so many little clay cups on the tray and who the hell was drinking that?*

"C'mon, let's go." Dewy left the kitchen, heading toward his room.

Madera dipped into the hallway but turned toward the back sunroom where Sofia and Adora gathered. Was this the coven's magic room? In spite of the salty personality clashes, she felt a powerful urge to join this group.

The sunroom's entrance was guarded with a swaying curtain of beads and ropes. Peering between these heavy curtains, Madera saw Adora and the Mediterranean looking man, Oscar. They were shaking out a cobalt blanket to place on the floor as if they planned an indoor picnic. The smell of warm coconut oil wafted from the room. Madera stared in, taking in the sunlight from the large windows and all it illuminated. Random supplies—buckets, folded towels, and a plethora of jars rested in one corner. In the opposite corner lay a treasure chest that looked like it was from another era.

Sofia must've been standing near the doorway. She turned to look straight into Madera's eyes through the curtains.

"It's not your time yet," Sofia snapped.

Madera's jaw clenched. Lamb's Ear mewed.

"Mad?" agitated, Dewy yelled down the hall.

Unlocking her eyes from Sofia's gaze, Madera turned around and, like a problem child, she skulked down the hallway to Dewy's room. "What the fuck is going on? Do other people live here?" she demanded.

"No. They're visitors." Dewy rolled his eyes. "I don't get involved and I don't think you need too, either. That's my *Tia's* business. My mom told me not to be concerned with all that—"

"—Your mom?"

Dewy's face tightened.

"Well, where is she? I wanna meet her. What the hell is going on?"

"Look, Mad, it's too much to get into and—"

"—Like, why? You know everything about me." Stepping toward Dewy, she snatched her bagged grapes out of his hand.

"Look. Let's just study for this biology exam." Dewy's voice was direct.

"No," Madera teased.

She took off her jacket and tossed it across Dewy's bed. Suddenly her mild frustration slipped away. Her head felt less heavy. Her pelvis grew warm. Maybe she got a waft of something from the sunroom, or maybe it was those nasty smelling cups. Whatever it was, she was drawn to touch Dewy.

Closing the door, Dewy ran his hands through his hair, he threw his own grapes on his nightstand and turned to face Madera. She inched closer to him, allowing the outside of her body to graze his. Madera felt him throbbing. Dropping her snacks on the bed, she pulled Dewy's neck down, pressing his mouth onto hers. His small, tight lips met her pouty mouth. It was a gentle peck. Pulling back, Madera licked her lips and tasted deep desire, like a breeze against thirsty skin.

Dewy leaned in again. This time he lifted her chin, cupped her cheek, and opened her mouth with his. Their tongues hungrily collided. With his left hand, Dewy tugged Madera by her belt loop closer to his body, making her feel what her touch did to his shaft, growing and thrumming against her navel.

As they kissed, a metallic taste invaded their mixing saliva, and Madera pulled her mouth from Dewy's. He wiped his mouth with the back of his hand and kicked his bedroom floor, cursing at the presence of blood.

"I'm so sorry. I don't know why there's blood. I mean, I'm not mad so I don't know why this is happening," Madera muttered, embarrassed and confused.

She took a seat on Dewy's bed and reached for a tissue on his nightstand to check her own mouth: absolutely nothing.

"I thought you were figuring this shit out?" Dewy whined, pacing back and forth, trying to deter his erection.

Madera huffed, finding it hard to focus on Dewy's eyes.

"I'm sorry, I think I need to . . . I gotta figure all this out first before I kiss you or . . . "

"Let me do all the kissing," Dewy pressed, "I don't care about the blood, Mad. I've wanted this since . . . do you really wanna know how many times we fucked in my head in this bed?"

Sitting down next to her, Dewy lips fell deeply into Madera's neck. Lightheaded and turned on, she fought the urge as soon as his left hand slipped between her thighs. Madera scooted off the bed.

"Dewy!" In heated confusion, she adjusted her shirt. "How are we supposed to study after this?"

"I don't want to study," Dewy said.

Swallowing her lust, Madera shook her head. She wanted him but she didn't feel in control. Something was off.

She buried her face in her hands. "I'm not cool with choking on blood at a time like this. And I don't really understand anything that just happened."

"I get it. I just never thought I'd be left blue balls and all in my own bedroom. Da fuck!" He snatched his pillow to cover a much larger lump than Madera imagined.

"It's like I really want to do something with you but it feels out of my control."

"I'm here! I'm here. You can control me, Mad. Seriously," Dewy said excitedly.

"Is it me, or do you think that Adora person released some kind of spell when we were in the kitchen?"

"*Adora?* Look, Mad, what are you trying to say now? Why? You're saying you wouldn't have kissed me if not for a spell?"

"I wouldn't say that. I just think she and I were fighting, energy-wise. She seems like the opposite of me. Like, if I have Mars energy, she probably has Venus? Venus is pleasure, right? I don't know, maybe I'm thinking crazy. But it's like she was softening the kitchen. Fucking casting vibes."

"Yeah, see, I don't know what any of that stuff means but it sounds like you're saying you'd have to be cursed to kiss me? Plus, she didn't soften anything on me." Dewy shook his head.

Laughing, Madera said, "No, I don't want to take this too seriously,

Dewy. But I can't do this until I . . . maybe this just means getting to Piggy sooner than later."

"Fuck Piggy, Mad! This is getting in the way of everything. This friend thing is cool but I'm always ready for more."

"I think we should just study over the phone or on our own maybe."

Madera fought against another urge to kiss her friend. Purposely she tried to override her desire to mount him. It wasn't the right time if blood was flowing.

"Whatever makes you comfortable, Mad. Just remember, you kissed me first." Dewy stood up and tossed the pillow onto the bed.

Sliding her jacket back on, Madera continued, "Adora said she was busy spreading love, remember?"

"She always says that," Dewy mumbled, frustrated.

"Well, she must mean it then."

On their way out the kitchen door to Dewy's car, they encountered Adora again. She held a ceramic bowl of water. Dewy slithered out the door, holding his jacket in front of him.

Madera, actually excited to see Adora, whispered, "Did you do some type of spell? A love spell?"

Adora's doe eyes brightened. "You're welcome?" she said hesitantly.

"Oh, no, that didn't go well. Some of us don't want a bloody kiss," Madera half-lied.

She honestly didn't think Dewy could turn her on, but her mind revisited his kisses on her neck as she made her way to the door. Plus, now she was curious about the number of times he thought of her in his bed.

"Madera, you didn't use your bloodstone?" Adora nodded at Madera's neck.

Madera clutched her stone as if to protect it. Sure enough, she completely forgot about its ability to lighten the tension. *I could've stopped the blood from flowing if I wanted? Fuck!* But she preferred to kiss Dewy on her own time, not Adora's. Maybe Adora sent the wave of desire to keep Madera from asking more questions about Dewy's mother. But Adora didn't give off conniving vibes. Instead, she stared into the kitchen cabinet of essential oils and batted her eyes. "You deserve a little fun though, right?"

"But Sofia says not to play around with your powers too much," Madera answered.

"Oh, Madera. She was talking to you about that. Everyone loves a helping hand from Venus," Adora smiled.

A little embarrassed, Madera walked through the kitchen silently, then outside to the car.

2 2

"Eerie prohibition photos!" Dewy scanned the ominous walls of the Whistler's Room.

For privacy, they sat at a round table instead of at the bar. Eddie greeted Dewy and Madera with free drinks as they settled onto the spinning stools. The tall, slender glasses wore lemon wedges at their rims and cherries at the bottom. Bars around town were pushing these honey whiskey cocktails for the autumn season.

This was the first time they'd seen each other since their bloody kiss a couple days ago. Dewy wore a tailored plaid shirt which Madera discovered in his closet a couple weeks back.

"You look good in that," Madera said, peeling off her coat.

"Don't tease. Have you figured that out yet—the blood?" Dewy tossed the mini straws from his drink. They dampened his paper coaster that advertised a local beer.

"Haha. You know that was a one-time thing, right?"

"We only kissed, Mad. We didn't do a damn thing . . . yet," Dewy said, taking a sip, trying to lock eyes.

"I can't imagine taking more than two classes this semester." Madera shifted, deterring her eyes from Dewy's gaze. Instead, she focused on Eddie's laughter across the room.

"Because you're working." Dewy took another gulp.

"This drink's good as hell so be careful. By the way, what's up with Thanksgiving this year? No one is talking about it. It's like two weeks away, right?" Madera changed subjects again.

"Man, fuck Thanksgiving. My *Tia* and I don't celebrate that. I'll probably stop by my dad's though. What about you?"

"Ugh. Maybe Amaryllis will burn the turkey again? Or maybe I'll make it. Come to think about it, Diane did invite me to Thanksgiving at her place when I visited. That's the kind of Thanksgiving I've been missing!"

Madera sipped on her cocktail. She spun the tabletop's black candle holder around, watching the white votive candle slide from side to side. Last night was the second night in a row she'd gone to bed with Dewy on her mind, and she was curious what a night like this could lead to. They planned on heading to the lakefront next to smoke. Dewy had packed a couple of *sarape* wool blankets in the backseat of his car, as well as two solar lanterns, sketch necessities, plenty of weed, and a music box. And, of course, munchies.

As if on cue to start a show, Catalina blew in the door, waved to Eddie, and strutted toward their little round table.

"Hi everybody! I love industry night. Drink big and tip even bigger!"

Catalina slid a neighboring stool over to their table. Dewy's eyes blinked in brief annoyance. Madera knew he was expecting some one-on-one time with her—and she desired that, too, mostly in the hopes of persuading him to go with her to Florida. She had a few dates she wanted to whittle down. Now, Catalina and her over-the-top flowery fragrance hovered all around them. Eddie dropped off her free drink.

"Thank you, darling!" Catalina said.

"Oh, please. Give me like twenty minutes and I'll be joining you guys," said Eddie.

"Yes!" Catalina screeched.

Elbowing Madera, Catalina nodded toward the corner of the bar and said, "Is that Officer Scott?"

Sure enough, Officer Richard Scott was sitting alone. He straddled a stool, reddened elbows stabbed the bar top as his chin rested on folded hands. Madera imagined a dirty gin and tonic sitting between his arms. She was surprised she hadn't smelled him when they entered the bar.

"Why isn't he at Hendricks? Amaryllis is working the bar," Catalina said.

"Maybe he doesn't want to be seen," said Dewy.

"Richard!" Catalina yelled across the room.

Madera and Dewy exchanged quick looks of annoyance as Richard turned, waved, and stood.

"Girl, he was fine right where he was," Madera muttered.

She hoped he wouldn't want to be bothered. They were like kids to him anyway, right? Richard had to be in his late thirties or early forties. But this was the same creep that flirted with her after sticking it to her aunt. Hot coal simmered against Madera's navel.

"The more the merrier!" Catalina batted her eyelashes at her coworker, then looked back to Richard and said, "Grab a stool."

He obeyed, plunking himself down across from Catalina.

Not once did Richard look Madera in the eye. When he spoke, he addressed the small group collectively, eyes lingering between the bouncy bottle blonde and Dewy. The cop's sour vinegar smell overpowered even Catalina's flowery scent as the foursome huddled around the table.

"Not Hendricks tonight, huh? At Hendricks drinking your Hendrick's." Catalina asked.

"Sometimes you need to change things up. I may pass by there later. How are you kids?" Richard looked solely at Dewy.

"I'm good. How about you?" Dewy leaned down to take another sip of his drink. The crouch made his six feet appear taller.

"Hanging in there. Can't complain. Got your eyes on the Bears this year?" Richard gulped his Scotch.

"Naw, I really don't follow sports except soccer."

"It's futbol," Catalina corrected. She raised her drink and asked eagerly, "Should we get shots?"

Madera's face tightened. Drinking shots with Officer Scott was last on her to-do list. She answered, "I'm good."

"I'll pass," Dewy followed.

"What are you studying in school, Dewy?" Richard asked, brushing off Catalina's question.

Madera could almost feel her parents watching her at this moment. Sometimes, she'd imagine them together, looking in on her uncomfortable moments. Was Adan just as bitter as she was about Richard snorting his line of cocaine?

"Still undecided, but I'm an artist at heart," Dewy said.

"Oooh, like can you make a portrait of me?" Catalina winked, then returned to scrolling through her phone.

"Well, I do draw people. But I like tattoo art and mixed media the most."

"What's mixed media?" Catalina asked.

"A mix of different materials, right?" Richard said, sipping his drink. "Those can be awesome. Sounds interesting."

"I'm sure! More interesting than arresting bad guys?" Catalina teased the officer.

"Probably not as exciting as arresting bad guys," he answered.

Madera's stomach churned. Her slicked-back ponytail was wrapped in its scrunchie too tight.

"Well, as long as you're actually arresting bad guys and not pulling a Phillip Hughes move," Dewy said.

All eyes watched Dewy: Catalina's with inquisitive ignorance, Madera figured he was feeling his drink, and Richard stared with study, as if searching for an invisible insect on Dewy's face.

"Who?" Catalina's head cocked to the side.

"How do you know the great Officer Phillip Hughes?" Richard interrogated Dewy.

Fever struck Madera like lightning. In a flash, the dark Whistler's Room felt like a swirling storm. Dewy's eyes tried to soften hers, but she was already too mad.

Richard began to cough.

"Oh, no! Not again!" Catalina's scream startled patrons.

Now, when Madera released her madness, her fever cooled as the agony she caused Richard increased. She was spoon-feeding him pain, transferring her heat onto him. Calling Phillip Hughes *Great* only hiked up his bloody sentence. Blood poured from Richard's nostrils and mouth. He discarded his bloody vomit into his near-empty glass.

Madera, Dewy, and Catalina hopped from their bar stools in unison.

"Holy fuck! What is going on?" Eddie's voice dropped an octave.

He rushed over, his hands full of bar towels.

"Get the mop!" He cried to the barback, who paused for a sour look before fetching a plastic trash can.

"He's sick!" Catalina said in between rushed breaths. "He needs to go to the hospital. Richard, you need to go to the hospital. Like—"

"—Shush! He has to get it out of here," Madera urged Catalina into silence.

The hospital was too close to the police department. She didn't need anyone questioning her. But why would they?

Eddie slopped up the blood from the table while Catalina guided Richard to the trash can. Chunks of blood spilled from his mouth as if he'd been shot in the back of the head and a bit of his brain came with it. He struggled to breathe as blood flooded out of his nostrils.

"Take him to the restroom!" a man at the bar hollered.

Dewy touched the nape of Madera's neck. His touch was cool. The hair on her arms tickled and her eyes grew wide. She turned to see Dewy standing rigid like a statue.

"Stop it," he mouthed.

Obliging, she rubbed her bloodstone to lessen the flow, and Richard breathed easier through little gags. As the flow stopped, he buried his face in a white linen napkin. Richard yanked a couple of ten dollar bills out of his wallet and nearly forced them into Eddie's palms.

"No, no, you don't have to—" Eddie said.

"—Yes I do. You're fucking losing business because of this!" Richard pointed at a couple of tables closing tabs as Catalina rubbed his back.

With her body temperature rebalancing, Madera moved to an empty table. Dewy followed, grabbing their drinks. "You're a magic genius, I see," he said.

They sipped their drinks and observed the withering chaos: Eddie's tangled expressions, Catalina's fawning, and the boiled vinegar officer blowing his nose

"This is what my *Tia* meant. You *do* have powers," Dewy huffed.

"Yes, I do . . . And he knows Phillip Hughes."

Catalina said her goodbye with a soft bat of her eyelashes in their direction as she led Richard from the Whistler's Room.

"You think she's going to sleep with him?" Dewy asked.

"I hope so. Gives more chance of Amaryllis leaving him. But I don't want her to be heartbroken."

"If she cares that much for him, shit, maybe she deserves the heartbreak. Dude's a creep."

"Dewy! You sound like me." Madera chuckled, finishing off her cocktail.

Stepping away from the front door, Eddie, with a clean towel draped over his shoulder and hands on his hips, shook his head. He lifted his hands and announced, "So terribly sorry! Next round is on us."

Then he mumbled, "As if twenty dollars is enough to cover this. Cops don't make money."

"No, they make misery," Madera shouted.

Eddie smiled brightly and threw her a kiss through the air.

23

MADERA DECIDED IT WAS BEST TO LEAVE THE WHISTLER'S ROOM. SHE didn't want to drink too much since learning that mixing alcohol and weed would alter her consciousness in a reckless way—She didn't want to barf up any more mini planets. And she'd rather leave room for the lakefront smoke session.

As they said their goodbyes to Eddie and stepped into the chilly evening, Dewy received a phone call from his *Tia* that plastered his feet to the sidewalk. Madera stared down the block to see whether Catalina broke girl code and sped off with the Dick cop—the same man who had called Piggy Hughes *great*. Like Madera, Catalina didn't drive. She was an Uber girl. Richard's car was nowhere to be found. Madera had her suspicions.

She turned to see Dewy still on the phone. He sounded agitated.

"Like, right now? You need me to drop the car off right now?" Dewy shook his head, turning his back to his friend.

Uncertain of the night's agenda, Madera unzipped her backpack purse, pulled out her lip gloss, and began lacquering her lips. The little bit of alcohol she'd had made her feel a bit naughty. *So exactly why were there two blankets in the car? One intended for under them and one on top?*

Or was it one for each? Madera wondered even though going to the lakefront didn't seem too promising anymore.

Maybe they would go back to his house and participate in a ritual with the coven? That sounded just as exciting. What if Adora was there to give her more advice, play with her powers, or make her some special kind of tea. She wondered if Sofia would get after her for casually testing her blood skills on Richard. Maybe going to his house wasn't ideal. No, she needed to settle on a date for Florida. *Fucking Dick cop knows Piggy Hughes!*

"What's wrong?" Madera asked as Dewy slid his phone into his back pocket.

"I got to drop something off for my aunt. And then I'll drop you off because she needs my car."

"Wait? Doesn't she have her own car?"

"Yes. But . . . Look, *they* need my car. See, this is what happens when your car ain't really your car. I need to get some real money, fast. Probably should just talk to my dad."

"What do you have to drop off?"

"Who knows. I have to go by Romi's house and grab something there and then take it to Humboldt Park. I can take you home after that. Then I got to drop the car off at home. You cool to ride with me? Or do you want me to take you home first?"

Madera shrugged. "I'll go with you."

Cruising down Lake Street Dewy kept the newest Kendrick Lamar album at a medium volume. A train rattled above them as Madera packed Dewy's little one hitter—the kind that looked just like a cigarette. It was the only one Madera was cool with smoking in the car. She rolled her window down a couple inches.

"Where does Romi live?"

"Ukrainian Village. Off Chicago Avenue."

"She's Latina or Black or like me? I thought I heard an accent," Madera asked.

"Panamanian. Romi is short for Romelia."

"Well that makes sense. I know you're not feeling this, but something is exciting about this little mission we're on," Madera admitted.

"I'm glad somebody's enjoying this."

"Well, I'd much rather be with you at the Lakefront," Madera confessed.

"I'd hope so."

Madera inhaled deeply off the faux cigarette, then exhaled slowly, the smoke trailing through the open car window.

Dewy turned the music off as they pulled up to the small, yellow house with a picturesque porch, like one on a 1000 piece spring puzzle box. Where Romi sat swaying on the porch swing. Her eyes looked heavy, even from across the street. She wore a black hair bonnet with a brown cigar dangling from her mouth. She looked comfortable and warm in her vivid coral jogging suit. Beside her was a large, black insulated food pan carrier that resembled a safe.

Standing up, Romi appeared taller than Madera remembered, maybe about 5'8". She had a short torso and long legs. She scanned the block swiftly as if she were looking out for someone else. Madera followed her gaze both ways. No one.

"I'll be right back," Dewy slid out from the driver's seat.

Madera was hoping to be invited but instead she studied the scene from the passenger seat. She saw Romi angle her head to look into Dewy's car. Madera rolled Dewy's window down even further to allow the words to flutter in. Once again, the thought of Richard and Piggy knowing each other settled into her mind. Disgusted, it was almost unbearable for Madera to hold space for this fact. She concentrated outside.

"Thank you so much, Dewy! Is that Madera?"

Romi rested her cigar in a standing ashtray to wave her arms up over her head. Madera waved back.

"Yes. Is this it? Just this right here?" Dewy nodded at the mammoth food container, grabbing its handle.

"Why'd you leave her in the car?"

"Because, I just came for this. Right?" he said, showing his irritation.

"Yes."

Madera recalled being high when she met Romi before the bloodstorm. She was drunk and high the night Romi called out her Mars energy. She hoped the woman wouldn't judge her for her current state now. *What was Romi's special power? What was in her cigar?*

Dewy picked up the container and started down the stairs. Romi followed. As they approached the curb, Madera caught flashing lights in the rearview mirror. Red, blue, and white swirled. A short piercing siren sniped through the air, then silence. Madera's eyes widened, her heart pounding as a huge Chicago Police SUV skirted and stopped just behind Dewy's car.

Staring at what her mother saw moments before her murder— flashing cop lights—

Madera anticipated a fever to overtake her. But instead, she felt frozen. Through her depths she searched out the fever, somewhere in her body, but nothing. She pressed her hands together. *Where is my madness? I should be Mad?*

Across the street, Dewy and Romi froze, too.

The cop's door slammed as Madera shoved the one hitter into the bottom of her black purse and zipped it up.

A round-bellied Latino cop approached Dewy and Romi on the porch. He tugged his belt up over his waistline.

"How you folks doing out here tonight?" The officer asked.

Locking eyes with Dewy from across the street, Madera found he was somewhere between pissed and puzzled, but certainly not scared.

"Just fine, Officer. What seems to be the issue?" Romi said with softness, folding her arms against her chest. She was a bit cautious with her confidence. Unlike Dewy, her demeanor had shifted.

"What's in there?" The officer nodded at the container.

"Food, Officer," Romi responded.

"Open it up, please. I want to take a look."

"Why? Didn't she just tell you what's in it?" said Dewy, matching the edge in the cop's voice.

Madera swallowed. Even a Latino cop might give Dewy a bigger break than fellow Colombians who looked more like Sofia or darker. This had to be why Dewy was unphased, so ballsy. She felt relieved. Perhaps he was just waiting for Madera to spill blood.

"Open it up, Dewy. We don't need any problems." Romi said with a huff. She sought after Madera's eyes across the street and mouthed to her, "It's okay."

A wave of ease washed over Madera. She was feeling lightheaded and defenseless, unable to wreak one drop of bloody havoc. Maybe Romi was preventing her? Or maybe she exhausted her energy earlier, churning the blood up and out of Richard? Just sitting there, Madera felt faint, doubtful she could put an end to anyone's life, like Piggy's, if needed. Maybe she'd have to continue searching for death potions. She needed a plan b if her blood magic wouldn't prove powerful enough. This fact frightened her more than the scene unfolding before her. She would have to seek outside help. She wanted to master it all herself and she was confident she could until now. Madera breathed deeply, trying to bring herself back.

Madera smelled the food from across the street as Dewy opened the black box. The cop lifted the plastic lid and steam wafted up into his face as he directed his flashlight over it.

"Okay. You can zip it up. Just got information that something was fishy over here. Not many big black boxes being taken to cars or sitting on porches at this time of night. Good night."

The cop nodded and walked across the street to his SUV. He gave Madera a weak half smile. Static voices crackled through the cop's car intercom as he passed. Dewy snapped the latches closed. The SUV sped off, and Dewy mounted across the street in long strides. Romi followed, her arms still pressed against her chest.

"Madera, nice to see you again. Sorry you had to see that. Especially with your past and everything," Romi said, shaking her head.

Dewy opened the backseat door of his Volvo and slid the container smelling of curry on top of the wool blankets.

"Thankful nothing came about that. Do you think someone called the cops on you?" Madera said.

"I have my suspicions but nothing for you two to be concerned with. Just some nosy neighbors that want to cause drama for us hood witches!" Romi laughed, stepping from the curb. "Thanks again. You got the address, right?"

Dewy nodded and opened his door, his face one tight knot.

"Hurry off now. But be safe! I know your *Tia* needs the wheels," Romi said as she waved.

As Dewy sped off, he cursed, "Fuck!"

Madera shuddered, retrieving the one hitter from her purse. The November wind snapped at her through the slit of the window. She watched her friend chew his bottom lip, shake his head.

"You want a hit? You okay?" she asked.

"Ready for this night to be over with. I'm a fucking errand boy and I can't stomach these mutha fucking cops! What was the purpose of that? Huh?"

"I get it. I wanted . . . I wasn't sure if I needed to do anything back there, but I felt drained and—"

"—You didn't need to do anything, Mad. I understand my privilege. But I'm still pissed. There wasn't any real reason to do anything he did. Not one." Dewy took a purposeful breath before continuing, "Do you think you're depleted from using your powers on Richard? Because that was intense."

Madera placed the wooden smoke box into the cup holder.

"I think so."

"You may have to rethink the Piggy dream. You can't kill yourself trying to kill someone else."

Madera didn't like those words, as true as they were. She also didn't like the fact they were coming from Dewy. *What the fuck did he know?* Maybe she just needed more practice. A series of foul cops back-to-back to build her stamina. The fact kept clinging to her mind: Richard knows Piggy, and he calls him *great*.

"I'm overwhelmed," Madera admitted. "I need . . . I need to get this Piggy thing figured out. I have to. It's the only way to move forward, Dewy. I gotta try harder. I gotta practice."

Dewy didn't speak. He sat in his own frustration as Madera numbed herself with a couple extra hits of marijuana. She stared out the window sucking up the urge to cry as they drove up to a larger house to drop the food off to Oscar.

24

November brought a return to standard time, giving Madera morning light to dress by. Today she took time to gel her hair into a high ponytail, add two-strand twists, and wrap it all into a tall bun—the same hairdo that her mother once wore. She looked like royalty.

She donned one of the many black blouses she added to her wardrobe from hosting at Hendricks. This one had long sleeves with ruffles at the wrists. She felt at home wearing black. She loved red, but as of late, wearing it might be distracting—might make her stare at herself in the mirror all day.

Borrowing another custom from her mother, she'd taken her famous worn-out maroon jacket to the dry cleaners. Its leather reawakened, and to Madera, leather always smelled like blood. Reaching for her bloodstone necklace that she kept in the white mug, Madera noticed a sweet little spider plant in its place. Its soil was still damp from its first feeding. Her aunt had put it in her room without her knowledge, perhaps when she was asleep.

Sweetness was needed. She'd awakened with some sour thoughts since last night's drama at the Whistler's Room and that unexpected drive with Dewy. The mention of "Great" Phillip Hughes. The blood in Officer Scott's glass, Catalina's flowery-scented hand rubbing that pig's back—the same pig that spat on Ms. Della. The same pig that ejaculated acrosse the hall inside her aunt. The same pig that snorted the naughty offering intended for her father. The same pig that spewed his own blood into the snake plant, Severus. Madera recalled the prayer she'd offered for Severus on Amaryllis' birthday. Good to know it had been answered by Richard's own offering; Severus had grown about four inches since. Madera found her bloodstone necklace among the devotion notes on her altar and clasped it around her neck.

In the living room Madera surveyed all the plants, plus Amaryllis. Legs stretched out on the gray couch, she faced east toward the altar, wearing her usual smiley face pajama coat. A lace prayer shawl rested on her shoulders and an almost finished cigarette hung from her mouth. A tug of war between peace and burden played on her face.

Madera spotted new lit candles on the altar, long and white. Did Amaryllis actually clean the altar? The candleholders held no drippy wax. Madera recognized the symbols of each element there. Fire burned from the chunky purple candle that reigned in the center. Air danced, shifting the smoke of the burning sandalwood, Amaryllis' favorite. A lit palo santo stick was stuck in the soil of the red amaryllis flower that Madera had given her for her birthday. A clear glass saucer of water sat in front of the purple candle. And a couple burgundy leaves, bits of earth, rested on top of the altar's frameless oval mirror.

Madera felt the gift of a cool breeze. She learned to encourage all things cooling after blood had flowed. Even last night after Dewy dropped her off, Madera opted for a cool shower—maybe the same type of shower Dewy was taking lately.

"*Tia?*"

"Yes?" Amaryllis lifted her head up over the back of the couch.

"Thank you for the little spidey."

"Oh, you're welcome. I know I said I was going to pot one for you when you found that mug. Then I forgot. But I remembered today. Everyone needs a little alchemy. Get it? Alchemy, the plant. Anyways, I need to talk to you about something."

"What's up?"

Madera sat on the green rocking chair. She figured where this was going. Richard must've told her what happened at the Whistler's Room . The sole thought of Richard's name coming out of her aunt's mouth heated her flesh. Clearly, her body was well rested since the fever was so easily accessible and automatic. That was a good sign.

"I heard about the Whistler's Room," Amaryllis whispered, looking over her shoulder.

Madera's ears perked, hearing a bit of shuffling in the hallway and then a man clearing his throat: *ugh*.

"He's here?" Madera said.

"To get some shit he left here. But he called me last night when I got off work."

"You know he left with Catalina?"

"Yeah, he told me. She walked him to his car. I can only imagine," Amaryllis sighed, releasing a billow of smoke. "But I honestly don't give a fuck. I mean, *he broke up with me* even though we were never official. We were just having fun."

"He broke up with you?" Madera pulled at her blouse ruffles. The rocking chair creaked. Then she clutched her bloodstone for a sense of calm.

"Well, he blamed me for giving him *blood-mouth-cancer*," Amaryllis said, her fingers arcing in the air in quotation. "Or that's what his dumb ass is calling it. And, I know it has nothing to do with me, but it probably has something to do with you."

Madera genuinely wanted to laugh. Little did he know. "With me?"

"I didn't tell him that. I did *not* tell him that. I just let him think I'm some kind of backwards witch. I don't care anymore . . . It's actually kind of fun."

"You can't forget how he was towards me, *Tia*." Madera rolled her eyes like a pair of dice.

"Oh . . . I've been talking to myself about that. Just been too dick crazy, I guess. I'm sorry. I am. Like, a woman has needs but I need to use one of those dating apps. Sleeping with your customers is not it."

"I'm sure there's much better out there," Madera stressed.

"What's up with that painting in your room?"

"Oh," Madera nervously laughed.

"What's so funny? I know you didn't make that. You *know* how to draw or paint. Well, better than *that* . . . "

"All right! Stop, stop, my mom made that painting. Diane gave it to me on Halloween," Madera said. She'd be damned if she allowed Amaryllis to talk down her mother's painting. That painting was pure passion, not to be judged for its artistic merit. *Damn*, Madera thought. She now understood Dewy's frustration last night about his car. Well, it wasn't his car—the same way Madera's apartment wasn't her apartment. Maybe she needed her own place . . maybe after her trip to Florida she'd start saving for one.

"So that's what she painted after she went to Michaels? What does it mean? What the fuck is going on, Mad?"

"Look, I really just want to—"

"—You really want to know where Phillip Hughes is? Huh?"

"Wait, what did Richard tell you?" Still whispering, Madera's heart raced.

"These were his exact words: 'then that grungy Mountain Dewy kid brought up my cousin, Phillip.'"

His cousin? Madera rocked back in the chair, watching her aunt finally take the hanging cigarette butt out of her mouth and snuff it in the ashtray on the coffee table. "His cousin?" she finally said out loud.

"—He's coming," Amaryllis whispered as she reached for her cigarette pack and placed her finger to her mouth. Madera was surprised her hand was empty of the usual beer or wine that accompanied her chain smoking. At least her aunt had enough sense not to be heartbroken. She wouldn't have to assume the role of consoling her over this worthless man.

Shoe steps clicked along the hallway, followed by the uniformed Officer Richard Scott. His shirt collar hung loose at his neck.

"I'm outta here," he announced as if leaving for work.

He probably was. His Walgreens plastic bag held a few items, including clothing.

Turning from him, Madera focused on the cool, clear glass of water on the altar as she visualized her body as a wall blocking his energy. She felt his heavy green eyes fixated on her. She refused to return the look. She squeezed her bloodstone so hard she was fearful she would split the stone in half or maybe even crush it. She had to keep from screaming, let alone making blood ooze out his ass. *Damn, Amaryllis better sage the place today.*

"Okay. Take care."

Amaryllis allowed Richard to saunter back down the hall and let himself out. The door clicked closed and his shoes clicked faster down the stairs until their sound faded away.

Madera leaned forward. "You were telling me . . . "

"One time, Richard told me that his cousin was a cop—here—in Chicago. I know he comes from a family of cops. He has a couple cop relatives downstate. But the one here was in service from 1992 until, *como*, a few years ago? When I heard that Dewy randomly brought up this cop's name, I figured there had to be more to it. I did my own digging and here are my theories. You tell me if I'm wrong, okay?"

Her aunt's voice held a sturdy edge, the way she imagined her father's voice sounding. Madera slowed her rocking to listen. "What are your theories? Hurry up because my mind is fucking blown that this man you slept with is related to Phillip Hughes."

"Phillip Hughes killed your mother. That's my first theory," Amaryllis said.

"That is not a theory. That is a fact! He shredded her stomach apart for speaking up— speaking up on all the hate!"

On the altar, the fat purple candle's flame flickered like a golden blade.

"Your mom knew, deep down, something was going to happen to her," Amaryllis continued. "She had a dream about your future. Maybe that you'd seek revenge? And now Sofia is helping you figure it out."

"Well, I wouldn't say you are wrong. Sofia isn't helping me do this. She just gave me a concoction that made me dream about the day of the painting. Just guidance."

"But what the fuck—Blood! Do you really know how to make

people bleed, Madera? Like what is that about? Why did it start? Did it start with Richard?"

"You just theorized why, right? Revenge, to say the least. But what did he say about Phillip Hughes?" Madera pleaded.

"Phillip will be in town next week for his mother's birthday. About a month ago, Richard invited me to her party. I'm not going now. Fuck him. I really need to pray about all this!" Amaryllis gestured at their living room altar.

"You?" Madera jumped up from the rocking chair.

"My little niece has special powers that make people bleed? How does one make sense out of that? I'm guessing you have to be in front of them, since you can't make it happen to Phillip, right? But it's not cancer, it's just blood loss. Right? What the fuck? Like, I need a day or two to process all of this." Amaryllis stood up and grabbed her pack of cigarettes.

Holding back an urge to curse, Madera slapped her forehead and tugged at her blouse's ruffles.

"Madera, can you promise me that you won't get yourself into trouble? Can you promise that?" Amaryllis squinted, her mouth hung open. "Please?"

"I didn't ask for this power, *Tia*. This wasn't by choice. I need to get it out of me because it's in the way of a lot of things. I believe that after I confront Phillip Hughes, things will get better."

"Did you see Richard? He looks like he is shrinking! I'm sure that's what's been happening, Mad. Listen, I need some water," Amaryllis said as she headed to the kitchen.

Madera bit her inner cheek. *Piggy is coming to town!* It was time to see Sofia.

25

THE NOVEMBER SKY WAS THE COLOR OF TIN. MADERA'S OPEN MAROON jacket welcomed the crisp wind to kiss her chest. Her combat boots, polished and shiny, caught the stares of a jogging couple as she strode toward Sofia's brown bungalow, chewing on two sticks of peppermint gum. Like her mom, Madera was infamous for chewing wads of gum at a time. Two sticks were never enough. But today she kept it at two because she didn't want to smack too much in front of Sofia.

Madera asked Dewy to work with her on a psychology project in about an hour, but she arrived earlier to talk to Sofia. As she approached the curb, she saw Dewy's car wasn't on the block or the driveway, but there was Oscar carrying a large, cream-colored sack of coffee beans from a gray van. His dark eyes jabbed at Madera's subconscious. *Where did his magic lie? What did he do with that food Dewy dropped off to him last night? Maybe he was just there to provide muscle when needed? Or pleasure?*

"Hey, Madera! Come on in!" said Oscar, dressed in hospital scrubs.

Madera responded with a nervous half smile.

She followed him into the house where he put the bag of beans beside Romi, who was shaking caramel syrup into a freezer bag of coffee beans. Madera found it rather bizarre they were doing this in the living room. On the coffee table sat bottles labeled with flavors: coconut, hazelnut, macadamia nut.

"Mars decided to slide through, huh?" Romi greeted her, draped in a stained white apron, rocking her hair in a mushroom shaped purple afro.

"Hi, Romi," Madera cleared her throat.

"Back-to-back days I get the pleasure of seeing you around. Not often Mars comes looking for help."

"Oh, okay. I guess you're right. Is Sofia here?"

Madera hadn't expected so many people to be around, and their busy motions made her anxious. She felt relieved when Sofia stepped into the living room carrying a huge, black tourmaline crystal in a clear glass case. Sofia surveyed the room with curious eyes and cradled the boxed tourmaline like a precious newborn against her ivory jumpsuit. She set it on the glass table beside her chaise.

Madera moved to speak, but Sofia interrupted. "Romi, you met Madera, right?"

"Oh, yes! How could I forget her!" Romi said smiling.

"Madera, what kind of tea would you like? Nevermind the question, I know what you need," said Sofia as she headed for the kitchen.

Uneasy, Madera took a seat on the couch. She watched Romi pull a black sharpie from her apron pocket and scribbled a date and the flavor onto the freezer bag.

"I'm going to pick up the food," Oscar announced as he dropped off another bag of coffee beans.

"Thanks, O!" Romi said as he walked out the front door.

Curious questions flooded Madera's thoughts. "Adora is Venus, right?" Madera randomly stated as if trying to impress a teacher.

"Whoa, you're smarter than a fifth grader!" Romi snickered.

"She put a spell on me and Dewy last week . . . and it worked."

"Yes, I heard, but I may disagree about it being successful," Romi chuckled, revealing a little gap between her front teeth.

"There was blood and—"

"—You learned something, didn't you?" Romi cut her off.

"What do you mean?" Madera asked. A whiff of macadamia tickled her nostrils.

"Even in this moment of intensity, you can make room for a good time—if you choose! The last Mars energy around this place was so full of aggression that they depleted themselves entirely. Balance is essential in honoring our planets. Sure, you are majority Mars energy, but—"

"—Oh, don't get her started on planets! She won't stop!" Sofia teased as she entered the living room. She set a vintage gray teapot with a matching dainty saucer and teacup on the coffee table. "This is a peppermint and chamomile mix. It'll calm your nerves" She handed Madera a tea cup and saucer. "Relax."

"That's a good mix," Romi chimed in, straightening her apron, "My planet is Mercury, by the way."

"What does that mean?" Madera asked.

"A whole lot of communication, process of thinking, travel. I go on and on, but I don't have time to talk about myself today, believe it or not. I'm really excited about the idea of—"

"—What's going on, Madera?" Sofia cut off Romi's rambling and sat down on her chaise.

"Would it be best if I left?" Romi asked.

"Yes, please," Sofia answered.

Romi took her apron off and twirled out of the room, the rattling chime of the sunroom beaded curtains echoing behind her.

"Um, I found out from my aunt that the cop that killed my mom will be in town next week."

Sofia's eyes held steady. Madera couldn't read them; they reflected her own expression.

"I'm not sure what to do, and as much as the idea of getting rid of him feels good, is it really what I should do? I don't want to get caught."

"I understand." Sofia cleared her throat. "But I can't tell you what to do. You have to step into your power. I do know that the universe will protect those that need it when justice magic is done properly."

"But wouldn't justice be bringing people back? Like, my mama isn't going to just raise from the dead."

"Exactly. Where are these doubts coming from? They don't feel authentic. But bringing your mother back is not the purpose. And you know that." Sofia half smiled.

"So, the purpose is . . . ?"

"You must answer that. Sit with it, Madera. Yes, there could be a very big day next week for you. I can tell this day is coming faster than you expected. Maybe that's why there are doubts. But the rambunctious energy you had in my kitchen the other day told me you are ready to set that man into a bloody mess. Now, do you know where Phillip will be?"

"No. But I'm sure I can find out. My aunt was invited to the party, but she broke up with Officer Scott today. I can find out."

"Got it. So can I. We always find our ways around here. But *escuchame*, Madera—listen. It was about fifteen years ago that I met my friend, Everett."

That name rang familiar to Madera, but she couldn't place it.

"He's a great friend of mine. A very close friend. Everett's lived so many different lives and seen so many different things. He *knows* justice magic. That's all he deals with. Well, most of the people I love are tied to justice magic in one way or another. But one day, long ago, he came to me and broke down crying like a child, a sad defenseless child. I held his face in my palms and he pleaded. He pleaded with me about how our magic is needed more and more to battle. Battle the system. He told me there's no other way. The hands in power have secured the future to remain in their power. The only way to break the cycle is to work our magic. To have *faith* in our magic. I believe him. I see it—everyday. It makes me mad. I get sad, too, but I remember that I have to . . . I have to keep pushing, I have to keep pushing justice magic."

Sofia paused to point to Madera's cup of tea, and Madera filled her cup with the brew obediently.

Sofia continued: "Of course, your mom will not come back, but you carry power that'll extinguish future possibilities of cases like your mother's. Think about it. I do believe that moving forward on Phillip will clear headspace for you. Take time. I know it's next week but you're too hot for fast answers right now."

"If I don't do anything next week then it seems like everything will remain the same until I confront that awful man? Including more senseless murders."

"You don't have enough blood magic or justice magic to counter all the corruption that the police force offers! There needs to be a team of you in every city for that to ever happen. You are young enough, passionate enough, and dedicated enough to spearhead such a thing— if that's what you want. You gotta want it. But like everything, Madera, your mother is your root, and the seeking out and properly handling her killer will stabilize and enhance your magic. How can one stand without a sturdy base? It's required, even for your happiness."

Sofia's eyes cast a blinding light and a chill raced down the back of Madera's neck as she straightened her posture with intention.

From the kitchen, Madera heard keys jingling. Perhaps startled by the movement in the kitchen, Lamb's Ear dashed in from the hallway. Dewy appeared with a pair of gym shoes in his hand. Madera was surprised to see him in workout gear—a sweaty long-sleeve thermal and basketball shorts. His calf muscles bulged and his brow glistened with sweat.

Madera was also surprised to see Dewy's eyes squint into a wince when he saw her. That didn't make sense; they were to meet in an hour or so anyway. *Maybe he doesn't want me knowing he's been working out? Maybe he found some other girl to release all his tensions with.* Madera suppressed a nervous giggle.

"You're here early. I thought I was picking you up," Dewy muttered.

"You're not the only one she comes to this house for," Sofia said, petting Lamb's Ear, who had jumped onto the chaise. "Did you have a good workout?"

"Yes. Hopping in the shower," Dewy said, barely audible this time, as he walked down the hall.

"Madera, remember the universe provides when things are needed. Believe it! If that situation with Dewy and Romi last night called for your magic, you may have had enough energy to conjure it. You got to *believe* it. And the universe also provides for us to seek wisdom and knowledge about those things. Don't be afraid to ask for help, but have faith in your magic and the universe that gave it to you —that is the first step!"

"Did Dewy tell you about all that?" Madera asked, eyes wide and tea cup held close to her lips.

Sofia smiled. "No. It just hopped in my mind. That happens sometimes."

TWO HOURS LATER, MADERA'S EARS WERE RINGING FROM THE psychology experiment she and Dewy were assigned. They were researching whether various music genres led them to different physiological responses. Dewy normally favored hip hop and Madera liked rock, but they had to listen to new age music by an Irish woman named Enya. They checked their pulses and jotted down their first thoughts and emotions. Madera was certain there was more to the assignment but neither of them cared to double check. Their minds weren't too concerned about class.

Madera slammed shut her notebook and stood up. "That was a snoozefest." She said sliding her pen into her twisted hair bun.

Standing up from his bed, Dewy laughed and nodded in agreement. He stretched his arms above his head and yawned as Madera watched.

"Ready to hit the road?" Dewy's question sounded tangled.

Dewy had a round mouth with a bottom lip just a bit more plump than his top one. To Madera, he was good looking, just not particularly sexy. He could pass as a tan twin of Kurt Cobain. His sandy brown hair was natty most of the time, and any girl would admit his hazel eyes were poetic; but Madera never really favored fair eyes. Physically, it was mostly his blunt facial expressions and strong Carib

Indigenous nose that drew Madera. And the way he ran his fingers through his hair, his unabashed natural charm, and his genuine concern for her. Dewy had stepped up his wardrobe and was working out since the first time their lips touched, but she didn't like Dewy thinking he ought to change for her. Even if it did make him more attractive.

"Sure, I'm ready." Madera slid her backpack purse onto her back. She grabbed her jacket as if to walk out into the cold without putting it on. But she was not ready to go. She wanted to see if she could kiss him with the absence of blood. Of course, it was her escalated passion that made her bleed last time she visited Dewy. Now, after listening to the music of a woman that seemed to sing with ocean birds, Madera was in the perfect tranquil state to slip a kiss onto Dewy's lips without repercussions.

She stepped in front of him. He pulled her hip in closer and dipped his head to meet hers. The kiss was long, soft, and endearing. Madera held one hand over the bloodstone before they pulled apart.

"Come on, let's go," she said before he tried for more.

A surprised smile slid across Dewy's face. "No blood?"

Madera shrugged. "I'm working on that. But we have to go slow."

Glancing up, Madera caught sight of Dewy's Frida Kahlo poster. Dressed as the little wounded deer, Frida exuded a calm sadness that Madera feared would shake the confidence out of her magic. Those somber eyes, the arrows, that blood, the pain—all signs of Frida's inevitable fate.

"I don't like her staring at me," Madera blurted out. Her lips curled at the sullen artist.

Dewy laughed, "I like deer."

"But do you like Frida looking defenseless? Isn't that a painting she made at the end of her life?"

Dewy paused, his hand caressing her hip. "Yes, but, like all art, it can be interpreted differently every time you look at it. Now, we can go . . . or we can stay?"

Biting her inner cheek, Madera stepped over Dewy's foot and out into the hallway, leading the way.

26

It was the day before Penelope Hughes' 85th Birthday Bash. "Location: River Forest. Bring your best wishes and dancing shoes!" Shortly after sunset, Madera sat on the rooftop, staring at the electronic Evite her aunt had forwarded her. The invitation was painted in sky blue and metallic gold pixels, almost as if the party was for a royal little boy.

Madera still hadn't any specific plans. The past week flew by and she was counting on the universe to bestow her some kind of direction. The desire to ask for help did not come to her. Maybe she just had to react on impulse tomorrow, which sounded more like her speed. *The forces will have my back, somehow, right?* She didn't know how long the calling would continue to wrestle and fester inside her. Sofia confirmed Madera's need to use her blood magic, her justice magic: there was no other way to battle the system.

On the rooftop, Madera sat on a gray blanket with her gray scarf around her shoulders. She lifted a bottle of South American Malbec and drank from it. She had fallen for its taste after Marvin had the Hendricks crew sample it. Its taste reminded Madera of the black currant jelly toast that her mother made her for breakfast. Toast with jelly and a banana. Toast with jelly and one boiled egg. Toast and jelly and some turkey sausage. Jelly toast was always on the morning table.

Staring out at the Chicago skyline, Madera reflected on how this all started; the Coffee Magician. The rugged look of his peppery facial hair appeared identical to the man she spotted at the Whistler's Room. Or maybe it was all in her head. Regardless, the small role in her life held enough weight that it kept revisiting her. Maybe Sofia knows why he keeps coming back to her mind. Sitting down cross-legged, Madera took a long chug from the bottle. She tugged at her necklace of shells and fake pearls, the one that once hung in her mother's Toyota. The one she normally kept inside an old Adidas shoe box under her bed near the letters from Diane. She decided to wear it tonight. Madera's mind settled on the necklace's history.

With half her tax refund, Constance had bought the beige 2001 Toyota Corolla from a Bella's Binge regular, Mrs. Peterson—an old lady the color of soy milk with a matching bob. She smelled of peppermint medication and so did the car—all the way up to Constance's death. Her mother kept Mrs. Peterson's green tree-shaped air freshener in the car and added the beaded necklace with shells and fake pearls around the rearview mirror.

Madera made the necklace on summer break the year before. Thinking of nothing special, Madera gave the long necklace to her mother. She simply plopped it on Constance's belly one Saturday morning as her mother lay across the multicolored chindi rug in their sunroom. Constance was watching the leaves on the tree outside with the breeze.

"What's this?"

"It's just a necklace. For you," Madera said. Constance smiled, held it tight, and kissed it.

Much too soon, Diane would place the necklace back into ten-year-old Madera's hands. "Do you want to keep this?"

Madera accepted it without words. She knew the necklace saw what happened to her mother. The unopened mail on the passenger seat and the broken orange umbrella on the backseat floor in the Toyota—maybe they didn't see it, but they sure did hear it. Madera kept all these things, hoping that one day, when she was ready, someone or something would tell her the truth.

Now, the necklace laid against Madera's abdomen, between her navel and chest. It framed her gold-chained bloodstone like a guardian.

Guardian. Madera laughed at that word. It was an odd word, like the word "orphan" which always sounded outdated and dusty, like a forgotten rural town after the young fled, leaving the elders to comfort one another until their death. To her, "orphan" described an old person who hadn't a single child, a niece or baby cousin, or anyone, to care for them. The words "survivor" or "striver" sounded more fitting for her situation. Maybe even "hero."

Madera stared at the black wine bottle with its red substance. A wave of rowdy wind slid into her mouth. She coughed, looking down at the street when a familiar voice hollered. Ms. Della waved her arms under the streetlamp. Madera followed the stairs down and outside to join her.

"You like being up on that roof?" Ms. Della asked as Madera crossed the street.

"I'm surprised you're still out here yourself. You're not cold?" Madera said, her black wool scarf hung loosely around her shoulders, playfully flapping like a pair of lazy wings alongside her makeshift cape, the gray blanket.

Ms. Della smelled like lilacs this evening, and her wheelchair was polished as if anointed. She wore a comfortable cream jogging suit with her short hair, hanging just above her ears, styled neatly. She held a handkerchief in her right hand.

"Ida down the block just did my hair. On my way back, I was trying to talk to some man that came up on your stoop looking around at the apartment names. He didn't say anything, but it looked like he was praying or something. It was suspect if you ask me. You know I have to keep my eyes on this block." Then Ms. Della patted her hair as if fishing for a compliment.

"Your hair's sharp . . . but what did this man look like?" Madera asked as she raised the wine bottle to take a quick swig.

"Older Black man. Not old like me. I'm sure he has nothing to do with you. Never seen you or your aunt with a Black person. You Black, right?" Ms. Della joked.

Madera frowned; it wasn't funny. She always felt her mother's murder separated her from her Blackness.

"Blackness is in your DNA. I see it," Ms. Della said reassuringly. "You've been wearing a lot of black, though. What's going on? What or who, should I say, are you mourning, baby girl?"

"No. I'm not mourning, really." Madera took another drink from the bottle.

"Then why you running around here looking like a witch, drinking red wine out the bottle? Ha! You do your thang, Madera. But be careful. You're still a lot better than those kids with them damn phones glued to their gotdamn faces. My God, that's why Jesus is going to come down because he needs to make sure these kids can still look people in the eyes. So many idiots out here. I tell you! It's 2015, we probably have another five years before this world crumbles," Ms. Della rattled, then glanced at her watch. "It's getting late now. Almost ten. I need to get my ass in the bed. But why are you drinking out the bottle? You sure you okay?"

Drinking from a wine bottle under a light post on a Friday could make her look like a sad-eyed bum. Madera replaced the bottle's cork.

Ms. Della shook her head. "Girl, you better get inside. Wait—there goes that man, right there," Ms. Della said and nodded in his direction.

The man's profile resembled the Coffee Magician.

Watching him stroll, Madera's insides bubbled. She placed the wine bottle on the pavement as he started to casually jog east, away from her.

"He's up to something. Not sure if I've seen him around before. May have . . . " Ms. Della mumbled as Madera took off, racing after the man down the one-way side street.

The long tails of Madera's black scarf became one with the small blanket and billowed in the wind behind her. She bounded down the side street but saw no one. Not one door closing due to some unexpected man running by. And not a sound: no sirens or dogs barking. Just a fat feral cat scooting across the street.

At the end of the block, she saw a black Volvo parked with the lights on, engine running. Madera jogged toward the car. Maybe she could ask the driver if they saw a Black man with bushy eyebrows sneaking around. Swifter than an alley rat, the car sped off. Madera stared as it drove away from her, trying to see if it was indeed Dewy's car.

"Mad? Mad!" Ms. Della hollered after her as her wheelchair squealed towards her.

"Damn it!" Madera huffed, out of breath. "I didn't see the license plate. That car went too fast. But it couldn't be Dewy. No. That wasn't him."

"Child, take a breath. Did you find the man? You know him, huh?"

"I . . . I don't know him. I mean, I do. Look, I need to call Dewy. Something's not right." Madera walked back toward her greystone apartment.

"I got your bottle if you want it. If you don't . . . I'll take it," Ms. Della said as she sniffed its contents.

"All yours!" Madera hollered.

Pale and frazzled, Madera found Amaryllis in the kitchen pulling a Sol beer out of the refrigerator.

"Well, you've officially lost your summer color," she said.

"Have you seen my phone? Can you call my phone?"

Ignoring her aunt's comment, Madera scanned the kitchen. She peeled off her scarf and blanket and tossed them onto a kitchen chair. She lifted a pile of mail and a kitchen towel. She peered behind a bowl of limes.

"*Espera*! What the hell? You expecting a call?" Amaryllis closed the fridge with her hip and pulled her phone from her back jean pocket. She opened her beer and took a sip with excruciating slowness. "*Relajate*, I'm calling you."

Frantic, Madera detected a muffled vibration coming from her bedroom. She darted to her unmade bed and fought with the heap of blue covers. "Can you call again?!"

"I am!" Amaryllis stood at Madera's bedroom door, her brows furrowed.

"Got it!" Madera fished the phone from under her bed.

"Are you okay?"

Amaryllis folded her arms, beer in one hand, phone in the other. She leaned against the door frame. Her black work blouse showed a red sauce stain on the collar. Must've been the marinara from the cheese sticks appetizer, Madera thought, finally catching her breath. With a huff, Amaryllis turned and left.

Dewy answered on the third ring. "What's up, m'lady!"

"Huh? You never call me that. Where are you?"

"At home. Why? You coming over? I can pick you up."

"What are you doing?"

"Just finished this bad ass fish scale drawing on my arm. Mads, this shit is dope. I can ink you up if—"

"—No. Look. Were you around the corner about ten minutes ago?"

Madera heard Dewy coughing. He was clearly hitting his bowl. "What? You talking to me? Remember when I drew those cat tails and—"

"—Yeah. But I'm not coming over now. Guess what? I saw the Coffee Magician. You know, the one from the train who had the—"

"—The white mug. That guy. Aww. That made your day, I'm sure. Where'd you see him?"

"Around the corner. No! Down the street. Ms. Della said she saw him on my stoop looking at the names in the apartment building. Like, why? Why would he do that?"

"Maybe he's stalking you?" Dewy exhaled a chuckle.

"Dewy, that's not funny. Why would he stalk me?"

"Because you're magic, too?"

"You think this is funny? You're not freaked out by this? Not one bit?"

"Mad, what do you want me to do? Huh? Go looking for him and see why he was at your stoop? I will if you really think this guy is being creepy, by all means, let me know. Or . . . are you drinking, Mad?"

"That doesn't matter."

"What do you need from me, Mad? I'm here. Always."

"Nothing. Don't need nothing. Just going to get some sleep. Bye."

Madera tried to yell but could only muster enough energy to toss her phone across the room and roll on her mattress like a child in a tantrum.

"*Tia!*" she whimpered.

Amaryllis returned with her Sol bottle in hand, dressed in a light blue pajama coat.

"That's new. Those pajamas?" Madera sat up with her elbows, trying to regain her composure.

Taking a swig of her beer, Amaryllis nodded with concern.

"Had to treat myself with some post-Richard jammies! But what the fuck is up with you, *sobrina?*"

"Ugh. I'm not sure what's going on but . . . " Madera stopped herself, remembering that Amaryllis didn't know about the Coffee Magician. Nor did her aunt know about the L trip where she first encountered him, being arrested by her cop ex-boyfriend. Madera had no energy to go down that rabbit hole today.

"Never mind."

"Listen, I've been thinking about tomorrow. I know I gave you the address of that party but how are you going to do this?"

Madera knew her aunt was genuinely curious. She hadn't given her the address for nothing. Amaryllis was capable of vengeful thoughts. She yelled passionately at thrillers on television, she made a handful of voodoo dolls just to practice her crocheting a few years back, and she practically hexed rude drivers on the road. She was really good at holding grudges, too—a trait she blamed on her Scorpio sun sign.

"I don't need to struggle trying to bail you out or anything, but your gift of blood shedding is untraceable, right?" Amaryllis asked.

"I have to believe that. It's their blood that leaks, not mine. And I'm not the one losing weight. I'd be dead by now if people were shedding my blood."

"So? What's your plan? Your tummy warms up and you concentrate on him and he starts bleeding? Is it enough to send him to the hospital?"

"I think I can manage it. Hiding in a shed or maybe at the corner of the block. I can't let myself be seen. Richard knows who I am."

She hadn't a clue what to do or what was to happen tomorrow. Should she take a page out of the Coffee Magician's book and follow Phillip Hughes to the airport and nab him as he waited for his flight? Where was his hotel? Should she pretend to knock at the wrong hotel room door and get his blood spilling as he opened the door? Maybe it would work best in the hotel elevator. Or what if he was staying at his mother's house? Would she pretend to sell Mary Kay and ring the bell?

"Listen, I'm here for you. I get it. *Tu sabes*, I love the idea of Richard suffering a bit, watching his cousin struggle with a worse case of blood mouth cancer than him. Maybe he'll think it's genetic!" Amaryllis said.

"Maybe," Madera added. "I know I need to get some sleep. I feel dizzy thinking about it."

"Let me know what I can do for you. I don't want you to feel . . . overwhelmed. Good thing you just have a short shift in the morning," Amaryllis said, then closed the door.

Madera was relieved to hear her aunt's enthusiasm for her mission, whether for her niece's cause or just to see Richard suffer. She rolled over, wondering if Ms. Della was enjoying her wine. As her eyes grew heavy, the Facebook profile photo of Phillip Hughes popped into her. But she preferred to fall asleep imagining Dewy inking her inner thigh with an intricate mandala of mini bloodstones. Bloodstones that would clog any chance of blood to flow from him or her during any moment of intimacy.

27

AT EIGHT IN THE MORNING, MADERA, WEARING HER CLOTHES FROM LAST night's rooftop visit, was awakened by the looming presence of Amaryllis. Looking excited and a bit perplexed, she held a small, unfamiliar gold and red treasure box, about the size of a bible.

"Someone named Romi dropped this off. She was maybe Dominican? Purple hair. You know her?" Amaryllis said.

If Amaryllis was going to invite herself into her bedroom, this was definitely a good reason to.

Wiping sleep crud from her eyes, Madera rose from bed. Her heart thudded against her chest as a warm rush covered her skin. She took a few deep breaths to lower her temperature. Today would play a heavy toll on her body, even while possibly validating her wildest dream. Maybe Sofia realized Madera needed more help than she was willing to ask for. After all, Romi did say, "Not often Mars comes looking for help."

Trembling, Madera took the box from her aunt's hands. It was lightweight and dainty. Inside she found a large bloodstone, about the size of a baseball, with bath salts sprinkled all around it. The salts, translucent like clear quartz, smelled of blood. The aroma fueled an urge to kill inside Madera as her mother's words echo in her mind:

Damn, evil souls dressed in uniforms. Does that mean we attack them? Does that mean we kill them? Life is filled with options for a reason, I mean . . . would it be easier to kill the ignorant than to teach them? They already hate us. They're already killing us. They already made up their minds with what they want to do with us.

A note underneath the bloodstone read: "Take a bath for at least a half hour with this stone and bath salts. Do this first thing in the morning, so that it will guide you in the steps you must take for your quest today. Always with you in spirit, Sofia."

Madera turned to her aunt, who stood behind her reading along, silently, uncertain. Madera knew Amaryllis didn't envy her niece's "calling" though she may hold some jealousy of Sofia's knowledge and guidance. She sensed a desire in Amaryllis' heart—the desire to become a proper witch. *Tia* always chased magic, but she'd never sought outside help in human form. *Ha, maybe, we have that in common,* Madera thought. Instead Amaryllis paged through books, listened to parts of podcasts, and sometimes put things on her altar. The side effects of working at Hendricks stunted Amaryllis' potential.

"I'll clean the tub and run the bath water," Amaryllis offered.

Once the tub was clean, Amaryllis brought in a timer and they agreed on forty-five minutes. As she ran the water, the crystal-like bath salts bloomed into red bubbles. The bath didn't smell like blood, but it sure looked like it, and that made Madera smile.

After Amaryllis left her to rest in her bath, Madera's mind began to wander as she thought of all she needed to do. She made a mental note to ask, at some point, for Sofia's advice on the Coffee Magician. Why did she keep seeing him—or was she hallucinating? Ms. Della saw someone last night. Also, Madera wasn't sure whether to call out of work. But something beckoned her to at least stop in for her short lunch shift at Hendricks. And all the while, Madera rotated the position of the bloodstone from sitting on her navel to being sandwiched between her upper thighs. Amaryllis suggested this, recalling what she knew about chakras. "Bloodstone is connected to the root chakra. It is the base. The drum. Home."

As she drained her bathwater, Madera awed at the loud gurgling of the drain. She felt her whole being open up, wide and wild, available to feel and take action where needed. Damp but wrapped in her towel, Madera prayed for protection. Leaving for the day, she kissed her mother's picture, rubbed her father's photo, and watered her spider plant.

~

"WHAT ARE THE ODDS WE'RE BOTH WORKING THIS SUCKY SHIFT? WHAT are the odds . . . isn't that like an expression?" Catalina laughed, her hair now back to a more natural blonde. She tossed a clean bar towel at Madera.

"Yes, it is. I'm actually more surprised that they ok'd for Ginger to work this evening," Madera joked.

"Big boobs, duh! Of course they did. What's your plans this evening?" Catalina said as she stroked her hair.

"Ah. Just a party out in River Forest."

"What! Me too. Well, I'm working one. Officer Scott's aunt is turning eighty or eighty-five or something. He asked me to come pour drinks for like a shitload of money, but I know that things went south with Amaryllis and him and everything. Trust me, he's not trying to get me in bed. Well, I don't think so. Plus, I don't break the girl code— and if he really wanted me, wouldn't he take me as his date and not as a bartender? You're like going to be in the *same* town, what are the odds? What's going on there?"

A sharp lump clogged Madera's throat. A purposeful swallow did not help. She rubbed her hands, moist with anxiety, against the sides of her thighs. This piece of intelligence must be why the universe sent her to Hendricks. She learned not only would she have to keep away from Richard, but from Catalina, too. How exactly does a twenty-year-old woman of color hide herself at some random old white lady's party in a wealthy suburb? And, Catalina might say, what are the odds of them being at the same random party?

"Oak Park. I meant Oak Park. River Forest is right next to it," Madera lied. "All the suburbs have names like trees. Sorry. A friend of

Dewy's is having a party there. Birthday. Twenty-five not eighty-five."
She forced a smile, but Catalina was busy gathering the menus from
their holder and didn't notice.

"What time?" Catalina asked. "Because if I'm done early, maybe I
can have a couple drinks with you guys or something. If that's okay
with the birthday boy? *Yo no se*. Never really hung out in the burbs like
that. That's what they call them, right, 'the burbs'? For like the
suburbs?"

"Yeah," Madera nodded. She sprayed Windex on a menu and began
wiping it clean with the towel.

"So, what time is the party?"

"I think eight. What about yours?"

"I have to be there at five. Ugh. But it doesn't start until six. I will
certainly want a drink after that. So, text me the addy."

"How long are you staying for?"

"Oh, I think until ten or eleven? Yeah."

"Are you taking the train?"

"Yea, it's like right off the Metra. He said that it's like a block away
like Bonnie Brand or Brae Lane or Bonnie Brae? Some double-B
name street. Ha! I said double B. I guess it's better than saying double-
D street," Catalina laughed at her own joke. "So, he told me to just
Uber it from the train and it shouldn't be more than like a few bucks."

"What are you wearing?"

"He said to wear what I usually wear here. Something black. I
mean, I will be serving old folks so I can't get too sexy," Catalina
moaned. "What about you?"

"Oh, I don't know yet. Always black."

"That seems to be your thing now, huh? Like, I don't see you that
much outside of here, but you never change into anything when you
leave or come with anything different on. So, all I picture about you is
black . . . like the color, your clothes. Didn't mean to sound racist or
anything. That was odd—What about your hair? You're not going to
keep it slicked back, are you? I really, really want to see you with some
hot red highlights. *Como* dynamite red, *tu sabes*," Catalina looked up
for Madera's approval.

"Oh," Madera shrugged. "Maybe one day."

"Are you okay?" Catalina's question sounded sincere.

A bit alarmed and aware she had to play it cool, Madera decided she would pretend to be sick, gradually, throughout the shift. Her co-workers would completely forgive her furiously nervous demeanor, and the ruse would keep Catalina from recruiting her for revelry. She would be home, too sick to go to "the burbs" to party.

"I think so. Tummy's a little queasy, that's all," Madera winced.

"I have some Tums. Want one?"

"I think I'll grab some soda water from the bar," Madera said.

She'd come to the restaurant with Amaryllis, who was working a double that day. A huge thermos of Hendricks Steakhouse's finest coffee—with a splash of Baileys—sat in front of Amaryllis as she organized her bar drawer, her chipped burgundy nails flipping through the dollar bills as she counted.

Madera watched her aunt with a bit of grief. She didn't want to lose her. She never really understood why Amaryllis felt the need to drink so much. She was a hard worker, she cleaned hard, laughed hard, loved hard, but why—why did she have to drink hard. That had to be a family trait, one shared with her father, who did everything hard, too, no? At this rate, Madera couldn't imagine her aunt's condition in another ten years.

"I'm not feeling well," Madera lied.

"Bullshit, you're just nervous. That bath wouldn't have done that," Amaryllis said softly, continuing to count in her head. She lifted her eyes to focus on her niece.

"Catalina's bartending at the party tonight," Madera mumbled.

"Really? So, another obstacle besides that fucking Richard? Look, I don't hold a job just to bail you out, so please, tell me what's the plan?" Amaryllis moved to stand hip-to-hip against her niece.

"Can I use your car?" Madera asked.

"What—when? Today?"

"I just want to visit Sofia for a little."

"You have a shift."

"I'm not feeling good," Madera spoke up, burying herself in the lie.

Amaryllis rolled her eyes and looked about to throw something. She threw words instead: "I've been pretty fucking patient with all this stuff you're into . . . and doing . . . and bleeding. I want all of this to be over. Actually, don't tell me what you plan on doing. I really don't want to know. I just want you alive and not in trouble. Can you do that for us? Please. Like, all we got is each other. *Me entiendes?*" Amaryllis swiped an angry tear before it could fall.

Madera took a deep breath and said, "I will. I will stay alive, and I won't get in trouble *if* you do us a favor."

"What? My car? Yes. You can use it. Just see first if you can leave now. They never really need two hostesses until two on a Saturday anyway."

Amaryllis flagged Catalina. They made the case for Madera's sickness and obtained the early dismissal.

"Call me," Amaryllis said sternly. "That's what you do. Call me when all this is over. I'll be heading out around eleven tonight. Okay? I'll Uber home. If I don't hear from you, I'll find you."

"I had another favor to ask . . . besides the car." Madera whimpered.

"Later," said Amaryllis.

2 8

Sunbeams penetrated the driver's window of Amaryllis' little blue Honda, sending a warm tickle along Madera's face. She put her hand on her cheek to cool it. The mid-November day was unusually sunny, perfect for scheming an early dismissal from work.

Madera parked Amaryllis' car down the block from Sofia's house. She hoped Sofia's guidance today would be clear and direct. She didn't want to leave the house still pondering what to do. Madera carefully put the car key in the inside pocket of her black leather backpack purse, exchanging it for her mother's necklace. She kissed the necklace and folded it down like a snake dancing into her palm. This necklace would witness the end of Phillip Hughes, the same way it bore witness to the end of Constance. She pulled it over her head, allowing it to rest against her black blouse—the one that held a golden shimmer.

Glancing up at Sofia's house, Madera was surprised to see Dewy walk out the door. She studied him—he walked like a jock now, his days at the gym already molding his slender physique—and wondered just how good he could make her feel. As usual, he wore his pumpkin-orange hoodie and gray sweatpants. He stood on his front porch and stared straight ahead, revealing his profile to Madera. Somehow nervous, she slumped down in her seat. *Why the fuck am I nervous about Dewy?* Was Adora playing around, projecting love vibes again? Now was not the time. She watched him type into his phone. A moment later her phone buzzed. Madera reached into her purse, eyes still pasted on Dewy's frame. Did he know she was there and was telling her to get out of the car? He faced the sun and closed his eyes, basking in its warmth.

She read the text: "Thinking of you on this sunny day. Be safe. I love you."

Madera's eyes welled with tears as if she imagined Dewy's voice speaking the words he just wrote to her. When she looked up after wiping her eyes with her wrist, she saw a woman standing behind Dewy in a charcoal trench coat, her red hair was short like his, and she held a cigarette in her hand. A warm wave swept over Madera as she recognized the woman; the middle-aged redhead from the Whistler's Room. She looked tired, dragged. Almost sullen now, Dewy brushed his hand through his hair, turned, and began talking to the woman.

A soft spark of jealousy flooded behind Madera's teary eyes as she squinted to get a better look. This spark quickly lost its flame once Madera understood why the redhead's eyes and her striking white teeth looked so familiar. She was smoking with pearly whites in her mouth? The only other person who did that was Dewy. This wasn't any woman, this was Dewy's mother, the fair *Colombiana* Dewy never wanted to talk about. If Sofia and this woman were indeed sisters, melanin had favored Sofia; her complexion was as copper as a penny, set off with a plump, pretty mouth. The redhead was a diluted version of Sofia, her skin like gouda cheese, a pinch darker than Dewy's. Her mouth, shaped like Sofia's, appeared thinner.

Already feeling like an intruder, Madera wished Dewy would leave. She needed to talk to Sofia: her counsel, her cup of tea. Time was running out.

Both Dewy and the redhead followed the noise of the car door as Madera stepped out. Their bright eyes, misty and calming, stared at her as if she were wearing wings. They didn't move, didn't speak, they simply watched as Madera strolled their way. Madera locked eyes with Dewy, whose statuesque posture gradually folded back into his familiar slump.

"Good Morning! Or is it afternoon already?" Madera muscled out a half-smile to soothe the awkwardness. "Hi, I'm Madera."

"Oh, yes! I'm Lila. I'm . . . Dewy's mom," said the redhead as she took a drag from her cigarette. "My sister's in there!"

Madera glided up the stairs and said, "Nice to meet you."

How does she know I'm here to see Sofia?

Dewy looked his friend up and down and shook his head briskly. "You came out the car looking like a superhero. This shit is wild. Amaryllis really let you drive her car?" Dewy laughed.

"Superhero?" Madera raised her eyebrows.

"Pretty much," Lila said.

"Wow, okay. That's cool. Yes, believe it or not, Amaryllis did. It's been crazy since I spoke to you last night." Madera smiled at her friend.

"Please, Madera, you can go on in. Sofia's here." Lila opened the screen door with unexpected force. She stepped past Madera to push open the main door and yelled, "Sofia, Madera is here!" She sounded excited, as if she'd won a scavenger hunt.

Madera gently closed the door behind her as she entered the house. Other people were in the front room; she felt the weight of their eyes. She found Sofia sitting upright on her chaise, bare feet crossed at the ankle, red mug of tea in her lap and a look of strained wisdom on her face. Romi, in a ruby sweater, sat on the couch, lips closed in a smile. Beside her sat Adora, aloof in a gray hoodie, who raised her red mug in greeting. She smiled, girly and big. And sitting on the floor, long legs stretched out, was the Coffee Magician.

"*You!*" Madera yelped, sandpaper in her throat.

"Madera, come in. Here. Sit next to me," Sofia said, bounding from her chaise like a young girl.

"Welcome, Madera. Why don't you sit? This will all make sense," said Romi.

Stiff with confusion, Madera edged toward the chaise where Sofia graced her with the lightest touch to her shoulder, guiding her to sit down.

Madera locked eyes with the Coffee Magician. "Wasn't that you in Dewy's car last night by my house? You took off right when I saw you!"

"We had a lot of duties to tend to yesterday. We were low on vehicles, so I used Dewy's," the Coffee Magician answered from his seat on the floor. Wearing a white t-shirt with a large red "M" on the front and blue jeans of a style many years younger than his face, he stared up at Madera. His dark, deep-set eyes, the color of java, lit up like fireflies, and for a moment she wished the numbness would vanish from her own eyes; This man had seen many things.

But he hadn't answered Madera's question. "Why've you been following me?" Madera's voice rang out. "Wasn't that you at the Whistler's Room last month with Dewy's mom?"

"—Oh no, you two pissed her off not telling her sooner!" Romi said, shaking her head.

"Well, we've been busy with a lot of assignments, Romi. Do not come for us," Sofia said, her voice turning sour.

"No, see," Romi said, hands open in explanation. "This happens a lot when you two connect on assignments. We should've told Madera last time she was here. Get her prepared, maybe? When cases reside at home, everyone puts things off, and then bam, today is here!"

Madera's eyes roved among the faces, searching for answers. "Does Dewy know about this?"

"No," Sofia and Romi answered in unison.

"Really?"

"No, Madera," Sofia said. "He hasn't any stake in what happens in this group. He has his reasons that have nothing to do with your case. You can address that with him later. Now, do you want to know what's going on? Because now is your time."

It seems things had changed since the week Madera had peeked into the back sunroom.

"Oh, I do. I wanna know!" Madera professed.

"It started ten years back when I saw your mother in Diane's basement," the Coffee Magician began.

Madera's blood raced, "Huh! My mom? And, how do you know Diane?"

"Of course I know Diane. She's prolific on the West Side. And, yes, I saw your mother. I knew of her. I heard she was quite dynamic. Then I saw her painting this messy, beautiful picture, right before her death. It was of a woman and blood. I believe you're familiar with this painting."

Somewhere deep inside Madera, a wound opened. She flashed her eyes at Sofia.

"It's okay," Sofia soothed.

The Coffee Magician continued. "Listen, to be straight with you, I'm just a guy that triggers and assists with prophecies. My name is Everett, by the way."

Madera remembered the name Diane had mentioned—*The guy looking through the basement windows!* "Of course . . . you're Everett," she said.

"The spirit guides me to tend to the prophecies I'm shown." Everett's expressive eyebrows rose and fell with his words. "Prophecies come to me in the most bizarre places. I'm talking about locker rooms, a car dealership, a children's Christmas' performance. But with yours . . . ten years ago I was walking down the alley, and the lights in Diane's basement drew me to the window. And your mother's paintbrush strokes revealed your prophecy to me. Each dab of paint, each stroke she made on that canvas: *Blood taken. Blood giveth back. Bloodshed to bloodshed, Out from the legs, the pain will be theirs instead.*"

Madera rested her head onto Sofia's shoulder and listened to the lullaby.

"The prophecy told me more than what your mother wrote down that day. She tapped into the prophecy without even knowing. I left that window knowing that in ten years, I would be looking for you, a young woman named Madera. I was assigned to trigger and care for your prophecy," said Everett.

"Trigger?" Madera's head was heavy, and her heart raced.

"Everett activates prophecies," Romi explained, adjusting her off-the-shoulder sweatshirt. "The prophecy in your case is your justice magic. Your prophecy is to play a significant role in undoing the pigs' control. But first, you must face your own past. You must take care of home first, your mother. The root. The red. "

Madera flinched. Prophecy sounded like surreal comic book talk, not West Side Chicago grit. Prophecy, a preacher might say, was purpose plus prestige or pressure, perhaps both. For the real stuff, you had to check out the Bible, where people got crucified or stoned to fulfill prophecies. *Well, death would be involved with this prophecy, right?*

"Prophecies are intended to be fulfilled. My calling is to make sure of that. The person who fulfills the prophecy is given more gifts and more power. For example. If you get rid of Phillip Hughes, you could use your gift of blood magic to help prevent more tragedies," Everett said.

"But—you saw my mom? You watched her painting and knew that I was going to be given this gift. So, you knew she was going to die? You did nothing to stop it?" Madera

"If I had that kind of control, I would save the whole world." Everett said, chuckling.

"—Not funny," said Adora. "I think we all could use a glass of water." She darted into the kitchen.

Madera lifted her head from Sofia's shoulder, the lump in her throat growing.

"Why?" She demanded of Everett. "Why was I given this prophecy —or whatever? Did you give it to me?"

"No. No, I don't have power like that. That's why I was laughing. I don't have that power. But I do hear things. When your mother was painting, I heard a deep, euphoric voice, one that sounded like it came from the sea, with an echo—That's what the prophecies sound like when they are delivered to me. That voice, what's behind it, is massive. It's the universe. That's a fast answer for you. And, well, the universe feels you are entitled to it. You were dealt it. I don't pick who it goes to. I don't make prophecies or what have you. I do know that I must listen to that voice when it tells me what to do, though."

"I understand, this may sound strange," Sofia inserted.

"It can sound creepy, too," Romi said. She settled back on the couch like a movie spectator. "If I heard some undersea voice chanting demands to me, I'm telling it to leave me the fuck alone. But we all have our gifts."

Adora returned with a tray of tall cups of water and served them to each person.

"Thank you," Madera said, finishing her glass in two large gulps.

"When I heard your prophecy," Everett continued, "I was told your birthdate. When you turned twenty years old last March, I searched for you and all the necessary parties that would be involved. It took me about six months. I found you in September. I planned to run into you on the L train. I sold loose cigarettes to get the officer to follow me and whisk me away. I triggered your blood flow. That's how I began nurturing your prophecy—Oh, and the white mug!"

"You know I have the white mug?"

"I asked Sofia to bless that mug for you. It holds nurturing energy. And I made trips to your apartment's stoop to nurture your prophecy. Just being in your vicinity, I nurture the prophecy. Now that you are much, much closer to fulfilling it, you finally meet me."

Sofia rubbed Madera's shoulder. "It may sound like an earful, but it's really Everett's duty. He's not the only one that nurtures prophecies. Another friend of ours, Rosie, just left to Zambia to nurture one."

Tears fell from Madera's eyes. "Did you know this too, Sofia? All this time?"

"No. I found out after you told me about your gift. Everett knew about the prophecy ten years ago. When I blessed that white mug, I didn't know it was for you. I knew it was for a prophecy. My duty at that time was to bless a mug. I bless many things. All the time. Our hands are overwhelmingly full over here. But the universe finds its way to connect our lives to fulfill our destinies," Sofia said.

Madera looked around the room again. Everyone was indeed connected. Romi with her ruby sweater. A red jasper necklace dangled against Adora's hoodie. Sofia's blouse showed a wild pattern of maroon swirls. And Everett's white t-shirt sported that red "M."

"My allegiance to my prophecies is so important that I had to withhold what I knew about you from Sofia. Eventually, she mentioned you to me. I thought it was pretty cool that you're Dewy's friend," Everett beamed, taking a sip of his water.

"Madera, your prophecy has been blessed since the beginning," Romi explained. "Justice magic is often criticized. So many of us want to live in the light without ever acknowledging the darkness. Justice magic is all about dissecting the darkness. Confronting it. Lifting the layers. Summoning justice by taking down the causes of injustice. Sure, an eye for an eye—many will say that isn't justice. It's sure not perfect. But let it show them that we do not play."

Madera looked at each of them and asked, "So . . . now what?"

29

Perched on the corner of a quiet street in suburban River Forest, the dark brick, Tuscan house seemed the ideal spot to gather generations of an upscale family. Its mistress and matriarch, Penelope Hughes, had it built twenty years before, in the mid-90s, a memorial to her husband who had succumbed to a heart attack after a long, stressful career as a Chicago police detective. Tossing money and orders at a lineup of contractors, she'd kept the place immaculate. Gardeners trimmed the evergreen bushes just below the front sunroom windows. Landscapers inserted a youthful, winding pathway lined with pebbles. Two ivory pots cradled colorful autumn mums on either side of an oversized wooden door beside stately oval windows.

In her front sunroom, Penelope sat with her legs propped up on a dark leather ottoman, mustering enthusiasm for her 85th birthday. The decor she updated over the years—new curtains in the bedroom, the mirrors in the dining room—were all in hopes of rejuvenation, but did nothing for her own body's ailments. Now the only thing she wanted for her birthday was relief from the pain. She lifted her arm and sighed, her wrinkled skin like dried rags on her bones. She wiggled her toes, testing the long-lived ache that plagued her joints.

Since she was a little girl, every year on her birthday she'd expected something dreadful to appear, a Grim Reaper draped in a dark cloak. This year, death might feel warm and inviting, a fair man surrounded by white light, arms reaching for embrace.

Penelope sat in her sigh, a dainty demitasse cup of espresso and brandy warm in her hands. Like her, the porcelain white cup was old and fragile and, if dropped, would shatter into pieces. Her quiet contemplation was broken with the break of the side door opening, followed by a jumble of piercing sounds—the click of high heels, a babble of young voices. When her children, Phillip and Kristine, and her nieces and nephews were small, Penelope dreamt of a Hughes family dynasty. Nowadays, with the world such a mess, she didn't understand why anyone would choose to have children. While once she had despised birth control, saying women were "playing with God," she now accepted that God made doctors and science for a reason. But mainly, that children were irritating, and why raise an irritant in a society that is only growing in darkness?

"Mom?" Kristine said, her heels clicked from the kitchen, resounding on the dining room's hardwood floors and into the sunroom.

"You know where I'm at!" Penelope hollered.

"I got your cake."

Kristine stood before her, and Penelope winced at her daughter's short, tight tangerine dress. At over 50 years old, was she still trying to tempt men? Once a coy, low-key office administrator, Kristine morphed into a free-spirited marketing director for an artsy ad firm, sporting a pixie cut and visible tattoos. Her only child, Michael, a boy whom Kristine birthed in her late thirties and out of wedlock, was away in Austin, also doing artsy musical things. To say nothing of his decision to date men. *A travesty*, thought Penelope. *That's what happens when the father isn't around much.*

Samantha, Penelope's niece, followed her cousin Kristine into the sunroom, swinging a shopping bag in her hands. She planted a red lipsticked kiss on Penelope's forehead. "Happy Birthday, Auntie Penny."

Samantha's fourteen-year old son, Theodore came awkwardly bearing a massive red velvet cake cloched in glass. Already fifty pounds overweight, he looked ready to devour every crumb. Reluctantly, under Samantha's eye, he found an odd spot on the oak coffee table and set the cake down. His eyes lit up when he found a triangle of salami sandwich on a tray.

"Shouldn't the cake be in the kitchen?" Penelope questioned.

"Yes. Mother, it will get there. I thought maybe you wanted to see it first?" Kristine bent over, finding a spot to kiss her mother's right cheek that didn't have Samantha's lipstick on it.

"—Oh, dear," Penelope gasped in disappointment as the boy bit into the sandwich. "That was the rest of my lunch. I'm full now, but it would've been best to ask, Theo."

"Sorry, Aunt Penelope. Happy Birthday, Aunt Penelope," he mumbled, as sandwich crumbs threatened to tumble out the side of his mouth.

"Yes, Theo. Slow down, you're not going hungry, guy! Why's our family filled with pigs?" Samantha joked, relieved her son had gone after the salami and not the cake.

Samantha could stand to lose a few pounds herself, Penelope thought. She had married a chef, he fed her very well. When they got divorced, she ate up her whole kitchen in consolation.

According to Penelope, Theo held the only potential in the youngest generation to become a law enforcement officer. She remembered being delighted when she saw Theo reading detective novels. So, why would Samantha swipe at Phillip, whose police academy diploma hung on the wall of the sunroom? Penelope took a long look at her niece's waistline and swiped back, "Pigs? Sounds like something street people would say."

"Some of the artists I work with are street people . . . and they're smarter than many," Kristine retorted. Samantha raised her eyebrows in silent agreement.

"Why do you always feel the need to correct me?" Penelope said.

"I'm sorry, mother. This is your day. I didn't mean to be critical. Do you like the cake?"

"It's nice" Penelope said without breaking a smile. "Anything is a treat when you get as old as me."

"Great," Kristine said. She picked the cake up and clicked her way into the kitchen.

"Wait, there's more. I have an 85th birthday crown for you!" From the shopping bag, Samantha pulled out a citrine and topaz tiara. "Kristine sent me a picture of your lacy blue birthday gown. Stunning! I figured this would pair just perfectly with it!" Samantha beamed, tucking her blond wavy hair behind both of her ears.

"It's very nice," Penelope said admiring the blue tiara. Then the pain hit her ankle again. She sighed and stared out the sunroom window. Penelope took a slow long sip of her brandy-tainted espresso, possibly the only thing making the day bearable.

Theodore took a seat on the other matching leather chair to join his look through the grand front window with his great aunt. "What's that bird?" He pointed to the bush outside.

"What bird? Samantha, go to the shelf and get my binoculars!" Penelope demanded.

"It's still there," said Theo. "Look!"

Penelope pressed the binoculars against the thin skin that circled her eyes. She gasped. "Oh! It's a red-winged blackbird! I just love these birds!"

"The red winged?" Samantha turned her head to see.

"Can I see your phone, mom?" Theo called out.

"For what?" Samantha asked.

"Can you look it up? The red-winged birds? You know I like birds like Great Aunt Penny. That's what you've always said!"

"Yes, ever since that birdie mobile you had when you were a baby." Samantha softened her voice like a young mother cooing to her child.

"Stop mom!" Theo rolled his eyes, impatiently holding his hand out for the phone.

"It's Phillip's favorite bird! I haven't seen one since the spring." Penelope announced as Kristine returned to the sunroom, "Kristine, isn't Phillip in town now?"

"He supposedly checked in at his hotel last night. I texted him, but haven't heard back. Absolutely nothing."

"Well, he'll be here. Remember how much your brother likes red-winged blackbirds?"

"Yes, mom. You've told me many times before." Kristine rolled her eyes.

As if posing for an audience, the blackbird flicked its tail and swooped to the top of the nearest tree, squawking all the way as it flew.

Theo looked up from his mother's phone. "Says here that the male blackbirds have red and yellow spots on their shoulders. The females are a dull brown and act shy. So that one must be a boy. They're mean! I think it was one of them that dive-bombed me in fifth grade when I was walking through Keystone Park."

"Oh, I remember that! My poor boy. Why do they do that?" asked Samantha.

"They're protecting their territory," Theo read. "Why Blackbirds are territorial . . . Says each male bird runs a territory. They might be mating with five or ten female birds. But they only help one with building her nest. They squawk like that to keep other male birds out. But sometimes the other males sneak in and mate with the leader's females . . . Uh oh."

Penelope leaned back on her chaise lounge and turned to Kristine. "Territory. Protecting their territory. I think Phillip likes these birds because they remind him of what your father used to say about protecting the neighborhood. He called them 'the warrior birdies.'"

"I don't remember as much about that as Phillip—he's older. All I remember is that dad was always away at night."

"Well, your dad was always wary of new people moving in the neighborhood. People that had nothing in common with us. People who would ruin the property values. He saw all that coming into the city around Maxwell Street and Roosevelt Road. He wanted to move our family out here to River Forest. But we couldn't afford it until he died, and I got the insurance." Penelope heaved another sigh and rattled her empty cup. "Before we could move out here, those boys attacked me at the playground and hurt my foot."

"That's how your foot got hurt?" asked Theo.

"Yes. Kristine was playing in the sandbox when it happened, but she was too little to remember, I guess. My Phillip was about six or seven years old," said Penelope. "They used to come down to our playground, young black boys from North Lawndale or Garfield Park, or even from Maywood. I don't know where they came from but . . . they really thought they could move in. They were swarming all over the swings, throwing basketballs," she shuddered. "They stole Phillip's baseball! They threw it back and forth among them, teasing him to try to get it back."

"What did he do?" Theo asked.

"He pouted, balled up his fists and started screaming. His face turned red, the color of a boiled lobster."

"Did they hurt him?"

"No. I marched over to them myself. One of them said to me, 'He didn't ask for his ball back.' I told them, 'Give him his ball back and get out of our park now!' That really startled those boys. They wanted to get out of there. One turned around and threw the baseball back over his shoulder, the ignorant little punk! And it hit me on the foot so hard I fell down in terrible pain. People gathered all around me thinking they should call the police, but the boys had run away by then. I somehow managed to drive to the emergency room with both children in the backseat and found out I had a talus fracture. You know it's bothered me the rest of my life."

"What did Phillip do?" Theo asked.

"He kept screaming so everyone in the park could hear, 'I'm gonna tell my dad!' And for weeks after that, he kept saying he was going to find those boys and beat them up. Kept telling me he would dive bomb them like the red-wing blackbird if they set foot in his turf, and I told him, 'That's right, son! Don't let any of those people intimidate you. Never ever. They don't belong here.' He said, 'I promise, mom!' I swear every time I see a group of N--Negro boys on the street, my foot starts hurting again."

"Maybe those boys were just teasing Phillip. Sounds like they didn't really mean to hurt you, Mother. So why can't you forgive them?" Kristine asked. "Maybe your foot will stop hurting, even."

Theo and Samantha swapped wide-eyed looks.

"That's a bunch of hocus pocus and you know it, Kristine. I'm surprised you would even suggest such a thing. You think I'm imagining this pain that I'm having?"

Penelope didn't wait to hear her daughter's response. She closed her eyes and soothed herself with the knowledge that Phillip had held his promise. With Phillip, Penelope knew that she'd done well. She raised someone fearless and aggressive, just like the red-winged blackbird. Even more than Phillip's father, it was she who'd led her son to wear the uniform that signifies a warrior-like mentality that would protect the innocent. *Kristine hadn't raised her son with that strength. She had no problem with Michael playing the flute when he should've been learning the trumpet.*

"Kristine, call and find out what time Phillip is coming."

"Sure, mother. I already said I texted and asked him to come by and help out, but—you know Phillip. The cooks and bartender should be here first. I expect the cooks in an hour."

"Mmhmm. I see. I sure hope these new cooks are better than the ones we had at the garden party last summer."

"That was three summers ago, mother." Kristine said. "We've had other cooks since, but none of them were available today. But then out of thin air, when I was getting my nails done last week, a woman with purple hair told me about these caterers. They have incredible reviews, so let's hope they deliver."

"Did you say a woman with purple hair? Dear God!" Penelope shook her head.

"Yeah . . . I probably should've left that part out," Kristine said. She picked up the empty plate that once held the salami sandwich, "Samantha?"

"What?" Samantha was studiously filing her nails.

Penelope brushed aside an ancient memory of a childhood fight, sometime after the park confrontation, when her son had given

Samantha a black eye. She didn't need to have to deal with such things today, not on her birthday.

"If we are a family of pigs . . . then we must be cannibals." Kristine winked at the tiny bits of salami Theo left on the plate. Samantha covered her mouth with her hand, and her brown eyes wide in amusement.

"I don't see what's so funny!" Penelope said. She sipped the last of her drink. "Why don't you bring me another espresso and brandy, Kristine?"

3 0

"It's time to get ready. We must feed your root!" said Sofia.

At two o'clock in the afternoon, Sofia cut up a handful of raw beets and ran them through her juicer. She boiled an egg and sliced part of a red pepper and set the sparse meal in front of Madera, who ate it standing right there in the kitchen at the butcher block island. Lamb's Ear rubbed against Madera's leg as she nibbled.

"Beet juice?" Madera had seen it advertised at a North Side juice bar once. It looked hearty. The color was certainly intriguing. She thought it couldn't taste as bad as that herbal apple concoction that Sofia first gave her.

"Yes. With lemon." With a quick stir, like Amaryllis mixing drinks at Hendricks, Sofia poured the red elixir in a glass. "Not only does it purify and strengthen your blood, but it empties you out. We are feeding Mars, your inner warrior, so you have enough fuel to get the job done. But you have to remain fluid. We don't want to clog you up with anger either," she looked up at Madera. "Only six or more hours to go."

The dusty smelling beet juice was sweet and grainy, while the egg and pepper combined to give Madera an acidic stretch of gas. "Urp," she said. "I'm stuffed or something."

"You did a great job, considering. Go meet Romi in the sunroom. She'll show you some yoga poses to help you digest."

Romi met her with a smile and a couple of exercise mats in front of the seven mammoth candles that dominated the sunroom. Each candle, as round and tall as a toddler, represented a color of the rainbow—the colors of each chakra. At night, they would be lit up to provide the only light in the room. Right now, the sunlight poured in on dozens of multi-colored clay pots hanging from the tops of the windows, overflowing with herbs.

"Now breathe!" commanded Romi. "Think of each breath like a square step. Three counts to inhale, three counts to hold, three counts to release and three counts to just be. Keep your mind on your breathing as you lie on the mat for your leg-lifts."

Madera breathed. She lifted. Her legs felt warm. She glanced at the row of candles. The red one, the root, Mars, captured her eyes.

"Did you know that Chakras align with celestial bodies? Sun, Moon, Mars, Venus, Saturn, Jupiter, and Mercury," Romi said. "Now we'll try triangle pose."

Madera stretched. Her tummy rumbled. Out came gas and a burp.

"This will loosen you up. You don't want to be blocked down there in your root chakra. You'll be taking on a lot of heat, a lot of energy, to use on Phillip Hughes."

Madera looked around and noticed that everyone seemed to have scattered elsewhere since welcoming her in the living room. "Where is everybody? Will they be ready when it's time to go? Where's Adora?"

Being Black and closer to Madera's age, Adora belonged on this expedition. Plus, her opposing energy would help for balance.

"Don't worry. Things come together when we have an assignment. Right now, Sofia's off finishing blessings and steeping ginger. Adora has an errand outside the house. And everyone else is getting dressed for their catering duties tonight."

"Will Everett have the big red M on his shirt?" Madera snickered, feeling honored to be acknowledged by such a vibrant human.

"Everett wears different clothes depending. He's a bit of an actor. He impresses people. I bet he made an impact on you when you saw him on the train. Did he cross your mind at odd times after that?" Romi asked.

"Yes! How'd you pick up on that?" Madera smiled up at Romi.

"Oh, Everett shines bright. Most of us are drawn to the Sun. I really wished Sofia told you earlier about the planets and the roles all of us play in the group. We missed some opportunities that could have benefited you—and maybe your *Tia*, too. Now, raise your arms up to the ceiling and then down to touch your toes."

"My *Tia?*"

"Yes, she's Mars, too. Our coven needs stable roots around here. You and Amaryllis both have a lot of Mars energy. But if it's meant to be—well, we'll see."

Vertebrae by vertebrae, Madera stood upright. "Did you see Mars in my *Tia* when you dropped off the box today?"

"Oh, yes, and some Neptune. We all resonate to some degree with each planet. But you and she are especially Mars. She has a heavy dose of untapped potential. She may implode if she doesn't get it out and put it to some use. You'll have time to help with that, I think?"

"It's crazy I come over here on a hunch to talk to Sofia, and then I find you all waiting for me."

"Mmhmm, you did have that bubble bath this morning," Romi said and winked.

"Wow, that did it?"

Romi laughed. "Oh, we were waiting for you. Sofia spent all week blessing the bloodstone you used in your bath. And finding the black dress she's got for you today."

"How does everyone have time to do this?" Madera said. "Do you all have jobs?"

"We're busy with a lot of jobs that are kind of our fronts. We own a coffee shop. Oscar runs it. Same with the catering business that Lila and Everett manage. Sofia helps me out at a florist shop. Adora, too. We make it work. There's a lot to learn, Madera. And a few more of us to meet, but all in due time."

Madera wasn't sure she could take all this in. The organization, the group, the coven or whatever they considered themselves; she did her best to stay afloat.

"What do you call this—this coven?"

"I call us the Rectifiers. But there's not one name. We're nameless. Sounds sad, I know. Everett and Sofia believe that until we have literature in our hands about who we are, then we shouldn't assign ourselves a name. I have some fifty handwritten pages at home about what I think we should be called and our vision, our mission. I'm not ready to present it to the team because we're evolving. I prefer to have all moving parts before I go any further." Romi exhaled and with her arms, she made a circle around her head. "Honestly, Madera, we are so busy that it's hard to really box us in. But justice magic is our specialty."

Everett came swishing through the beaded curtain wearing a white chef jacket. Oscar followed in the same. And then a third chef—Dewy's mother, Lila, red hair pulled up in a tiny, tight ponytail. For once, her smile seemed carefree. They stood in a straight line, like three cutout paper chef dolls.

Everett doffed his chef hat and bowed to Madera. "At your service, ma'am," he grinned. "We are the chefs for Penelope Hughes' 85th birthday party tonight. We're leaving to set the food up, of course. We still have a couple dishes to make there. Everything else you need to know, Romi will fill you in, okay? Best of blessings."

"I'll drop her off at the proper time. Let me know of any detours," Romi told the chefs. They turned on their heels, ready to march out to fulfill their duties.

"Everett?" Madera called out.

"Yes?"

"What happened when Officer Scott arrested you on the train?"

"Oh, we bailed him out. It wasn't much of anything," Lila responded.

"Officer Scott's going to be at the party tonight. Will he recognize you? You know, from the train?"

"I have ways of being inconspicuous," he answered. "See you soon."

The beads clapped and swayed as the chefs left the room.

Romi turned, nodding at Madera and said, "I have some more prep work to do. Sofia will be back with a special cup of tea for you."

The beads rattled again, as Romi departed and Dewy stepped into the sunroom.

He had taken off his hoodie and wore a wrinkled white t-shirt with his gray sweatpants. He looked like he'd be pretty comfortable stretched out on a couch after eating some chicken noodle soup. Madera wasn't quite sure if she wanted to pounce on him or curl up with him.

"I have some good news. Off topic though," Dewy sat down on Romi's mat next to Madera. He smiled and ruffled his hair.

"What's up?" Madera inched back from him. She felt heated with passion.

"I'll be training at the tattoo parlor two blocks down."

"Dewy, that's dope! Congrats. They fell in love with your art, huh? Of course."

"Thank you. We can talk later about it. But . . . um, you finally met my mom today," Dewy cleared his throat.

Madera giggled. "What's the big deal about her? Is she supposed to be kept hidden?"

"No. Look, Mad, her field work leads to some iffy places. See . . . " Dewy paused, taking a breath.

"What?" Madera squeezed his hand. He was cool to touch, nervous.

"My mom got pregnant with me because of a prophecy. I'm not the prophecy but the prophecy belonged to my father's ex-wife. It's some super wild shit, but my mom had to play a mistress—and get pregnant —in order to set my dad's ex-wife free."

Madera's mouth hung open. An aching warmth stemmed from her heart. One that cut her sudden horniness in half. "That's crazy! What the fuck, Dewy?"

"Found out when I was twelve. Messed me up. That's why I stay out of coven business."

"Do you and your mom get along?"

"For the most part. She is my mom. I love her. She lives where we went to pick up the food. You know, when the cop came? Sorry 'bout the lie. I didn't want to talk about it while being an errand boy. But the house is my mom's, not Romi's. Most of the catering business happens there. But I'm best with my *Tia*. I would feel too involved with their business if I lived with my mom."

Prophecies are serious, Madera realized. She pictured a twelve-year-old Dewy learning the news he just told her. *How small he probably viewed his life to be. Hopefully he doesn't feel that way now.* A wave of dizziness fell upon her, then dissipated. Maybe a force in the room knew Madera didn't have the energy to carry Dewy's story. She stored it for later.

She caught him staring at her longingly. His eyes softened and his chin lowered. He slid his hand from under hers and placed his on top. His thumb caressed her pinky.

"So—Everett was the Coffee Magician?" smiled Dewy. "Of course he was. Everyone loves Everett. Sorry if I gave you a hard time about it. I thought this magician was some random dude you were infatuated with." Dewy flashed a wide smile. "Not the sun in the sky, himself. Don't tell anyone about my jealousy around that. They'd run with that one for days. Especially Romi."

Madera smirked playfully and ran her hand up Dewy's arm, "Don't worry about it. But, um, after all this, let's stay the night together."

Dewy smiled. "Hope that's not sympathy talking . . . or Adora with her Venus?"

"Adora's not even here!" laughed Madera.

The beads rattled again. Sofia brought in a cup of steeped ginger root and black hooded dress on a wooden hanger.

"*Dejala*—leave her alone, Dewy! She needs to focus on today. We're not feeding her Mars for you!" Her eyes flashed gravely. "Drink it up fast," she ordered Madera. "Mars brings a lot of energy. And it can be sexually aggressive. Different from Venus," she said.

Dewy winked at Madera and leaned in to whisper, "Whenever you want. Your choice. Mars? Venus? Something in between?"

Reluctantly, Dewy headed out the door.

Sofia grimaced at the friends' exchange as Madera harnessed her breathing techniques to cool herself down. As if in trouble, Madera took the mug from Sofia and blew on it to cool it down.

Sofia checked Madera's shirt size tag and said, "Right. This dress should fit you perfectly. You'll be wearing it under your kitchen scrubs when you leave here. It's been blessed. It makes you invisible under the night sky. Remember, you will only be invisible outside, where it will be dark anyway. So don't think people can't see you indoors."

Romi came back in and noticed Madera's eyes on the turquoise candle, the candle that represented the throat chakra. She moved the candle closer to her, then lit them all with stove matches. The friction that flourished as the flames ignited whooshed.

"Have you expressed it yet?" Romi asked as she watched Madera observing her actions. "Your prophecy? We welcome you to do that now."

"Welcoming? To my prophecy?" Madera asked.

"Yes. And we'll have to talk about welcoming you to our group after tonight. Maybe in a week or so. If you're interested," said Sofia.

"The waiting game isn't that helpful, Sofia," Romi said.

"Well, what do you want me to say, Romi? Madera's head needs to be on her mission today. *Tu sabes.*"

"Welcoming Madera into our world is a big deal. Remember how Charles depleted himself? He got so entrenched in his planetary energy that he burned the old coffee house down and then died of a fucking heart attack. Mars is so strong that—"

"Charles' story is not Madera's story, Romi—I will not have you frighten her with it. We can't rely on Madera to hold the weight of Mars' energy all by herself anyway. We need others, too. Mars, the root chakra, the drum, is extremely vital in justice magic. Extremely!" Sofia turned to Madera and said, "Being on the verge of fulfilling your prophecy opens the possibility for you to help us here in the future-Madera. But I won't pressure anyone to be a part of anything. I will not." Sofia's eyes blazed.

"So . . . what is everyone supposed to be doing tonight?" Madera asked.

"*Escuchame*, Madera. Romi is a little anxious and we all are kind of excited."

Lamb's Ear set off a delicate clapping of the beads. Romi bent to pet the Russian Blue cat.

"I understand. Thank you," Madera muttered.

"Just so you're clear, my role is to prepare you. Adora and I are both behind the scenes. Adora will be with you the entire time afterward. Romi will do the middle part, the transportation. Oscar, Everett, and my little sister, Lila, will be onsite with you. As I'm sure you've gathered, we are already many steps ahead in supporting this very important prophecy. Sorry, I didn't speak up to you about this earlier, but I knew you were going to make your way to us, just fine."

"But I'm the one with Mars energy?" Madera asked.

"Everyone has every energy in them," answered Sofia, rolling her eyes. "But we each have one planet we resonate with. I'm closest to the Moon."

Of course, Madera chuckled to herself. Sofia is comforting, instinctual, and moody.

"Now, let's focus," directed Sofia. "You're going to wear your dress tucked into your pants. When you're at the party, you'll go to the bathroom and change. Place the catering garb in this empty paper bag. Lila will be there to tell you what to do and when. Romi will go over these details with you in the car. Then, you'll fulfill your duty," Sofia said proudly.

Falling back into a seated position on the mat, Madera raised a still-unanswered question. "I did tell you that Catalina, she's a hostess at my job. She was asked to bartend there tonight. Richard asked her. What do I do when I see her? Or him?"

"Oh, don't you worry. The chefs will take care of that. Their job is to keep both Catalina and Richard from you. Now, let us know when you're dressed."

Sofia and Romi both pivoted and departed.

Soon, the sun faded and the autumn moon cast soft beams of light into the back sunroom. The colored candles and their flames, heavy and vibrant, stood strong like soldiers at watch. The smell of Eucalyptus filled Madera's nose as she eased into the cool, black cotton dress. It felt like being wrapped in a baby blanket. She admired her figure in the mirror, then pulled the bulky off-white catering uniform over her dress. As she put on a small black tourmaline necklace next to her bloodstone, as Sofia advised, an overwhelming sense of protection rushed over her. Next, she pulled out the shell and pearl necklace. Finally dressed, Madera gazed at the turquoise candle, realizing she hadn't found the words to voice her prophecy yet.

Sofia came back in and adjusted Madera's garment. Her usual cup of piping tea sat on a cream pedestal beside her, its wild steam dancing in the full-length mirror.

"You look ready! Here, I have these for you, too." Sofia opened a small jewelry box to present a pair of rose quartz stud earrings. "These earrings have helped many people—including me—to maintain balance and peace."

Madera placed them into her ears.

Sofia patted Madera's back and laid a modest, motherly kiss on the back of her shoulder. "The kiss is from your mother." Sofia's eyes brightened through the mirror's reflection.

Madera's eyes welled up with tears, but she blinked them back. "Thank you."

"Your mother is a tough cookie. Strong in her ways. She may not be easily accessible as a spirit, but she does force her way in when essential," Sofia said.

Madera's eyes softened. *That sounds just like mama.*

"She looks ready to me," Sofia said to Romi.

"Brilliant. Let's do this," said Romi.

But Madera wasn't completely confident. She'd seen the prophecy through her mother's abstract paint strokes, and she clearly heard the interpretations from the justice magic squad. But Madera needed to put her own voice behind it. It was her prophecy after all.

"What am I supposed to do?" she burst out. "I mean, I know how to use my powers. But I need to voice my why."

"What are you going to do, Madera?" Sofia asked.

Facing her reflection in the tall mirror, Madera's nostrils flared.

"Well . . . at first I wanted Piggy Hughes to feel what I felt. Pain. Sadness. That struggle you know, when your loved one, your *mother* is killed. But that would mean I would have to kill someone he loves. I wouldn't do that. Hell no, plus he's too heartless to feel for others. You know what? I . . . I want him to feel what my mother felt when he took her from me. That's more important. It's what my mother felt, Constance Maria Miller, and everyone else he killed. People who are constantly dying at the hands of hateful cowards. Some of them claim to represent the state, the people. But the power they possess is wrong. This pig, this coward, somehow felt threatened when he saw my mama. Threatened by her dark skin, her strong womanhood, her assertive voice. I . . . I can see it! I can see him!"

Madera's eyes grew wide then nearly closed in focusing at the scene playing before her. As if looking through a dirty window with the wrong pair of glasses, Madera squinted at her reflection in the mirror. Her hands curled into fists. She saw it now, right now, in her mind's eye: the wee hours of April 10th, a decade ago. She smelled the spring night, spunky, wet, and fresh. She saw it clearly now.

"He's burly and gross and staring at my mama. She's in that blue jean dress, the simple dress she used to love. I hear her. She's talking to him. 'Why is it a big deal? Just write me a ticket? Why do you hate us so much?' My mama is scared. She's not backing down and she is afraid of what will happen. She can't back down though. She has to speak the truth. That's how she raised me, to speak up and be honest. I owe that to her and to myself.

"Now she's standing there. In front of this sour beast. I feel like I'm in her skin—I am! His eyes are looking at me. My heart, *her* heart, is racing. My mama, so vulnerable, something he could never be. She says, 'Your legacy is already tainted by the hate you feed. We thrive and smile and live our lives all while knowing ya'll don't give a damn about us. And you have the nerve to stand there yelling about my damn taillight. Just write me a ticket!'

"He's shouting, talking over her. 'Enough! Are you done? Enough!' I see him, he's pulling out his gun now. My mama is still talking. 'Damn broken taillight? Write me a ticket. Do the decent thing. Be a human being and treat me as a human—'" Madera covered her face with her palms, clawing her forehead.

"He's shooting her in the stomach. Blowing her wide open! She's thinking of me. I can see she's thinking of me. She's holding my face in her mind and—shit!" Madera hollered. "Again. He just shot her again. Her stomach. He just punctured the life out of her that fast. She's on the ground! Such a simple coward move took out an entire vibrant person . . . " Madera wailed.

"Now it's chilly. It's getting cold. No, she's cold. She's cold with my face in her hands in her mind. She's gone. He killed her!"

Madera blinked. She rested there for a good two minutes before turning from the mirror to face Sofia and Romi. "I will return the pain he gave her and everyone else he harmed. Simon Spears, the deaf kid. A woman whose arm he broke. Dear God, I can see them all. That's what I will do. He will feel all the pain. Ugly pain. Afterwards, I have to join you. I will find those that intend to bring harm to the innocent by harming them first. The blood will be theirs." Madera spoke freely, the lump in her throat gone. The flame on the turquoise candle flickered brightly.

"Well, I'm glad you got the words out," Sofia said, her eyes glistening like a child's. "This is what you've been waiting for. It's what your mom's been waiting for, too."

Madera's face lit up in awe. Right before her eyes, she witnessed her mother's death. She wore her mother's body. Like the beginning of Madera's existence, Constance's flesh cradled her daughter's flesh. Madera felt ready.

"Come, get in my car." Romi took her arm.

3 1

"OH, HEY! I'M CATALINA! I'M YOUR BARTENDER FOR THE NIGHT."

A woman in a tangerine dress held the front door open. "Of course! Welcome, welcome, come on in. This is my mother's house," she said. Her short brunette hair hugged her head as if exquisitely painted on.

Stepping inside the glamorous home, Catalina felt small and conspicuous in her short black dress, her jaw clenched and for once, nearly wordless.

"Let me show you where you'll be. I'm so glad my cousin, Richard, got you to do this. I *really* didn't want to get just anybody. Always best to go with who you know." At least this woman had confidence Catalina could do the job.

The whole house smelled of butter, garlic, and fresh seafood. Recorded piano and violin music and the crooning voice of Frank Sinatra, boomed from speakers near the ceiling. The woman led Catalina down a long hallway, heels clicking on the wooden floors like a teacher strutting down a high school corridor. A chipper kind of teacher, one that would lighten up the room with humor if need be. Clicks of someone that loved to please. The breezy way she swung her glass of white wine took the edge off Catalina's nerves.

"I'm sorry, what's your name?" Catalina inquired.

"Oh, I'm Kristine. Forgive me, I'm all over the place. I wouldn't be all over the place if my brother had come to help me, but . . . this is life! I'm the daughter of the birthday girl, Mrs. Penelope Hughes. So glad you found the place okay. You came from the city, right?"

"Yes, Wicker Park," Catalina spoke.

"That's a fun, youthful place! I sang some Karaoke down there this past summer. Well, there's the bathroom." The gold-trimmed fixtures gleamed as they walked past.

In the spacious dining room, a long oak table was surrounded by twenty heavy wooden chairs on each side and one at the head and foot. A golden runner draped down the center of the table. The tall windows along the wall illuminated the floor-to-ceiling tapestries and reflected the immaculate, green yard in the mirror between them. *What a great shot this room would make for Instagram!* Catalina rummaged for her phone but stopped herself from shooting a picture —at least until all the food was set out. Only a charcuterie of cured meats, dotted with bites of cheese, stuffed olives and oversized grapes, was set out on a silver platter.

"The cooks are already making this home smell so heavenly!" Kristine squealed, taking the last swig of her wine. She snatched up a bottle of sauvignon blanc from a wooden hutch and topped off her glass.

The dining hall opened into a large parlor hung with another Italian tapestry. "This is the party room, and there is your bar." Kristine indicated with a broad sweep of her arm. "It should be stocked with everything you need. If you run out of something like ice, I'm sure one of the chefs will assist you."

When Officer Scott asked Catalina to bartend for the party, she imagined herself behind a little roll cart bar or maybe walking around with a tray of champagne flutes—not presiding over a massive oak bar almost as large as the one at Hendricks. All her co-workers would envy her for this high-class gig. But was she up to it? Unlike restaurant customers who trickled in all evening, partygoers would be doing things together, which meant they would all be mobbing up and demanding drinks at the same time.

"How about I show you the kitchen?" Kristine beckoned through an arched doorway. The oversize kitchen in the rear of the house echoed the paint theme of the home's tapestries in a soft, Tuscan palette.

"Everyone, this is Catalina. She's our bartender tonight. If she needs anything, you all can help her," Kristine announced.

Three white-clad chefs lifted their heads and nodded in unison. Catalina first caught the eye of the sexy, dark-eyed Mediterranean-looking cook who seemed right at home in the Italian decor. He was lathering up his hands at the island sink. Bending over the oven, hands in potholder mitts, stood a woman with dark red hair so striking that Catalina immediately filed the color away in her mind—maybe she'd dye it like that for the holidays. The redhead looked familiar, maybe as a patron at Hendricks. But she stayed silent in her greeting.

"Of course. We got you if needed," said the third chief—a tall, older Black man wearing thick-rimmed glasses. "Excuse me, Kristine?"

"Yes, Everett?"

"I have an apprentice coming here in a couple hours to help with—"

"—I know this sounds awful, but make sure they use the same door that you did," Kristine pointed to a white door in the kitchen that led outside. "I just don't want the guests to be like, 'who's this person?' if your apprentice comes through the front," she rattled. "My goodness, I probably sound racist or something. Dear God, not the case! I don't even know what color your apprentice is to even have said that. I should probably slow down." Kristine stared into her glass as Catalina cast her eyes to the floor. Not knowing any better, she had come through the front door. She couldn't bear to see the cooks' reactions.

Kristine ducked out of the kitchen. Catalina followed, wishing she could rewrite the woman's words. But Kristine stopped at the bar and launched into a new stream of party prep talk.

"We only drink wines and basic cocktails, beer and such. It

shouldn't be too complicated but there is a blender down there some-where if someone asks for a fancy drink. My little cousin, Theo, filled the bar with ice earlier. I think it's enough. Please double check." Kristine glanced at her watch. "I'm going to help my mother get ready now. Be back soon. Guests should be arriving in thirty minutes."

The guests soon arrived, piling in as Catalina anticipated. Soon, six or seven were lined up at the bar waiting for a drink. She moved deliberately with slow and steady pours—She had other tactics to compensate for her pace. Opening the top buttons of her blouse, she pouted her mouth and leaned forward.

The dining room table was now filled with brass chafers, baskets of bread, and two trays of thickly sliced, juicy fruit. About four dozen people ranging in ages from ten to one hundred shuffled back and forth between clutches of conversations, snacking around the dining room table, and bouts of dancing in the parlor. Kristine had pulled out circles of chairs for the guests to rest in. Up and down the hall, preteens were kicking an array of sky blue and ivory balloons like soccer balls. The action was so hectic that Catalina had missed her perfect hashtag #food photo.

In an overstuffed chair near the bar sat an elderly lady, hair pinned in a high bun under an elegant crystal tiara. Catalina noted a hint of drama in the woman's stone blue eyes. This had to be the birthday girl, Penelope Hughes, regal in a delicate, lacy teal dress, her crinkly porcelain doll face made up with a light rouge. She smiled softly and often.

A familiar male voice startled Catalina as she finished serving a round of drinks: "There she is!"

"Hey Richard!" Catalina smiled. The last thing she wanted was for Officer Scott to slow her staggered rhythm any further. She wanted to come off as #professionalaspossible. Richard could be distracting and talk anyone's ear off, but she knew she had to be extra nice to him because he got her the gig. Worse, she recognized a flirtatious glint in his eyes, the same look he used to give Amaryllis.

Catalina quickly made Richard's drink, Hendrick's on the rocks, as he stood puffing up and pushing forward his broad shoulders to cover the recent shrinkage in the muscles there. A cold, sharp quiver ran through her body as she recalled the amount of napkins Eddie used to soak up his chunky blood.

"I do hope you've been helping yourself to some drinks. That's how you all do it in this industry," Richard said with a wink.

"Not yet. But maybe soon." Catalina played along.

Kristine clicked her way up to the bar. "Hey Rich! Honestly, what do you think of this recessed lighting? And this Tuscan theme my mom's been expanding on for decades?"

Catalina briefly glanced up at the ceiling; she thought the lights were nice.

"Sorry, I've never been a fan of the Tuscan Mafia look," Richard snorted.

Catalina passed Richard his drink, meeting eyes with a stout-bellied man she'd served a moment ago. The ceiling lights reflected off on the man's balding head. He looked a little like Kristine but with tight, thin lips and a smugness that shone across his icy blue eyes. His nostrils had a natural flare as if constantly sniffing something out. He wore a navy blue suit, and his tie was pearl colored spotted with blue beach badges.

With his left hand, the bald man wiggled his ear at Kristine. "It's all god awful, but Mom's got about a decade left at the most. You think she cares about the state of her ceiling lights?" the man said, his right hand cradling his scotch and water.

Catalina strained to maintain her smile as she spotted crumbs of food floating in his glass.

"I didn't ask you, Phillip. Just save it." Kristine rolled her eyes. "I'll have whatever dry white you have, Catalina."

"Of course," Catalina batted back.

"Hey, Catalina, this is my cousin, The Great Phillip Hughes. Kind of like a champ in my field. Phil, this is Catalina, the prettiest hostess you'll ever lay eyes on," Richard winked again.

"Nice to meet you," Catalina swallowed nervously.

"Hot damn, nice to meet you, too." Phillip slurped his drink, staring at the soft space between Catalina's unbuttoned shirt.

"Don't harass the help, for goodness sake." Kristine said turning back to the men, "And listen, about the recessed lighting, Mom is the one asking about it. I think she knows she doesn't have much time left. She's put all her effort into this house all these years. Now she wants me to get this place presentable to sell after she passes. This is what she wants. But, Phillip, if you want to advise her about the house please have at it. You're the one with the influence."

"Oh, the baby sister's whine time has been activated!" Phillip chuckled.

Catalina delicately cleared her throat and slid Kristine her white wine.

Clearing bottle caps from the bar, Catalina noted Phillip slurping his drink, his eyes ogling her chest again. A chill crossed her neck. She turned and refastened all the buttons she'd undone.

By now, guests had eaten all of Penelope's cake. The food, particularly the charcuterie tray with rolled salami, was completely gone. Close to fifty people danced and swayed to the Rat Pack's greatest hits of the '50s and '60s. Collars were loosened. Wine glasses were fogged from soiled fingerprints.

Having shaken and poured a series of cocktails for a flirty group of men, Catalina sensed a lull and sipped her first vodka and tonic behind the bar, satisfied with her work so far. They wouldn't be complaining about her slow speed. She was even feeling Frank Sinatra belting "My Way" through the speakers.

The voice of Phillip Hughes jarred her thoughts. "This is the last song of the night! We have to play this one again! This is the end-of-the-night song! Come on, who programmed the playlist? No DJ, huh, Kristine?" Slurring his words, Phillip flapped his fat ear again at his sister.

Earlier, Phillip pulled Richard into a headlock, spilling the contents of both their drinks on the floor. Catalina had cleaned it up while Phillip stared at her backside. When she stood up and turned around, he winked and pursed his lip.

"You're playing that song at the end of the night, Kristine!" Phillip demanded.

To the right of the bar, Kristine sat beside her mother who was taking her time with her last bites of cake. Penelope looked up at Kristine and said, "You can replay 'My Way' at the end."

Catalina cringed. *Why did so many mothers often favor their son's interests over their daughters?* Not once did Catalina see Phillip attend to his mother the way Kristine hovered around Penelope all evening. If it wasn't her, it was Samantha, the soft-spoken woman in the yellow dress.

As Penelope finished her cake, Phillip wrapped his left arm around her, forcing her into a hug. He sniffed the fragile old lady's neck and muttered, "My mother. My darling old mommy."

"Give me space!" Penelope shouted. Catalina watched the old birthday girl jab her son's round torso with her bony elbow.

Phillip stepped back, tottering. He caught himself, securing his left hand onto the edge of the bar as the glass in his right hand swayed and sloshed his scotch and water onto the floor.

Kristine scooted Penelope's chair from the toxic puddle. "Maybe drink some water, Phil. Take a time out."

"Get off it, Kristine! It's a spill. That's all. *I'm her kid*, I always shock my mommy," Phillip tried to joke, his eyes glossy, his shirt splattered with oil spots from the food.

"Give me a paper towel. I'll help," Samantha said scurrying behind the bar, wearing an embarrassed smile. She took a wad of towels from Catalina and squatted on the floor to soak up her cousin's spill.

32

"Everett, your apprentice is here," Lila announced, smiling through closed lips as Madera stepped inside the River Forest kitchen.

Like a winter coat worn on a too-warm day, the chef garb carried a nagging heaviness on her shoulders. Already, Madera wished she could put it into the empty brown paper bag that rattled in her hand. A kitchen window reflected Madera's nervous face, her hair gelled back in a slick bun. The dime-sized rose quartz earrings snug at her earlobes. She remembered what Sofia said: balance and peace. She pressed them and felt the calm flow through her. Her skin glowed from the concoction of oils in her morning bath.

"You can place the bag on the stool and wash your hands, please," Everett said, pulling out one of the chunky leather brown stools from under the kitchen island where he chopped vegetables.

As Madera washed her hands, the smells of the kitchen wafted around her: cured chorizo, the leathery scent of port wine, and then the inevitable—vinegar. *Fuck, maybe Richard's close by.* She stared at the gaudy camel-colored backsplash behind the sink. Madera reminded herself to breathe, creating a square; *three counts to inhale, three counts to hold, three counts to release, and three counts to just be.* A wave of tranquility washed over her.

Lila assigned Madera to wash the long serving utensils, dry them, and place them into a bin. This duty kept Madera completely out of the view of the doorway that led directly to the party. Music and waves of chatter and laughter flooded in from the dining hall. The three caterers kept busy wrapping and storing the untouched food in aluminum pans.

"Romi and I will take these to the Seven Lullabies preschool tomorrow. Fancy hors d'oeuvres for four-year-olds, huh!" Lila noted.

"Children in our community should be familiar with good food, too. Especially those veggie wraps," Everett agreed.

"Time to broadcast the play-by-play," Oscar said smiling.

He was packing a tray of bacon-wrapped shrimp while keeping his eyes on the door to the dining hall and the crowd in the parlor. "Catalina is blocked by a crowd of men," he announced in his best sportscaster imitation. "Richard is one of them, but he's nowhere near us. Went to the restroom ten minutes ago. Shouldn't come by our way. Not sure about Catalina. Negative on taking a break yet."

Madera laughed then cleared her throat, talking just loud enough for the coven cooks to hear. "If Catalina comes in the kitchen, I'll say I was playing sick because I was nervous about this gig tonight and that I didn't want to tell her about it because I was embarrassed that I work two jobs. She knows I'd have no interest, except the money, in catering at a party where Richard Scott is at. I think I can make Catalina promise me that she won't tell Richard I'm here. I hope she listens." Madera scrubbed a pair of tongs in the hot dish water.

"Sounds like a plan," said Oscar, "but I don't think Catalina will get that far over here. We'll catch her at the door if need be. The lights are still low since cutting the birthday cake. I'm surprised the old heads aren't complaining. How can they see?"

Lila wheezed a laugh out—identical to the one Dewy gave when he was high.

"Oh, Kristine is headed our way," Oscar alerted as the growing, steady rhythm of clicking heels sounded.

"I figured you all were wrapping up. Great, guys. Thank you. My mother really loved it all," said Kristine.

"Absolutely. Most certainly our pleasure," Everett responded with an extra layer of charm.

Madera swallowed at the sound of the unfamiliar voice. Curious, she peeked over her shoulder at the woman in charge of the party. Where had she seen this Kristine before? She looked so familiar. Like Kristine's heels on the wood floor, it clicked: Roosevelt Road. Near the podiatrist's office over a month ago now. With the old lady who must be her mother—and the mother of Piggy Hughes. Madera bit her lip.

As Kristine's heels clicked away from the kitchen, Madera felt the rose quartz earrings squeeze her earlobes, sending a wave of serenity through her body. *Damn,* she thought. Any emotion unhelpful to her cause was instantly defused.

"She didn't glance your way. She's tipsy. Remember to rest in your breaths," Lila said.

Even though she took this advice, Madera clung to the thought of Officer Phillip Hughes. Madera was now under the same roof with Officer Piggy Hughes. They were both hearing the same Rat Pack Las Vegas songs, smelling the same garlic, seafood, and pork. Within these walls stood both Constance's daughter and her murderer. A person who gave Constance many reasons to live, and the person who took her life away.

Oscar nudged Madera's left arm: "Bathroom break." He reached to take over washing the dishpan.

Madera stepped back and locked eyes with Everett.

"Now's the time," he said.

"All clear. Take this and change in the bathroom," Lila said as she handed Madera the brown paper bag.

INSIDE THE BATHROOM, MADERA LOCKED THE DOOR AND FACED HER reflection in a mammoth gold-framed mirror. She released a pent-up sigh that edged into a wail.

Madera unbuttoned her chef's coat and peeled off the white pants to reveal the small black dress beneath, hanging an inch above her knees and her sheer red tights. She realized her feet hadn't felt their usual nervous sweat. Madera rubbed the black tourmaline stone that hung a couple inches below her bloodstone. Her mother's shell and pearl necklace weighed heavily around her neck.

The memory of the map on her mother's belly came to her. That map was ripped apart by bullets, saturated in blood and pain, violated and shredded to receive no medical care. That map was left in the middle of the road, grazing dark pavement, cooled by the mist of solemn early morning breezes until its blood, once radiant, departed.

Madera carried that map of her making. She could still feel its rough roads, the bounding terrain that grew wild and sweet like victorious tree roots. *You extend from me, baby girl. Your roots lie right here, with me.*

Her mother's pain welled deep down inside her own flesh, planting a tree that bloomed in the blood of its suffering. The name Madera was hers, as was this story and this body that pulled the blood of others. Her trauma, heavy and dark, was ready to rumble. Her desire, potent and fluid, was eager to unleash through the tainted body of Piggy Hughes. Somewhere in that Tuscan room, blood would spill.

The bathroom door swung open into the hallway where Lila was waiting. As she took the paper bag of chef clothes, Lila curled her pinky into Madera's and escorted her back to the kitchen. Blood, with the taste of old sulfur, a heavy metallic energy, skirted along Madera's tongue; a sample of all the gunpowder that Piggy Hughes foolishly fired throughout his career.

In the kitchen, Madera positioned herself behind the three coven cooks who stood like pillars facing toward the parlor and dining hall, chatting the chatter of caterers, gesturing at the table filled with steamers. Everett mumbled about trays and food temperatures. In the hall and parlor, the drunken partygoers danced.

Madera peered out between Everett's and Lila's shoulders and spotted the shrunken, formerly brawny frame of Officer Richard Scott in front of the bar swaying his head to Elton John's "I Guess

That's Why They Call It The Blues." A flush-faced Catalina mixed a cocktail behind him.

Near the edge of the bar, closest to the center of the room, Madera zeroed in on a sweaty head. There he was—the man whose comfort always mattered at others' expense. A putrefied soul in a body painted with privilege. These were the rules; he was a true protector, the blueprint for what mattered. His kind required constant reinforcement. Anything or anyone that stood in his way were to be removed by any means deemed fitting.

"Blood taken. Blood giveth back. Bloodshed to bloodshed," Lila chanted softly. "Out from the legs, the pain will be theirs instead. Blood taken. Blood giveth back," Oscar joined Lila. "Blood taken. Blood giveth back. Bloodshed to bloodshed. Out from the legs, the pain will be theirs instead." Everett took to the chant: "Paint the city red. Paint it in blood. Blood out between the legs. Let the pain be theirs instead." They all had learned Constance's words, the words she wrote after painting the picture. Blood was about to spill out from the legs, onto the town.

As the words faded, a red-hot fever ran from the top of Madera's head to the nail beds of her toes and unleashed a wave of blood. A powerful wave controlled by her presence alone.

As if struck by lightning, Phillip Hughes' cocktail glass leaped from his hand. Blood, thick and dark as chocolate, ran out of his eyes. It poured from his nose, his mouth, and his ears. It choked him. It soaked him. With both hands, he tugged at his neck, fighting to make an audible sound.

Madera stared at the results of her work from the kitchen. The blood wrath rocked Piggy Hughes, his knees folding beneath him. Blood filled the whites of his eyes and bright red tears poured forth. He crumpled to the floor with a thud, sending horrified children running down the hallway.

"Phillip!" Richard's eyes bulged in terror. He jumped to his feet as his cousin continued to struggle on his knees in a puddle of blood.

"Call 9-1-1!" he shouted.

The partygoers awoke from their alcoholic stupor, fumbling for their cell phones. Richard tried to lay Phillip on his back to attempt CPR, but the bald man thrashed in his own blood as if he were drowning. Richard turned toward the crowd, scanning for a culprit. The music clicked off as the quick silence soon became sprinkled with screams, screeches of chairs against the floor, and the clattering of dishes.

In the kitchen, Madera dived deeper behind the chef pillars. She saw Penelope rise stiffly from her chair, clutching her tiara, and hobble toward her bleeding son. The old woman flung her arms in the air, and her jaw fell open to release a piercing wail. Beside her mother, Kristine dropped her glass of wine. It splattered into crystalline shards on the floor.

The blood pouring from his ears connected with the blood from his nostrils; a scarlet face mask crowded his overflowing bloody mouth. Phillip Hughes yearned to scream. Bubbles of blood babbled from his lips as his eyes made tears worn on horror clown faces. His large, stubby fingers clawed at his neck as he writhed on the floor. Barely aware of his mother at his side or his cousin desperate to save him, his throat locked up as if choked by a beast. He tried to lift his arms, but his muscles would not work.

He knew who sent the blood: a woman, black or brown or something in between. He saw her ducking behind a chef in the kitchen, her eyes locked on him. And those eyes—deep, but not dark—they went red, bright, like a demon. She was a demon, Phillip believed, making his blood grow hot with steam and gush out of his body.

He knew this woman. He saw this face before. Years ago, near Kostner and Roosevelt, a woman in a blue jean dress. A woman too confident, too strong, too alive. Her screams, 'Just write me a ticket' had gotten in his way. She wasn't challenging him about a ticket, she threatened his way of life, his rule in the world, the correct social order he understood he must defend. He had to get rid of her. He had no patience for her kind. She wasn't deserving of life if that was how she was going to treat someone like him. He was doing the world a favor by eliminating someone that didn't know their place. And now she was here—somehow—stirring the raw copper and zinc of every bullet he distributed into the flesh of the innocent throughout his illustrious law enforcement career through his own body. His ears rang with all the gunshots he ever aimed at bodies he deemed unworthy—bodies in all shades of brown. The thunder bombarding his eardrums until he heard nothing else.

He coughed once more before his eyes, soured and bloodied by hate and pride, rolled back into oblivion.

~

"BACK UP, MADERA," EVERETT COMMANDED.

Madera obeyed, watching the scene from farther behind the chefs. With wet eyes and her face red in terror, Catalina stood frozen behind the bar. Her chest heaved as she tried to catch her breath. As Phillip lay limp and bloody on the floor, Richard stood nearby and wiped his brow, then swung his fist up in the air as if to strike an invisible spirit. "What the fuck!" he hollered as if a beast within him released. He spun around and his eyes met Madera's.

From the kitchen, Madera watched Richard's mouth drop into a perfect O. "You!" he screamed. "You! She did it!"

Richard bounded toward the kitchen.

"Out. Now," Everett ordered Madera in a pinched voice.

Oscar's hand latched onto Madera's right shoulder. He pulled the hood of the black dress over her head and led her toward the back door.

Richard saw me. Richard saw me was all she could think as Oscar pushed through the door.

Outside, sirens echoed through Madera's ears as she spotted Romi in the black Cadillac parked across the street. She skirted along the side of the house, praying Richard wouldn't find her. Red and blue lights flashed across the front of the house, circling like hungry flies, their reflections spilling onto the side street. Unlike the day Constance's body was left sprawled out on the cement like a fallen tree branch, all three emergency teams jumped to the cell phone alerts

—the ambulance, the fire truck, and the police. This was the way of the suburbs.

Scurrying across the dark street, Madera heard the car door unlock as she reached for the handle. Inside, the heat of the car overwhelmed her as she groaned. The tires were rolling before Madera could close her door. Madera's mouth hung open, her bottom lip numb. She thought of her own body depleting. How was she able to hold on right now? But she really wasn't holding. She felt herself floating. Her temperature rapidly dropped, and her fingertips became stone cold. The chill followed down her fingers and into her hands, then her wrists and what she thought was an overheated car wasn't even warm at all. The only way out was to close her eyes.

Madera envisioned her mother standing over the collapsed body of Officer Piggy Hughes, nodding her head at the bloody mess.

33

CATALINA STOOD PARALYZED FROM BEHIND THE BAR. SHE STARED AT Phillip on the floor. Face down with his left leg bent, he looked just like a chalk silhouette in a crime scene. But this wasn't a crime, just a man that bled to death. Catalina wasn't sure if anyone realized she was still there. She wasn't even sure if she was really there.

Next to Phillip's body, Samantha held Penelope, who rocked back and forth, eyes shut tight, her mouth open in a silent cry. Across the room, the young teenager Theo stared blankly. Catalina's gaze fell on Richard, now in the kitchen. His eyes were blazing as he screamed at one of the chefs.

At the kitchen doorway, Lila bypassed the arguing men and darted straight to Catalina.

"Are you okay, dear?" Lila asked.

"What is he saying over there?" Catalina managed to mouth the question.

"Nothing but nonsense, unfortunately. That poor man."

From the kitchen, Richard screamed at Catalina, "Catalina! You know Madera! You know her!" He pointed at Catalina and stalked toward the bar.

Catalina flinched at the sound of her name. But her mind held still at the name of her coworker. Madera? One moment Officer Scott was upset that his cousin choked on his own blood and now he's talking about Madera? *Madera?*

Catalina rasped, "Madera? What . . . what does this have to do . . . What about Madera?"

"Oh, he thinks he saw someone in the kitchen with us," Lila said. "I have no idea what he's talking about. None of us do. We're packing up in the kitchen. It's time for all of us to leave. I see you're in shock. Rightfully so, dear. But, here, let me help you. Where are your things?" Lila began looking around.

"Madera?" Catalina questioned again, confused as Richard stared, his green eyes hostile and determined. Catalina's jaw locked up. She shifted her head around looking for Madera. *Why would she be there? She had taken off work early at Hendricks and was at home sick.*

Before she could answer a wave of medics and police interrupted Officer Scott's closing approach. The EMTs flocked toward Phillip and crowded around his bloody body, towing their stretcher.

"Sammy, please take my mother away," Kristine ordered. Her orange dress was flecked with blood. Samantha helped Penelope, now wailing, off her knees and out of the room. They, too, had been doused by Phillip's blood.

"Officers! I'm Officer Richard Scott, CPD. I'm the cousin of the victim," Richard said, breaking his gaze from Catalina to address a young, round Asian officer and a heavily bearded White man.

Catalina unglued herself and began scanning around the bar for her coat and purse. Her hands trembled. *What was he yelling about Madera?* She looked behind her as a chill crossed her spine. She took a deep breath. Catalina recalled the times Richard had thrown up blood at the Whistler's Room and Hendricks. And now Madera had left work today because she was sick. She prayed it wasn't contagious.

Lila turned to Catalina as the officers talked. "I don't know what he's yelling about. I think he may be hallucinating. He's probably in shock."

"Maybe? Madera is a coworker of mine."

The two women paused their stilted conversation as they heard Richard giving his account of the night to the two officers.

"You can call me crazy all you want, officers. But I've dated this witch that works at Hendricks Steakhouse in the West Loop. She . . . she did some pretty awful things to me that made me cough up blood like Phil did. It was her niece, Madera. Madera is her name. One awful name, you can't forget it. A Black Mexican or whatever. I think she's twenty-two or something. I'm not sure if her last name is Guitterez like Amaryllis. Amaryllis Guitterez is the bartender that . . . hey, Catalina, over here. She knows them, too! What's Madera's last name? They are witches and they're doing some kind of voodoo or something that makes people bleed out their mouths and, ever since I've stopped dating this woman, I haven't—"

"—Richard, what the *hell* are you talking about? Witches? Have you gone mad?" Kristine blurted out. She had been conferring with the EMTs and now faced the two confused cops and her cousin.

"Kristine, you don't know. See . . . *you don't know*," Richard insisted. "You don't know this woman but—Catalina, don't get weird on me now, answer me, baby girl. Please, answer me. Did you see Madera here?"

Catalina's mouth dropped open. She spotted Lila pulling out her purse and coat from underneath the bar's sink. *Madera?*

"No. No, I didn't see Madera," Catalina mumbled, even more confused.

"Listen, Officer Scott, did anyone touch your cousin? Did you hear a shot? Anyone around him at the time he collapsed?" The bearded cop asked.

"I was. I was around him and so was everyone else! And no shots, no," Richard said.

"The woman that you said you saw in the kitchen, was she near your cousin at the time he collapsed?"

"No, she was in the kitchen, staring at us and—"

"—No, officer. There wasn't anyone in the kitchen but me and the two other chefs," Lila inserted. Catalina peeled her eyes from the cops' exchange and stared gratefully at the daring woman beside her.

"Ma'am, can you follow me?" The young officer asked, wearing a calm face. Lila passed Catalina's coat and purse to her. She headed to the kitchen with the officer. Catalina heard the muffled voices of Lila, Oscar, and Everett reassure the policeman that no, nobody else was in the kitchen besides them. Some kind of apprentice was supposed to come but was a no-show. Sliding her purse over her shoulder, Catalina watched as the other officer went back and forth between Richard and Kristine, debating how a spell could make a man die.

"But why would some strange woman want to hex my brother? He doesn't even live here, Rich." Kristine massaged her forehead with her fingertips.

"Her friend! The Madera girl has a friend and he mentioned Phillip's name randomly at a bar in the West Loop a week or so ago. Yes, that's right. I know it. There's definitely something fishy going on and I will not back down!" Richard hollered.

"Officer Scott, what you said sounds a bit far-fetched, to be quite honest. An autopsy will be done. If there is any evidence there, we will certainly look into the matter. All respect though, sir. All respect. Let's just make sure we send the guests home and we get this scene cleared up, okay?" said the bearded officer. Then he turned to Catalina. "Miss, you can head home now, okay? Everyone should leave."

"Oh, yes . . . Get on out, Catalina—Thank you," said Kristine, pulling a wad of cash from her brassiere. "Here's your pay. . . My goodness, just head home, okay?"

Catalina stepped out from behind the bar. Still in wild disbelief, she clutched her coat like a worried child holding its blankie. She stuffed her earnings into a purse pocket.

Lila rushed to her side, "Come. Did you drive? I can take you home if you need a ride?"

Dumbfounded, Catalina nodded, taking Lila's hand. "Can you take me to the train?"

"Done," Lila reassured.

Catalina took one last look at Richard, who bit his bottom lip and stared at the dead body of his cousin, The Great Phillip Hughes, being lifted onto a stretcher.

34

SMELLING LIKE MARLBORO LIGHTS AND WHISKEY, AMARYLLIS SLAMMED the Uber's car door, sending the terrier next door to Sofia's house into a barking frenzy. She spotted her little blue car a few houses down; odd to see it parked there. It felt like days, not hours ago, when she lent it to Madera . . . *who is—here?*—she hoped.

She felt a damp heat at the front door of the bungalow. Amaryllis couldn't tell if it was radiating from her or from the house. Underneath her small leather jacket, her collarbone was moist. Biting her inner cheek, she knocked on the door like a hyper child, hoping her niece would answer. She rocked back on her feet and cracked her neck. Amaryllis now wished she'd called Dewy before showing up like this. Again, she released a rapid pounding on the door.

Romi, the same woman with the purple afro who brought the bath salts, answered the door. Her dark eyes lit up, "Amaryllis! Great to see you—"

"Is my niece here?"

"Um, well, yes, she is." Romi stepped aside as Amaryllis marched in.

The house was steaming hot. The windows were wide open and

standing fans whizzed a hot breeze across Amaryllis' face—*bizarre for November. What's going on here?* "Madera? Mad!"

"Shush, please! Wait—you have to be quiet, okay? She's resting. You want to see Madera healthy, then you gotta give her some more time. Okay? please?" Romi said, wide eyed.

Amaryllis folded her arms against her chest and stared at Romi. "You're for real, huh?"

"We got back here twenty minutes ago. She's lying down right now. She needs to—"

"—Where's her bag? I need my car keys. Is Dewy here?" Amaryllis' gray eyes twitched.

Dressed in a pajama suit as red as the core of a ruby, a woman stepped in from the hallway. *She has to be Sofia,* Amaryllis guessed, finding this woman's quiet vibrancy as intimidating as a preacher at a Sunday school. Big curls, vivid brown eyes, and a piping hot black mug in one hand. In her other hand was Madera's black purse.

"I'm sure *tus llaves*—your keys—are in here." Sofia's voice was brittle, tired. "I made you some tea. You should sit and sip until your *sobrina* is ready. If you want her safe, *sientate*— sit. Or leave."

Grabbing Madera's purse, Amaryllis said, "Oh! no! I'm not leaving without Madera."

"Then, here you go," said Sofia, grinning, handing the mug to Amaryllis.

Amaryllis wanted to snatch it from her but the gesture wasn't worth getting burned. She missed her chance to snatch the purse. Lips pursed, Amaryllis took the tea with both hands like a cautious child. The mug was heavy in her hands and carried the smell of lavender. Unexpectedly, her mouth began salivating for it. She hovered her mouth over it and blew.

"Just tell me what I need to do to get her home as quickly as possible?"

"*Espera*—wait. No more than fifteen minutes." Sofia took a seat on her chaise, "*Soy* Sofia. Nice to meet you, Amaryllis."

Amaryllis sat beside Romi on the couch and said, "I know about you. Can't say I'm thrilled some *bruja* is helping my niece seek revenge."

"Oh, but this is more than revenge," Sofia said, still smiling.

"Well, it started that way," Amaryllis snapped.

A man stepped into the living room, carrying a plate of multicolored peppers and settled into a cross-legged position on the floor. He was a clean-shaven Black man probably in his early fifties or older. His sable eyes stared into hers. They held galaxies.

Amaryllis eyed him skeptically as the questions raced out of her mouth, "Who are you? Were you there tonight? What happened?"

"I'm Everett. And you're Amaryllis. Nice to meet you."

Someone with a pudding-soft smile peeked her head in from the hallway, "She'll be out in five!" She scurried back out.

"Is she talking about Mad? She's gotta be. Damn, how many witches are there?" Amaryllis demanded.

"Her name is Adora. And, yes, she's talking about Madera. She's with her. She's caring for her. I think you should drink your tea," Sofia cleared her throat, reaching for her own mug.

"But she looks so young! Why is she taking care of Madera?"

"Amaryllis, your niece fulfilled her prophecy tonight," Everett said chewing on his peppers.

"What the fuck does that mean? Did she kill that man? Huh? What happened?" Amaryllis' words tumbled out.

"Yes, Officer Phillip Hughes is dead," Sofia said.

"She did it? My fucking niece killed a man?! What?! No . . . no . . . no! We want to be good people!" Amaryllis shook her head. She put her tea on the coffee table and clutched Madera's purse to her chest. She rocked with it, reaching for her tea again, not quite sure where to put herself. Her insides wanted to explode, her body urging to break out, but instead, she rocked. She felt hot.

"How did she kill him? Does anyone know? Like, she gonna be locked up for this shit? No one's going to come after her, will they?"

Everett sat his pepper plate between his legs. "Madera is fine. Officer Phillip Hughes got what was coming. His death has meaning and will spread throughout police fraternities like wildfire. Especially here in Chicago, when cases of spontaneous blood flow coming from cops may soon be on the rise. They may get scared and hopefully change their ways," Everett tried to refrain from snickering as Romi caved into it.

Between laughs, she spoke, "I wasn't even there but I can imagine it! Probably quite the show!"

"All this weird magic shit . . . " Amaryllis mumbled, grimacing at Romi. She took a larger sip of tea, sat it down, and peeled off her leather jacket.

"Magic isn't some exotic belief in our heads—it's real. If you tend to it like a garden, it grows. We are just showing Madera her tools," Sofia said.

Amaryllis nodded as a slow swarm of translucent mini dragonflies and little crescent moons and suns fluttered about the room. They glowed like dust particles in a sunbeam. Amaryllis blinked hard. *What the hell is in this tea?* She thought as the fluttering images dissipated.

"I don't know what you put in this tea, but I'm seeing things. You guys say you are showing my niece her tools, huh? You're implying there's a future with this? Really?" Amaryllis rested one palm on her head.

"On a lighter scale," Romi said.

"*Ay Dios Mio*! Seriously? What am I supposed to do with some magical niece doing all kinds of madness to who exactly, other people that have killed others? Or does Madera even want to do this? Huh? Have you asked her?"

"We don't force anyone. That's how bad magic takes over," Sofia said.

"Preventative justice magic! Stopping them in their tracks. And, Amaryllis, if you want to learn more, the door is open here. You may benefit from learning to use your energies. They're ready to burst," Everett said smiling as he popped a bright red pepper into his mouth.

"Do you care for a plate, Amaryllis?" Sofia asked.

Amaryllis took another sip. "No, thank you."

Does this strange man really see my potential? Why are these people so calm? How has Madera dealt with all this? I want to see her! Where's Dewy? Amaryllis' thoughts clattered in her mind like kitchen pots.

"Specific planetary energies run deep in families," Romi said with urgency. "Families share more than blood. They share energy. You have Mars energy like Madera. We can use more of that around here."

"Let's not go too far with this," Sofia warned.

"If Dewy is with Mad now, then I ought to be there, too!"

"Dewy doesn't get involved with this business. Adora's the only one with her," Sofia stressed.

Amaryllis leaned back against the couch, feeling like she was sitting on a delicate cloud. Startling her, a sleek gray-blue cat hopped onto the couch. Amaryllis gasped, then giggled.

Suddenly Adora burst into the living room: "I need her aunt!"

Everyone scrambled to their feet.

"What is it?" Amaryllis begged.

"Come with me!" said Adora.

They all hurried down the hallway.

Amaryllis fought the dreamy, sedated feeling the tea had given her. Adora drew aside the beaded curtain to the back room as Amaryllis hurried to her niece. On a pallet, Madera was lying still, face up, eyes closed surrounded by gigantic candles and music that sounded like an alto voice humming a lullaby. Falling onto her knees, Amaryllis touched her niece's forehead—she felt cool like a chilled balm.

"What's wrong with her?"

"She's getting too cold! She needs your warmth," said Adora. *"Please!"*

"But, how?"

Sofia moved the red candle closer to Madera's body. She folded her hands in prayer in front of her face.

Allowing her intuition to lead, Amaryllis lay down, her side pressed against Madera's. She put her cheek against her niece's and shut her eyes tight. Tears ran down her face.

"Mi sobrina, can you hear me? Get up, Mad!"

Madera didn't move.

"Her heart rate is off. She exerted too much energy during the bloodshed," Adora said.

"Amaryllis, you gotta stabilize her! Share your energy!" Romi urged.

"Let me turn off the fans!" Everett said, running out of the room.

Amaryllis glanced up to see the three women staring down at her as if she embodied a secret key. She knew she had a well of energy right now, but it felt too angry, too painful. It needed a bit of softness —no, it needed love. Pushing her fear back, Amaryllis searched her heart. With one hand, she cupped the bloodstone around Madera's neck.

A feeling rushed through her—a feeling of being better than she ever thought, of embracing the armor it takes to raise a child. She called it forth, intense and hot as it was, up out of her heart. Surging out as pure energy, it mingled with the house's own warmth that greeted her at the door. The soggy heat slid out from her skin and dripped onto her niece, forehead to forehead. Heavy tears spilled out of Amaryllis' eyes as she thought of her niece when she first met her— a small, terrified ten-year-old. How tightly wound Madera was. Her heart shattered by the death of her mother—the murder of her mother. How could a young girl stitch her life together without that strong love around? Amaryllis remembered trying to mimic what she'd imagine Constance gave her. Amaryllis understood that was the wrong thing all along. Sobbing, Amaryllis released her own trans-forming power. Her intensity was rooted in love. Love that didn't know exactly how to operate but was there. Loud and ready to pour out of her and onto her niece.

Madera exhaled a calming breath and Amaryllis felt it tickle her chin.

"Come on, Mad! Get up!" Amaryllis yelled, sobbing onto her niece's shoulder.

Gingerly, as if aggravated by an alarming light, Madera's eyes blinked open.

"*Tia?*" Madera's voice was meek and dry.

"Mad!" Amaryllis wrapped herself around Madera, lifting her up to feel her, completely, in her arms.

"I'm good. I'm here." Madera's gargling little child laugh started weak, then gathered strength as it spread throughout the room.

"Yes! Yes, you are!" Adora touched her red jasper stone and sighed.

Amaryllis helped Madera to her feet and smothered her niece with more warmth, gracing her with the energy she needed to thrive.

"Come on," Amaryllis said, taking Madera's arm. "Let's get you home to rest."

35

Around 9 a.m., Madera woke up to the sound of her aunt pressing the flat's door buzzer. As always, Amaryllis held it long enough to let in a family of ten. With a dry mouth and a sore back, Madera sat up in her bed. Her back was sore from resting on the palette in Sofia's back sunroom, or maybe it had something to do with what her body went through. She was pleased to be waking up. But who was at the door?

Madera pictured Richard with a crew of cops armed with guns, mounting up the stairs, spreading the scent of pickled bologna. It was too early to know whether to freak out or laugh. Peeling off her pajamas, her back cracked in sweet relief. She pulled on her navy yoga pants and a black zip-up hoodie.

On the altar, the pictures of her parents stared up at Madera. She picked up the picture of her mom, adorned by the shell and pearl necklace. Her mother's smile vibrated through the photograph, as if she were humming Madera a lullaby. She clung onto the sound of her mother's humming, wishing she could wear it on her body like the rose quartz studs she still wore. She would give her mother's humming a volume dial and a play button, to choose whatever setting she may desire. Madera smiled.

Less than twelve hours ago, she drowned a man with his own blood, fulfilling her prophecy. She had avenged her mother, bringing justice for Constance Maria Miller and all others that Piggy slaughtered. Madera held no remorse, just deep knowledge that things were different. There was one less evil in the world. She placed her mother's picture back onto her altar, hopeful that Piggy's other victims smiled back, somewhere in another world.

She looked at her father's image. It was time to frame his picture, Madera believed. Deep down, she knew most of her Mars stemmed from him. She and Amaryllis, Adan's sister, were kin in that way.

What about herself? Who would Madera be now? Having ended one foul pig, she was ready to target other deserving officers. But she still felt weak and in need of rest. She didn't want to use that amount of aggressive magic on someone again; it was too dangerous. It scared the shit out of Amaryllis—at least that's what Amaryllis said about a thousand times on their way back home last night. Maybe she could use magic in a different way—to stop them from making hateful choices. With the tired, corrupt structures of law enforcement barely functioning, preventative justice seemed like a smart path.

Madera smiled at her mother's painting that leaned against her wall. Since she wasn't sure who arrived, Madera turned the picture around, knowing she would have to find it a suitable location eventually.

Heading to the living room, Madera smelled the fresh scent of *Palo Santo* spreading out into the hallway. The plants were damp and happy. Her aunt must've given them misty kisses from the spray bottle. Madera realized she'd forgotten to brush her teeth.

Amaryllis sat on the green rocking chair with her skeleton coffee mug, dressed in the gray jogging suit that matched the color of her eyes. She blew out a puff of smoke. "We have a visitor. Are you feeling better?"

Madera turned to see Catalina sitting on the couch. Her brown eyes looked worried, circled by grayish bags. Snug in a black trench coat, Catalina waved lightly. "Hey Madera! I tried texting you this morning. I needed to see you because some crazy stuff happened last night. You *would not* believe it."

"I'm feeling a little better," Madera forced a fake cough.

"That party at Officer Scott's aunt's house was terrible." Catalina glanced at Amaryllis for reassurance.

"Yes. It's sad! Horrifying," Amaryllis declared.

Madera stifled a snicker as she joined the act. "Really? Why? What happened?" Madera asked.

"Officer Scott's cousin, the son of the lady whose birthday it was, died! He bled to death on the dance floor, in front of everyone! Like, you know how Richard has been losing weight and coughing up blood? I hope he doesn't die from the same blood disease. This man had blood coming from his mouth and ears and eyes and . . . it was like a horror film. It happened so fast but so slow, too. It was really freaky. I thought I was having a nightmare."

"What? That sounds crazy." Madera's mouth dropped. She shook her head as Catalina rattled on.

"But, the craziest thing was Officer Scott kept saying you were there and blaming the blood thing on you, like *you* killed him!"

"Me? Wait, what? Me?" Madera pleaded.

"I know it sounds crazy. It was very crazy. I tried to look into his eyes to see if he was possessed, but he just looked so angry. But how could he think you would do that? How could anybody do that?"

"Me? What? I'm so sorry to hear this, but why did he say he saw me?"

"No one knows, Madera. I didn't see you. No one saw you. The cooks that took me to the train, said they didn't see you, but Richard thought you were with them or something. His family and the police were looking at him like . . . it was really creepy. It was like he wanted to just call women witches. I was thinking about it last night because I couldn't really sleep . . . and it just made me think of how men love to call women that disagree with them witches. And it made me think of your mom and how she died and Richard probably thought that you may have a reason to hate him just because he's a cop. But . . . I think your gut feeling about him has always been right. He's just a creepy cop—I see that now. And you knew from the very beginning. That's probably why he wanted to blame you or Amaryllis, I don't know! I think I need to see a therapist about this. I'm so shaken up that I called off work today," Catalina said, shaking her head.

"Thanks for coming to tell me. I hope he won't try to come over here." Madera shivered.

"The fuck I'd allow him to come in my place and blame my niece for some off the wall thing! Like, he ought to arrest himself for thinking such nonsense," Amaryllis said, ashing her cigarette.

"Oh, I don't know, Madera. The experience was *bien loca*! So crazy! I just wanted to tell you this before you got word of it. You know, I don't think Richard will be at our bar ever again. I think he needs to get his mind right. He should be too embarrassed to come in anyway. Like, what if you're the hostess one day when he tries to come in? I don't know, but I think we may be done with him as a customer," Catalina said.

Madera slid onto the couch next to her and patted her shoulder as Amaryllis said, "You should stay for breakfast. I can make some *chilaquiles*."

Madera's eyes lit up. That was one Mexican dish Amaryllis did cook very well.

"Oh, *pues, gracias*," Catalina muttered, staring at the floor.

Madera could tell Amaryllis felt rather proud of herself. To wake up on a Sunday morning and make a pot of coffee over a lukewarm martini was exactly what the universe ordered. Maybe it was something in the tea Sofia gave her last night.

Madera touched her own frayed bun, becoming more cautious of her morning breath.

"Sorry, I haven't brushed my teeth yet," she admitted, facing the other way as she spoke. In chorus, the three women laughed only to be startled by another buzz at the door.

Mug in hand, Amaryllis leaned to peek out the front window. Was a S.W.A.T. team ready to bust in, guns in hand? She shrugged. No one was there. She took a deep breath, leaped into the hallway, and pressed the buzzer call button.

"Who is it?" She demanded.

"Dewy."

Madera excused herself, slid her boots on, and hurried down to the second floor to greet her friend.

Wearing a blue hoodie, Dewy held a gift bag in his hand.

"Damn, there you are. How are you? Wanna go for a drive? How come you came down here?" He asked too many questions too fast.

"Catalina's here. She just popped up. She's not a bit suspicious but filling us in on the party last night." Madera found herself whispering.

Dewy's eyes flinched, "Oh . . . this is all a lot. I'm glad the big one's over with. Here's your consolation prize," Dewy said, passing the bag to his friend.

"My what?" said Madera.

"It's from us. Well, I added something in there. A couple others did too."

Madera smiled as Dewy ruffled his hair.

"Let's go sit on the stoop for a bit. Catalina's staying for breakfast. Maybe you can, too? By the way, if Catalina asks, you were at a friend's birthday party last night. And I was supposed to go with you, but I got sick."

Out onto the greystone's front porch, the chill of late Chicago autumn nipped at them. They sat down on the top step together. Madera released a big exhale and watched as her breath took on the shape of a little cloud. Taking Dewy's hand into hers, she grinned.

"You've been using a nail brush, huh?"

"My mother told me it would be Mars that would get me to take care of myself," Dewy said smiling. "Open your gifts. They're from the house."

Madera raised her eyebrows and peered into the bag. She pulled out a book about the planets. "Oh, this must be from Romi! I want to know—which planet do you connect with the most?" Madera smiled.

"Neptune. Saturn. I've heard them both about me and my mom. Delusional at times? Um, yea. Dreamy, on another plane, but restricted? That's all Romi's stuff, really. She's the main one with the planet talk. But Raven has . . . never mind."

"Raven? Who's that? I never heard that name before."

Dewy only nodded toward the gift bag in her hand.

Madera pulled out another book. It was about the police force, its history rooted in slavery and the brutality it still inflicts daily throughout the country. She flipped through the pages. At the bottom of the bag, Madera found a red sketchbook from Dewy, plus two new bloodstone crystals.

"Who doesn't like an extra sketch journal, right? Had to get it in that color. We have some more sketch and smoke sessions in our future," Dewy said.

"This is dope. Thank you. I'll have to stop by later on and make sure to—"

"—My *Tia* told me she doesn't want to see you for a week. She says you need to rest. We should have our sketch and smoke sessions here at your place this week . . . when Amaryllis is working so we can be alone, if you want?"

"Yes, I'd love that," Madera said.

"Sure," Dewy said, trying to snuff out his excitement.

Madera swayed her leg to meet Dewy's. As expected, a rush of lust teased her. The connection was magnetic.

"Look, I wish you were with me last night and I'm sure I'll have the energy to let you know about it sometime . . . but . . . thank you. Like, I'm not getting mushy here, Dewy, but you are a ride or die for real. And I love you for that."

"Madera, I love you madly, and that's all you need to know. But how are you feeling? Like, you seem cool as a cucumber."

"Isn't it odd? I know! It feels like my mama finally settled into the spirit world last night. And I don't have that anxiety that comes when you think you *should* be in trouble. Even when I imagine something crazy, like cop cars swarming down the street. As soon as I think I feel nervous, I realize that I'm really not. It's like, a true fearlessness."

"That's really dope. I hope it stays that way. My *Tia* and my mom, all of them, are really good people. They're for the people. They fight for the good and as many cases of justice magic as they've been working, there's probably only a handful that haven't worked out. But that's out of like more than twenty years of cases. My *Tia*'s been doing this for some time."

"Yea, well, I feel like I'm in good hands. I know I wouldn't be able to feel this fearless if my mama wasn't satisfied. I know it doesn't bring her back and that's not what it's about. Now, we got to scare the hell out of these Piggy clones."

"Well, I'm here for it. Come on, let's get inside. It's cold as hell out here," Dewy said standing up.

"Yeah, well, last thing I heard: Hell is not cold," Madera teased.

"Only Piggy Hughes knows for sure!" Dewy joked, picking up the gift bag for Madera.

Her child-like gargle laugh was carried by the wind, sending its aroma underneath Dewy's nostrils.

"Mad, you haven't brushed your teeth yet, have you?" Dewy scoffed playfully.

"No, I still got all those root veggies on my breath. Leave me alone before I kiss you."

"Yo! Now I may be okay with that. I was fine with the blood, remember?"

Laughing, Dewy followed Madera inside.

ACKNOWLEDGMENTS

To the Rebels, Magicians, Lovers and Warriors combatting injustices daily, you are golden.

Big hugs to my loved ones, especially my husband for supporting me on this journey.

Special shout out to Bonni McKeown, you helped me in many ways. Mad appreciation for author Montrez for making sure I didn't make a fool of myself. And, to my editor, Elena Marinaccio for your brilliant work.

Much love to the readers that get lost in the world of books as it is difficult in a world with a low attention span.

Dear Daughters, may you always remember that you can accomplish anything at any time as long as you leave room for rest.

As always, I thank my ancestors, this wide universe and the Spirit up high!

ABOUT THE AUTHOR

Am Bornfree is a proud native of the Midwest - from Flint, Michigan to Chicago, IL. She lives with her husband and two creative spirited daughters. A self-proclaimed Astronerd, Am Bornfree has been a student of astrology for years. A lover of the arts, Am enjoys making one-of-a-kind holiday wreaths as well as playing with paint. She is currently working on Book 2 of the Revolt Occult Series which centers the character, Adora.

For more book news and updates visit:

http://ambornfree.com/

instagram.com/authorambornfree

Printed in Great Britain
by Amazon

77224844R00145